**"There is no need to be sarcastic.
I was paying you a compliment."**

He glanced away. "Perhaps we can do naught but brangle when we're together."

Oh, but once they had done more than that. Perhaps that was at the root of their arguing, a little voice whispered in her head. She forced her mind away from the thought. "Have you said all you wish, Stowe? Richard really will be waiting for me."

He nodded and stepped back, glancing up as he did so. And then he stopped, his gaze returning upward. "Well."

Tess looked up as well and saw a kissing bough. It was beautifully made, of evergreens decorated with velvet ribbons of scarlet and green, making the mistletoe berries that descended from it glisten that much whiter. In fact, she realized, the entire room was decorated, much as the drawing room had been, with pine boughs that gave off a strong, clean scent, and more ribbons. She wondered how she had missed that before. She wondered how she would remove herself from this situation. "The decorations are beautiful," she babbled, stepping back, as he had, only to be brought up short when he caught her hand. "Stowe—"

"I fear there's no help for it, Tess." For the first time since his return to Yorkshire, she saw the old gleam in his eye, the one that had attracted her so, seven long years ago. "We seem to be under the kissing bough." And with that, to her immense surprise, he bent his head to hers.

BOOK YOUR PLACE ON OUR WEBSITE AND MAKE THE READING CONNECTION!

We've created a customized website just for our very special readers, where you can get the inside scoop on everything that's going on with Zebra, Pinnacle and Kensington books.

When you come online, you'll have the exciting opportunity to:

- View covers of upcoming books
- Read sample chapters
- Learn about our future publishing schedule (listed by publication month *and author*)
- Find out when your favorite authors will be visiting a city near you
- Search for and order backlist books from our online catalog
- Check out author bios and background information
- Send e-mail to your favorite authors
- Meet the Kensington staff online
- Join us in weekly chats with authors, readers and other guests
- Get writing guidelines
- AND MUCH MORE!

**Visit our website at
http://www.zebrabooks.com**

AN ANGEL'S WISH

Mary Kingsley

ZEBRA BOOKS
Kensington Publishing Corp.
http://www.zebrabooks.com

ZEBRA BOOKS are published by

Kensington Publishing Corp.
850 Third Avenue
New York, NY 10022

All Kensington titles, imprints and distributed lines are available at special quantity discounts for bulk purchases for sales promotion, premiums, fund-raising, educational or institutional use.

Special book excerpts or customized printings can also be created to fit specific needs. For details, write or phone the office of the Kensington Special Sales Manager: Kensington Publishing Corp., 850 Third Avenue, New York, NY 10022. Attn. Special Sales Department. Phone: 1-800-221-2647.

Zebra and the Z logo Reg. U.S. Pat. & TM Off.

First Printing: October 2001
10 9 8 7 6 5 4 3 2 1

Printed in the United States of America

One

"Papa, I've decided what I want for Christmas."

"Hmm?" David Fairfax, Marquess of Stowe, glanced into the Bond Street shop window at the display of jewelry. Christmas was coming, all too soon. Already signs of it were everywhere, from the sweet, spicy scents of cinnamon and ginger wafting from bakeshops; in the armloads of packages borne by shoppers and footmen alike; even in the suddenly frosty air, so unlike London's usual winter damp. Not like winter in Yorkshire, where it was more likely to snow, and the best activities for a winter's afternoon could be found indoors. No, not like Yorkshire at all, he thought, and determinedly dragged his thoughts away from that subject to stare instead fixedly at the jewelry. He'd have to be thinking of a present for Emily, a ring, perhaps. Yes. Why not a ring, along with a proposal? He couldn't say he loved her. He'd left that violent, volatile, and altogether unreliable emotion behind with his youth. He did, however, like her. A widow, she was pleasant, supportive, and a trifle plump. If she was no great beauty, at least she was a comfortable person to be about. And she liked Jennie. That was the most important thing.

"Papa." Jennie tugged impatiently at David's hand, drawing his attention away from the window bedecked in holly and red ribbon. "You're not listening to me."

"I'm sorry, poppet." He smiled crookedly down at her. "But I was attending to you. You know what you want for your Christmas presents this year."

"Present," she corrected impatiently. "Only one."

"Indeed? Then it must be very special."

"It is. I want—" She stopped, took in a deep breath, and continued on in a rush. "I want to see my mother."

It hit David hard, like a fist to his midsection, and for a moment he was robbed of breath. "Jennie, I'm not sure if that's possible—"

"I've been thinking about it, you know," she interrupted. "I know you want to give me a new mother. I know you've been seeing Mrs. Granfield. I do like her, Papa, really, I do. But why do I need another mother when I already have one of my own?"

Dear lord. David briefly shut his eyes. Cool, rational, reasonable. He had a little logician on his hands, and well he knew it. At times, he didn't know what to do with her. Even in her earliest years, Jennie hadn't gone into any of the childish pouts or fits of temper he knew children could use when they wished to have their own way. No. She used logic, and the way she thought at the age of six sometimes scared him. "I don't think it will be possible," he said gently.

Jennie fixed him with a direct gaze, unnerving in someone her age. "Why not?"

"Your mother lives very far away, in the country," he improvised. "She won't want to come to town."

"Can't we go there? I know you have an estate there, and that that's where you met her. Nurse told me."

Dear lord, he thought again, looking down at this

daughter he loved more than he had thought it possible to love any child. "No, Jennie."

"Why not?"

This time he was forced to meet her gaze. Logician or not, when all was said and done she was still a child, a child who knew nothing of divorce, of broken marriages. Of broken hearts. "Jennie." He went down on one knee before her, heedless of the damage done to his biscuit-colored buckskins or the stares of other people, caring only that he met her at eye level. "Your mother and I are not the best of friends."

"Oh, I know that," she said, with careless scorn. "But she doesn't know me, Papa. Maybe she'll like me."

Remembering Tess, David rather doubted it. "You know that she and I decided to live apart. I explained that to you a long time ago."

"Yes, but we could stay at Stowcroft, and she could stay where she lives, and I could visit her."

"No." He rose. "It's out of the question, Jennie."

"Papa, my friend Elizabeth's parents live apart. So do Katherine's. But they still see their mothers. They still have their mothers," she went on with quiet force. "Why can't I?"

His face stony, David walked beside her. There was much he could tell her, if he wanted to. Because, he could say, as much as he once had loved Tess, he now hated her with equal ferocity. Because she was the last person in the world he wanted to see. Because, even though he had expressly forbidden Tess to have anything to do with Jennie, he was surprised she had never made a push to see their daughter. She was as heartless as he had come to believe. He couldn't say that to a child, though. "It's out of the question."

"Why?"

"Jennie, wouldn't you rather have another angel figurine? That crystal one we saw?"

"That would be nice," she said without enthusiasm.

"And we could have guests for Christmas. I can invite friends who have children—no." He frowned. Christmas was not like any other time of year. Those who were socially minded stayed in town for the Little Season; others repaired to their country estates, usually with a party of family and friends, to celebrate the season. *Hmm.* Now there was a thought. While David had always tried to make the day as special as possible for his daughter, the truth was that they were, essentially, alone. His family had always been small, and so there were no aunts, no uncles, and no cousins. He also rarely saw his mother, which was something else that wasn't going to change. Perhaps a house party wouldn't be so bad. "Jennie," he began, and stopped. No. To go to Stowcroft at any time of year would be hard; at Christmas, with all its memories, insupportable. Nor would any house party completely isolate him from Tess.

She looked up at him. "What, Papa?"

"Nothing."

"Oh. Wait! Papa, you could invite friends, but to Stowcroft."

He sighed. "Jennie—"

"Oh, it would be ever so much fun. Does it snow in Yorkshire?"

"Yes." Snowy days; Tess with her cheeks pink and her eyes sparkling from the cold and an impromptu snowball fight, which had led to quite something else; a winter's afternoon, spent inside, away from the stormy weather. *No.* Determinedly David dragged his thoughts away from memories of the past.

"Then we could all play outside. Oh, Papa, please. Please say yes."

"Jennie—"

"Please?"

Damnation, he thought. He'd always found it difficult to refuse Jennie when she looked up at him as she did now, her hazel eyes huge and pleading. He wondered if she knew what effect those darklashed eyes had on him, or the effect they would have on young men in the future. The thought made him shudder. "People may have other plans already."

"How will you know, unless you ask them?"

He set his lips. Damn. She wasn't going to give up on this. He knew his daughter. She'd persist until she got her way. To give her her due, though, it was only rarely that she did that. And maybe, he thought, weakening, it wouldn't be that bad. Guests would help, especially people with children, for Jennie's sake. Nor would he have to see Tess very often; Jennie's nurse could bring her to Harcourt Manor, the Harwood estate, where Tess lived. It could work. It would be two difficult weeks for him, but he could endure them.

He looked down at her, to see her watching him with that same pleading look, and let out a gusty sigh. "All right, poppet. We'll go to Stowcroft," he said resignedly, and wondered just what he'd gotten himself into.

London's cold dampness didn't prevail in the Yorkshire hollow where Harcourt was located. Instead, the air held a crisp coldness that made Tess Harwood feel quite invigorated after a morning spent bringing Christmas baskets of food to the estate's poor families, as well as Stowcroft's. Once out of her carriage, she entered the house with a light step. Christmas was coming. It was usually a difficult time of year for her, and yet for some reason she felt lighthearted about it this year.

"There's a letter for you," her brother Richard reported as she walked into the hall of the old manor house and began undoing the fastenings of her cherry red velvet cloak.

Tess turned to him, startled into a smile. She received letters so rarely. "For me? Why, whoever could it be from?"

Richard's face was dour. "I've a guess. It's franked by Stowe."

Tess paused in the act of handing her cloak to a footman. A letter from David. Her spirits plummeted. "Oh."

"Do you want me to deal with it?"

"Of course not," she said briskly, crossing the hall to him and taking the letter. "I can't imagine what more he could do."

"I can. If he learns you've been going down to London—"

"And how will he? No one knows me there."

"I've always warned you 'tis not a good idea."

"You know my reasons."

"Which are also unnecessary."

"To me they aren't." She glanced quickly at Bailey, their butler, standing poker-faced and motionless in the hall. "I don't think this is quite the place to discuss it."

"My study, then," he said, and walked away, opening a door farther down the hall for her. Inside the room a Border collie jumped up from his snooze before the roaring fire, wagging his tail excitedly at the sight of his master. "Tess, I'd rather spare you any more pain."

"I am an adult, Richard. I grew up six years ago."
She held out her hand. "My letter, please?"

"Are you quite sure?"

She glared at him. "Richard. Of course I am."
Men, she had learned, could complicate one's life
dreadfully.

"Oh, very well," he said after a moment, handing
her the letter with bad grace. "But I warn you, I
can see no point in his writing to you after all this
time but to hurt you."

"Oh, Richard, do go away," she muttered, breaking
the wax seal on the letter. From David. Once that
would have sent her into transports. Now it inspired
only dread.

A few moments later, she lifted stunned eyes from
the paper. "Jennie wants to meet me."

"She has no idea who you are, then?"

"No, none, I told you that." She scanned the brief,
terse letter hungrily for news of her daughter, but
none was forthcoming. To meet Jennie formally, at
last. To be able to hold her and love her as a mother
should.

"And I suppose he wants you to go to London."

"No. He's coming here."

"The devil he is!"

"Yes. He and a party of guests will be coming to
spend Christmas. From the week before, until just
after Twelfth Night."

"You can't let him."

"How can I stop him? It is his estate." She
paused. "I'm only surprised he didn't come back before now."

Richard snorted. "He won't be welcome."

"He probably doesn't care, if he even knows."

"He'll be furious when he finds out, you know.
That you've been to London."

"I know."

"He might even manage to keep you from seeing her at all."

She glanced away. Oh, lord. A life with no chance of ever seeing Jennie again would be beyond bearing. "He has that right."

"Dash it, Tess, are you going to stand there and tell me you're just going to let him do this?"

"How do you expect me to stop him?" she demanded, finally angry. "You know as well as I he always did as he pleased."

"Yes." Richard sounded grim. "And what he pleased hurt you a dashed lot."

Tess concentrated on carefully folding the letter back into its neat creases. " 'Tis in the past."

"Tess, if he does anything to hurt you, I'll—"

"What?" she said, alarmed. "Richard, you can't do anything. Please. Promise me you won't."

"Dash it, Tess—"

"Promise me?"

He stared at her, and then, apparently no more immune to the expression in her eyes than her one-time suitors had once been, snorted again. "Oh, very well. But, mind you, Tess, let him say one word about you and I won't be able to keep my promise."

"I know." She had little doubt he'd keep it in any event, not with his ready temper. "Thank heavens it will only be for two weeks. I think—I hope—we can hold on that long. Now." She tucked the letter into her pocket. "I'll go up to get ready for luncheon."

In Tess's room, her maid was ready with hot water for washing, and a brush to repair the damage done to her hair by a morning spent mostly outside. Tess dismissed her, though, going instead to stand by the window and look blankly out at the garden, bleak and sere now with winter. Beyond were the eternal moors, the rolling hills that rose in folds and valleys of land, a painful sight at any time of year, but more so now. It had seemed so certain that she'd never see David again. Now, it seemed, she was wrong.

David. Just thinking of him brought pain. Thus she had carefully steered her mind away from any thoughts of him in the past years. Such difficult years they had been, too, especially in the beginning, when she had been so full of doubts and regrets about what she had done; when she had been so lonely. Eventually, though, she had achieved a measure of peace, and then contentment. She had even come to believe she was happy. Now she knew how wrong she'd been. Never had she been peaceful, not really, or contented. Never had she been happy. David's letter had brought that plain truth home to her by great force, even if she'd always known it, deep inside her.

The worst of it was, it was her fault the marriage had ended. Oh, her reasons had seemed good enough at the time, even noble, but that was before David had forced her to instigate divorce proceedings, thus negating all her efforts in his behalf. It was before she'd known there would be a child involved, and look where that had led. The very last thing she had ever wanted was to wish the same fate upon her daughter that she herself had suffered.

Well, it was far past mending now. Even if she told David why she had behaved as she had so long ago, she doubted he'd believe her. There was too much between them, too much time, too much hurt. She suspected he was no happier about the situation than she was, but Jennie, strong-willed Jennie, had undoubtedly forced him to it. Part of her couldn't help but be glad. The rest of her, though, was, quite frankly, miserable.

Sighing, she turned away from the window and went to the basin, splashing water that had long since cooled onto her face, in preparation for going down to luncheon. Once David and Jennie left, she would manage. She had before; she would now. She was much stronger than she had once thought. The real problem was posed by the two weeks surrounding Christmas, she thought, lowering the towel and looking at herself in her mirror. How she would survive them, she didn't know.

In London, David had received a letter from Tess, as terse as his had been, acknowledging his plans for the season. Warmer, more forthcoming letters had come from the people to whom he had sent invitations for the house party. The Duke and Duchess of Bainbridge would be coming with their infant son, along with the Viscount and Viscountess Sherbourne, whose daughter was just a year younger than Jennie and whose son was just an infant. Also present would be Lord Adam Burnet and his wife, with their baby daughter, Lord and Lady Walcott, with their son, Nigel, and Mr. and Mrs. Fosdyck. Jennie was delighted at the thought of having so many playmates. He wondered if she would be so happy if she knew that he also planned on inviting Emily Granfield.

Several days after deciding to spend Christmas at Stowcroft, he was admitted to the drawing room of Emily's home on Upper Brook Street. In spite of the address, it was not a fashionable room, he thought, looking about at the furnishings which had been stylish perhaps ten years ago. No one, however, could accuse Mrs. Granfield, in her gowns chosen more for comfort and practicality than for style, of being fashionable. Perhaps that was one reason why he liked her so much. There was no pretense with Emily, he thought, bowing over the hand she extended to him with a smile, no chance that she might lie or even dissemble. One knew where one stood with her. If he didn't exactly love her, well, he'd long ago found that emotion to be an overrated commodity. He liked her instead, and that, he thought, sitting across from her in a comfortable padded armchair, was more important. So was the fact that she liked Jennie. It was why he was seriously considering marrying again.

"I haven't seen you in an age, David," Emily said as she handed him a cup of tea, the closest she would ever come to a rebuke.

"Yes, well, I've been busy," he said, and went on to tell her all that had happened over the past few days. Emily's eyes opened wide when he told her of Jennie's request, but otherwise her face was placid. "I didn't mean to neglect you."

"Oh, I didn't mean that at all, David. But do you not fear that Jennie will be hurt?"

"Of course I do." His voice was grim. "She has no idea what her mother is like."

"Except that Tess never comes to see her."

David looked at her sharply at that; she almost sounded waspish. But then, he supposed even Emily would feel threatened at the thought of his former wife. "Emily, I've a favor to ask you," he said, setting down his cup so that it clinked in the saucer. " 'Tis why I'm here."

Emily continued placidly on with her needlework. Crewel this time, he thought. Emily always had some sort of needlework going, in contrast to Tess, who had been too lively and impatient for such things.

But he would not think of her now. "Anything, David. You know that."

"Yes, well, this is a difficult one. I'd like you to come to Stowcroft, too."

Emily looked up, dismay on her face. "Oh, David, I don't know—"

"I know it's a deucedly difficult spot to put you in, but I wouldn't ask if I didn't think it necessary. If Jennie is hurt, she'll need both of us."

"No. She'll need you."

"And I need you, too." His brows drew together. "I don't want that woman to get any ideas from my presence."

"Do you think she will?"

"I wouldn't be surprised. She's never married again, you know."

"Yes, I know. But then, I suppose that would be unlikely for a woman in her position."

He shrugged. "True. I still half expected it to happen, though. Since . . ."

"Since?"

"There was someone else," he said, admitting at last to a bitter truth that only his solicitor knew.

"Oh, David. What a terrible thing for you."

"I know. And for Jennie."

Emily's eyes widened. "You're not saying—"

"I don't know." He stared into the depths of his tea, cooling in his cup. "I never will, now."

"She doesn't look particularly like you, now you mention it."

"No, nor like Tess, either, if that's what you're thinking. I can't think of anyone in my family she resembles. Except in her disposition." He smiled. "My grandfather was like her. Logical, and stubborn. Once he made up his mind, he rarely changed it."

"David, is there any chance you can persuade her against this?"

He shook his head. "I doubt it. Even if I could . . ."

"What?" she prompted.

"I'm not sure I would."

"What!"

"She was bound to ask about her mother someday. This might be the best way to do it, for me." He looked up at her. "I've found myself doing things for her I'd never do for anyone else."

"Why?"

"She's my child," he said simply, and, placing the teacup and saucer down on an inlaid side table, rose. "But I can't expect you to feel the same."

"Oh, no, David, I care about Jennie—"

"But I can't ask this of you. It isn't right. I realize that now."

"Can you not ask your mother? I know you rarely see her, but—"

"No." David's face had hardened, and he paced to the window. "She is the last person I'd ask."

"Why is that?" Emily asked.

"We are estranged. We have been for a very long time."

Emily frowned a little. "But can you not make it up?"

"No." He looked out the window, though he saw little of the passing scene. "I've hardly seen her since I was a child."

"As to that, I rarely saw either of my parents until I was old enough to make my come-out. 'Tis the way of things, in our circle."

"So it is. But did your mother ever actually tell you she didn't want you?"

"David!" From the shock in her voice, he presumed she had looked up again. "She didn't!"

"Oh, she did."

"But that's terrible, David!"

"I shall not burden you with the details, but it's one of the reasons I've decided as I have about Yorkshire. Jennie needs to see her mother. As to myself . . ." He turned and gave her a strained smile. "I've managed to go on."

But he remembered every detail of that long ago, terrible day, when he had suffered the first of the two worst rejections he would ever receive. He remembered slipping out of the nursery with a painting he'd done as a gift for the mother he adored. She was beautiful and always smelled so fragrant, and on the rare occasions when he saw her, when she came into the nursery or brought him out for her friends to see, she always had a smile for him. This day, though, when he had gone to her sitting room, only to find her with a man he knew now had been her lover, no smile had graced her face, unless he counted the way she'd laughed when he offered the painting to her. The laughter had quickly vanished when he had accidentally touched her dress. *Get your grubby paws off me,* she'd said, and then, to the servant she'd summoned to take him back to the nursery, *get him out of my sight.* That was when he'd launched himself at her, told her he loved her; that was when she'd laughed again. *Don't be silly,* she'd said. She didn't love him, she never had. She'd never wanted him, or any other children, for that matter, but Stowe must have his heir. And then she'd told the servant to take him away again, and that time, he'd gone.

David returned to himself to realize that Emily was talking. "Excuse me, Emily? I didn't hear you."

"I said I cannot like it that you are going to expose your daughter to such an influence."

"Who?"

"Her mother. So." She had risen as well. "I shall go."

"I really cannot ask it of you, Emily."

"Perhaps, but you need me there. So does Jennie." She faced him, her chin set at a determined angle he'd never quite seen before. "I meant what I said. I do care about her."

"I know you do." He looked at her, frowning. "You are sure of this?"

"Quite sure." Her hand on his arm, she smiled up at him. "After all, 'tis only for two weeks."

"True." He covered her hand with his. "Thank you, Emily. I do appreciate this, more than you know."

"Anything I can do, David. You know that."

"Thank you," he said again, bowing once more over her hand. "You're a good friend."

"Always."

The warmth of Emily's response, and the way she smiled at him, went a long way toward easing his worries, he found, as he stepped down onto Upper Brook Street and began walking along, swinging his walking stick. If Tess had been exciting, emotional, passionate, Emily was a haven of sweet reason and comfort. With her beside him, he could get through the visit to Yorkshire. At the very least, it would give Tess warning that he had no desire to begin anything with her again. And, when he returned, he would propose to Emily. It was, he thought, high time he did so.

Immensely cheered by the idea, David strode toward New Bond Street. In spite of Jennie's request, he'd try to find her an angel for her collection, as he'd been doing since her birth. It was a custom that just recently had become special to them both. 'Twould be foolish to ignore it this year simply because Jennie had finally asked about her mother. Tess was not going to change their lives, he told himself again, firmly.

Quite determined on that, and that he would enjoy the holiday no matter what, David turned at last onto New Bond Street—and came face to face with the man he had always suspected was Jennie's real father.

Two

For a moment the two men were still, taking each other's measure, until the other man spoke. "Stowe," he said, with every evidence of pleasure in his voice, in his wide, ruddy face.

"Rawley," David answered, his voice clipped. "I can't say I expected you to be in town."

"Business. Looking into new markets for the wool crop, you know. And," he chuckled, "even we provincials have to visit our tailors occasionally."

"Ah." True, Rawley was provincial, being a prosperous sheep farmer on his extensive, meticulously kept estate near Stowcroft. Perhaps, though, his estate wasn't what kept Rawley in Yorkshire. Perhaps it was a person instead, one particular woman. The thought angered David more than he would have expected. "If you will excuse me—"

"Surprised we never see you in Stowfield," Rawley interrupted. "Your estate manager seems to be a good man, but happens Stowcroft needs the master's attention."

"My work is here."

For a moment, Rawley's face was blank. "Eh, politics, bain't it? Aye, and your daughter."

Had he imagined it, or had Rawley's voice actually

taken on a sardonic tone under the lapse into Yorkshire speech? Eyes narrowed, standing perfectly still, David studied the other man, looking for something familiar, anything, with no success. Not the shape of the face, not the hair, nothing. Jennie had hazel eyes, like himself, but so did many other people. The origin of the rest of her features, though, was shrouded still. "Yes. *My* daughter," he said. "If you will excuse me, I must go—"

"Have tha heard from our Tess lately?"

The question brought David to a halt as nothing else could have. Oh, he knew that referring to someone as "our" was only affectionate Yorkshire usage, but coming from Rawley, it was infuriating. "As it happens, I have," he said, and had the brief satisfaction of seeing Rawley's eyes narrow. Very brief. So. Rawley was apparently still in the running. Why that should matter, though, was something that puzzled him.

"She didn't tell me."

"Didn't she?" He smiled. "Then you don't know that I will be seeing 'our Tess' "—he laid stress on the last words—"within a few days."

Rawley's eyes opened wide this time. "Oh, aye?"

"Aye. My daughter and I will be spending Christmas at Stowcroft."

Rawley went very still "Eh, tha'll come for Christmas again, then?"

That one went home. In spite of himself, David stiffened. "Yes."

"What does our Tess think of this?"

David only returned his gaze. Not for a moment would he give Rawley the satisfaction of knowing that Tess's note had sounded less than welcoming. Apparently, she wanted this reunion no more than he did. He only hoped she wouldn't hurt Jennie. "She's looking forward to Christmas, I imagine."

"Oh, aye." Rawley looked away, frowning. "Happens I'll finish my business here, then, and return home."

Damnation. Look what giving into the temptation to goad Rawley had done. Now the man would be near Tess. Uncomfortably near. "Indeed. Your sheep must need you."

"Oh, aye." Rawley nodded. Odd, how fashionably he was dressed. David hadn't noticed that before. The coat was cut looser than fashion dictated, but still it had come from a master tailor. Why would a provincial like Rawley care about his appearance? "Silly creatures, sheep. Some will wander onto the moors in winter, no matter what you do." Rawley straightened, holding his gold-knobbed walking stick lightly. "I look forward to seeing you again, then. And our Tess, of course," he said, and, with a nod, ambled away, leaving David in tense, smoldering silence. Oh, no, the man would have nothing to do with his Tess. Not if he had anything to say about it.

His Tess? His brow furrowing with annoyance, David at last turned, striding on quickly, angrily. He had lost the desire to call Tess his long ago. Foolish to let Rawley get the better of him as he had, to get his back up over something that was essentially nonsense. Tess was a free woman, just as he himself was free. She could do what she wished with her life. Except where Rawley was concerned, he thought grimly.

Damnation, David thought again, and turned back himself. Bad enough that he would have to encounter Tess again, and at all times of year, the time that always resurrected his worst memories, even beyond those of his childhood. Bad enough that Rawley had, if David's suspicions were correct, played a significant role in what had happened seven years ago. Worse, infinitely worse, that the man would be there now. His presence would only make a difficult time that much more difficult. All the more reason, then, that David must be very careful around Tess, that he must not let himself fall prey to her wiles again. No, he was going to Stowcroft for Jennie's sake, he reminded himself. For that, and that alone. He would do well to remember that.

Rawley, however, would do well to remember something, too, David decided, muscles in both sides of his jaw clenching now. Tess was not in any way his. He would not have her. Of that, David was quite resolved.

At Harcourt Manor, all was in readiness. A fire burned brightly in the hearth in the morning room, which both Tess and Richard preferred to use in the winter rather than the chilly drawing room, as it faced south. Richard's old Border collie lay before the fire, head on its paws, and though the Christmas greens would not be brought into the house until Christmas Eve day, Tess wore a bit of holly pinned to her crimson merino gown. Last night the note she had been both awaiting, and dreading, had finally arrived. David and Jennie were at Stowcroft. They were to pay her a call this afternoon. At last, she would meet her daughter, with no subterfuge, no hiding.

Something quivered in Tess's stomach at the thought, but her hands, automatically sketching a picture of the fireplace rather than, as usual, a frock of some kind, were remarkably steady. Only the fact that she shifted in her chair from time to time belied her nervousness. What would Jennie think once she realized who Tess was? Would she hate her? Did she hate her anyway? No, she wouldn't think that way, Tess thought, momentarily pausing in her sketching and playing with the charcoal. Jennie, after all, was the one who'd asked to see her. That David had agreed was proof that he loved their child. The thought relieved her more than she would have expected. Of course he loved Jennie. He was her father, after all.

As she had the thought, though, she shifted in the chair again. She herself was proof that parentage often had nothing to do with love. Duty, perhaps, and sometimes not even that, but not love. She could have spared Jennie so much, if she had only realized, seven years ago—but there, that was well-trodden ground. Going over it again would solve nothing.

The sound of carriage wheels in the drive made her lift her head sharply and drop the charcoal. They were here. For the first time, nerves threatened to overcome her eagerness, and she felt an almost overwhelming desire to bolt upstairs. Instead, she stayed seated, to all outward appearances a picture of calm, as Bailey brought her a tray with David's card upon it; as he opened the morning room door a few moments later and intoned David's name. Only then did she jump to her feet, dread suddenly forgotten in a rush of eagerness. She was about to see her daughter again.

"Madam." David stood just inside the door, looking so much as she had remembered him, his sandy blond hair neatly trimmed, neither his frame nor his height above average, that for a moment she was disoriented. Suddenly she was young again, meeting him for the first time, the sight of him blocking all else from view. It was another Christmas season, seven years ago, and from the first moment she had been lost. She still was. Heaven help her, she thought, she was still in love with David.

David shifted position, and Tess suddenly returned to herself. All that was past. If she'd needed a reminder of that, she had it in the way he looked at her, so coldly, so sternly. The David she remembered had had an eager, open expression. Not so this man. One thing was the same, though. He was alone.

Disappointment, cold and deep, filled her. "Jennie didn't want to come?" she asked, though her throat was tight.

"Jennie is at Stowcroft," he answered, coming farther into the room. In spite of herself, Tess moved back a pace.

"But I thought—"

"You thought wrong, madam."

"You didn't bring her?"

"Not today. Not until we've discussed a few matters." He moved toward a sofa. "May I?"

"What? Oh, yes, of course." She waited until he was seated, and then crossed to the bell pull. He had changed. Studying him without seeming to, she returned to her chair. Older, of course. That was no surprise. After all, it had been more than six years since she'd seen him. Since he'd taken Jennie from her. No, she would not think of that, she told herself sternly, and returned to studying him. There was more to the change in him than mere age, though. He had a remoteness that hadn't been present in the man she loved, a coldness. His total absorption in whatever activity he undertook, whether learning about his estate, or meeting people in the village, or going up on the moors with her—no, she would not think of that!—seemed to have changed to a cold stillness. His face might have been chiseled out of stone, so emotionless was it, and the only hint of movement she could see was his breathing. Oh, yes, he had changed. Not for the first time, unease prickled at her spine.

"Bailey, tea, please," she said when the butler came in. "Unless you'd like something stronger? I know 'tis a cold day, and—"

"Nothing for me, thank you."

That cold voice again, as if he were talking to a stranger. No. Likely he'd be more friendly to someone he didn't know. Lowering thought. "Oh, that's right, you never did enjoy tea. There's coffee—but, no, you said nothing. I'm sorry." She smiled at him apologetically. "I still tend to rattle on at times."

His answer was a raised eyebrow. "As you say."

Daunting, indeed. She hoped he wasn't this way with Jennie. However had the child had the courage to ask him to come here? "Thank you, Bailey." This as the butler returned, bearing the silver tea service that had been in her family for years. "But, of course, you didn't come here to hear about me. Tell me about Jennie."

"She is a child. She thinks as a child and acts as a child. Except"—and here, he smiled for the first time, though it was a small smile—"she is perhaps the most logical, and at times the most daunting person I've met."

Tess lowered her teacup without sipping. "Really?" she said, intrigued. "In what way?"

"When she thinks about something, A leads to B leads to C. No leaping about for her. When she was four, she wanted a puppy."

"Understandable," she murmured, sipping at last.

"Yes. But do you know what her arguments were?" This time, his smile was broader. "She understood that a dog might be uncomfortable in the city. Thus, point A. We could set up a house for him in the garden. Which led to point B. A dog that lives outside would naturally bark at strangers. So, point C. He would protect the house from intruders. Point D. If he could stand guard at home, then he would be a good guard for her as well, when she went walking with her nurse. All leading to the final point, which was that I would be vastly foolish not to get a dog, under the circumstances."

Completely charmed, Tess had set down her cup and given up all pretense of drinking. "She would make a formidable opponent in Parliament."

"That, she would. Of course, being four, she couldn't quite counter my arguments."

"Which were?"

"That a dog who would be unhappy in London would be unhappier in our small garden, that his barking would disturb the neighbors, that if he barked at anyone, how would we know who was an intruder and who wasn't, and that it wasn't done to scare people in the park. And, if that wasn't enough for her, I was the father and I said no."

"Unfair of you, David," she said, relaxing, forgetting for a moment all that had passed between them.

He raised his chin, looking at her coolly. "Quite."

"Yes, well." Tess looked down at her skirt, to see that she was pleating it between her fingers. Judging by the creases, she had apparently been doing so for some time. "She does sound charming."

"She is. And, as I said, a child. Which means I do not look kindly on anyone who hurts her."

This time Tess set down her cup with a thump that made it rattle in its saucer. "And you think I would?"

"I think it possible."

"Not my child!"

"Your child?"

"Yes, my child," she said, thoroughly angry now. "I may have had to give up all claim to her, but you know as well as I do that it wasn't my choice."

"And you should know by now that after what you did I wasn't about to let you near her," he snapped back.

Now she knew what his anger looked like, and it was a cold, cold thing. It made her blink. "Let us not fight." She was suddenly weary. Once this man had meant everything to her. "I assume you came today for a reason."

"Yes." He rose and paced to the hearth, leaning his elbow on the mantel. She supposed that was an outward sign of his agitation. Oh, yes, he had changed. The David she had known hadn't kept himself under such rigid control. Had she done that to him? "I wanted to discuss the terms under which you and Jennie will meet."

"Very well." She nodded unsmilingly. Let him see that she could be quite as cool as he could, quite as rational. "That is fair."

"Thank you. I will not allow unsupervised visits between you and her."

"David—"

"I don't recall giving you leave to use my name."

She gestured impatiently with her hand. "Very well. Stowe. What do you think I'm going to do to her?"

"I put nothing past you, madam."

"That isn't fair!"

He tilted his head. "Isn't it?"

"No."

"As you say. No unsupervised visits."

"Very well." She sighed. "Will her nurse be with her, then?"

"Sometimes. More likely, I will be, especially in the beginning."

The weeks to come were suddenly fraught with danger. How would she be able to act naturally with Jennie, if David were present? "Very well."

"No visits by you to Stowcroft."

"You actually trust me enough to bring her here?"

"More than I wish to see you there," he retorted.

That hurt. "And if Jennie uses some of her famed logic to suggest otherwise?"

"I will not agree. I do not give in to her every request, madam."

She leaned forward. "David—Stowe—is she happy?"

He took a moment to answer. "I believe she is."

"In spite of the situation? In spite of everything?"

"I cannot make up to her for her mother's lack, of course, but I do my best."

That hurt, too, but she would die before she let him see it. She had so wanted to spare her child. Instead, she had brought so much upon her. "I am glad."

"Are you."

"Yes." She sat back. "Is that all, Stowe?"

"No. Visits will not last for more than an hour—"

"Oh, please!"

"—unless I feel that things are proceeding well. Then I will consider lengthening them."

"How generous of you," she bit out. "You might remember that Jennie was the one who asked for this, not me."

"Believe me, I cannot forget. Do you think I'd be here, else?"

"No." More weary than ever, she closed her eyes for a moment. "No, I'd not expect that."

"Good. So long as you don't forget it yourself."

No danger of that, not when he was so cold. The impetuous young man she had loved so deeply, so disastrously, was gone, replaced by this controlled man whose only sign of the tension that made her squirm in her chair was a twitching muscle in his jaw. "When will you bring her here, then?"

"Tomorrow, for tea. If that is agreeable."

He wasn't asking permission; that, she understood. "It is."

"Good. I believe we have discussed all we need to."

All except something which he could not possibly know. She considered telling him, and then, as he continued to look at her coolly, discarded the idea. If he knew beforehand, he would likely veto all future visits, no matter how much Jennie pleaded or reasoned. "I believe we have."

"Good." He waited until she had tugged on the bell pull again; waited until his hat and greatcoat with its many capes were brought to him. Then, nodding at her, he took his leave as abruptly as he had come, leaving her feeling battered and shaken.

David. Oh David, she thought, slumping down into her chair. She had known this visit wouldn't be easy, but she hadn't expected it would be this difficult. He was so different, changed out of all recognition. That he resented, even hated, her, she could well understand. She could only hope he didn't take out that resentment on their daughter.

Sighing again, she rose. No, not their daughter, not so far as he was concerned. Jennie was his, apparently, and his alone. Understandable, perhaps; he'd had her to himself since she was born. Understandable, too, that he wouldn't wish Jennie to see her, given all that had happened in the past. The fact remained, though, that she was Jennie's mother. He'd best reconcile himself to that. Nothing was going to change it.

She'd best reconcile herself to something, too. The next two weeks were going to be difficult, indeed. How she would get through them, she didn't know.

The trees along the drive finally thinned, and suddenly there was the house. Jennie leaned forward to see out the window, though her nurse, sitting opposite, clucked in disapproval, and she could sense her father's tension. Harcourt Manor, where her mother lived. After all this time, she was going to meet her. Oh, she did hope Mama would approve of her! Jennie knew, quite without bitterness, that she was not a pretty child. Even if she hadn't heard things said about her when people thought she couldn't hear, there were mirrors to provide the evidence. She thought her eyes might be nice, but nothing else was. Her nose was too big, her skin too dark, her hair, manageable only in braids, far too thick. Not the sort of daughter most people would want, she thought. No wonder Mama had stayed away from her for so long.

Jennie studied the house for a moment longer, and then sat back, hands folded on her lap in the pose her nurse considered meek, and thus proper, for young girls, but which now hid her own tension. Stowcroft had been a disappointment, apparently a welcoming half-timbered manor house on the outside, but inside dark and old and just a little musty. Harcourt, built of thick stone blocks, was even more forbidding, making her fear, more than ever, the welcome she would find inside. What if Mama didn't like her? Mrs. Granfield didn't, for all that she pretended to Papa that she did. Jennie could tell, from the smile that only ever reached her lips and the high, thin voice, as if Jennie couldn't hear her. Mrs. Granfield was also one of the people who had commented disparagingly on Jennie's appearance, though not in Papa's hearing.

Jennie didn't know much about her mother. She knew only that they didn't share the same name, which she still didn't understand, in spite of Papa's explanation. Once they had divorced, he had told her, Mama had not been allowed to keep his name, because he was a peer. If Mama disliked her because of that, if she was like Mrs. Granfield, Jennie didn't know what she'd do.

The carriage came to a stop. Jennie jumped down before the step was let down, in spite of her nurse's sniff and her father's reproof. Couldn't they tell how important this was? Too important to stay inside a carriage, fidgeting with her frock and squirming on the seat while she waited for Papa's assistance. She'd run up to the stairs, too, if she dared, though this time something other than paternal disapproval held her back. Now that the moment had come, she was suddenly reluctant to enter the house.

The front door, already hung with a pine wreath, was opened by an aged man, who bowed in response to Papa's greeting and went away, carrying his card. In spite of her nervousness, Jennie looked curiously around. But it was much nicer inside than out, she realized, much warmer, and not because of the fire merrily burning on the hearth in the hall. The flagged floor was covered by a worn, yet still colorful, Turkish rug, while opposite the hearth stood a small mahogany table, much burnished and polished.

Above that was a painting, a portrait of some unknown person. One of her ancestors? Jennie looked at it with renewed interest. When she'd made her Christmas request to Papa, she hadn't thought about having other relatives, but of course it was reasonable to assume that she did. Aunts, uncles, cousins—just the thought of it made her shift from foot to foot. Oh, there were people coming to Stowcroft who had children, but this was different. Cousins. Family. Until this moment, Jennie had never realized she felt the lack.

A door at the end of the hall opened, and the butler returned. "If you'll come this way, my lord, Miss Harwood is waiting in the morning room."

"Thank you," Papa said, in the clipped voice Jennie knew all too well meant he was angry, and, his hand on her shoulder, urged her forward. Excited, yet scared, she trotted in the butler's wake. What she had been waiting for all this time was finally going to happen. She was going to meet her mother.

The butler bowed again as he opened the door for her and Papa. There was a fire in here, too, and from in front of the hearth a dog raised his head in lazy curiosity, his tail thumping. Jennie had again the same sense of warmth and care as she'd had in the hall. This time, though, it barely made an impression on her. All her attention was focused on the woman who was rising from a chair across the room. She exuded the same sense of warmth, from the cheerful red wool of her dress to the equally bright red ribbon that bound up her curls. Curls that, Jennie realized with a sudden shock, she'd only ever seen hidden before. Because she knew this lady. Oh, yes, she knew her quite well.

"But—" she began.

"Oh, Jennie, hello," the woman said at the same

time, going down on one knee, her arms held out impulsively.

"But." Jennie looked up at her father, and then back at the woman. "But you're the angel lady."

Three

David's head jerked up. "You've met?" he said, staring accusingly at Tess.

"You call me the angel lady?" Tess said at the same time, smiling delightedly down at Jennie.

"Yes, because you're so pretty and you sparkle so. Like the crystal angel we saw once. Remember, Papa?"

"Yes," he said, though his jaw was clenched. Only Tess had this effect on him. Only she could make him so angry he wanted to yell, to rage. Yesterday he had nearly lost control of himself several times, which would, of course, have been fatal. Tess would be quick to pounce upon any weakness.

"Yes." She faced him now, her gaze opaque. "I have chanced upon Jennie several times in Hyde Park."

"Chanced upon?"

"Yes. Surely you have no strictures against my going to London?"

"Papa, what does that mean? Strictures?"

"Rules, dear." Tess smiled down at Jennie, but her gaze returned to David. "Restrictions."

"Why would Papa want you to obey rules?" She looked from one to the other, and her grip upon

David's hand grew tighter. He could almost see her mind following its logical path. "Papa, did you tell my mother she couldn't come to London?"

He looked hard at Tess. "What have you said to her?"

"Nothing, Stowe. Nothing of which you would disapprove."

"Yet, in spite of everything, you managed to circumvent me."

"Papa!" Jennie's tug on his hand was suddenly more urgent. "Is Mama not supposed to see me?"

He looked helplessly down at her. "Jennie—"

"Did you say she couldn't?"

"Well?" Tess said, cool, ironic. "Are you not going to answer her, Stowe?"

"You did, didn't you?" Jennie pulled away and stared accusingly at him. "But I thought—"

"Oh, Jennie." Tess had gone down on one knee. "Did you really think I'd deserted you?"

"Yes," Jennie said, and both of them, looking very much alike in spite of the lack of physical resemblance between them, turned to stare at David.

David's collar suddenly felt much tighter. "Jennie, if I could explain—"

"I'd never do that, Jennie." Tess got to her feet, still glaring at David. "What have you been telling her?"

David ran a hand over his hair. "Nothing."

"Don't be mad at Papa," Jennie said earnestly. "He didn't say anything. Really."

"I see." Tess's brow was wrinkled. "Well. Why don't we all sit down? 'Tis much warmer by the fire."

Jennie looked up, smiling, as Tess's hand rested on her head, and David's stomach twisted. "Damnation, this is all your fault," he said, his voice very low, as Tess preceded him into the room, Jennie beside her.

"Mine?" Tess watched as Jennie bounded across the room to pet the collie, who looked up suspiciously at such a greeting. "I don't recall that I wished to give her up, David. Or that I wanted her to think I'd left her." The accusation in her eyes made her look, again, uncannily like Jennie. "Yes, I went to London against your wishes, and I'm glad of it. I'd've never seen her, else."

"I've a mind to bring her back there, now."

Tess sucked her breath in. "You'd do that to her, only to spite me? I didn't think even you could be so cruel."

"Even I," he sputtered, following her as she turned on her heel and stalked into the room. "What do you mean by that?"

Jennie looked up, her face wary. "Papa, please don't get angry. It always gives you the headache. And please don't be like Katherine's parents," she added to Tess. "They always fight when they're together, too."

Tess sank onto the floor beside Jennie. "We're not precisely fighting, Jennie."

"It's all right." Jennie shrugged with a nonchalance David hoped was feigned. "I expected it."

"You did?"

"Yes. Since you don't live together, I realized you mustn't get along well."

That left both Tess and David momentarily speechless. David cleared his throat. "It's a bit more complicated than that, but—"

"Why won't you let me see Mama?" she asked, finally asking the question he'd been dreading.

Again, David had the feeling that his collar was too tight. "There were a lot of things that happened, once," he began, carefully. "It seemed like the best idea at the time."

"Oh." She looked Tess, whose head was bent. "Mama, did you—"

"Sometimes things happen," Tess interrupted before Jennie could ask the inevitable questions that would damn him for all time in her eyes. "They aren't what we would like, but there's nothing we can do about them."

Jennie looked unblinkingly at her. "What things?"

Tess shook her head. "Things you wouldn't understand just yet."

"Why not"

"Because they're not logical, and you," Tess smiled and touched Jennie lightly on the nose, "are a logical person."

Jennie smiled, finally, tentatively. "Will you tell me someday?"

"Maybe."

"Oh. All right. What's the dog's name?"

"Shep, even though he never was much of a herder," Tess said, and David sagged in relief. Now, why had she done that? One word from her, just one, and she could have ruined everything between him and Jennie. He rather thought he hated her for that. "You must be excited about Christmas, Jennie."

Jennie raised shining eyes to Tess. Odd, but she rarely looked at him that way. "Oh, I am. It's ever so nice to be out of town. Does it snow here?"

"Oh, yes. I'm rather surprised it hasn't yet, but I hope we have it for Christmas."

Jennie clapped her hands, startling Shep, who woofed. "Oh, I'd like that ever so much! Could we have sledding, do you think?"

"Yes, and I imagine the pond behind Stowcroft is already frozen over for skating."

"I've had someone check that," David put in, feeling very left out of this conversation.

"Thank you, Papa." Jennie's glance at him was no more than polite. He had a long way to go, it seemed, before he earned her forgiveness. "I never can do things like that in town."

"How do you celebrate Christmas there?" Tess asked.

Jennie's face was glowing. "We buy presents for everyone, those that St. Nicholas doesn't visit, that is, and on Christmas Day we have a big dinner. Cook makes a plum pudding and I help stirring—may I do that here?"

"Of course."

"Then at dinner it comes out all on fire."

"It sounds exciting."

"Sometimes. We don't have many guests, though, and no other children."

"No? Why not?"

"Everyone's gone to visit their own families. But this year"—she brightened—"we're having guests to Stowcroft, and there'll be lots of children. Some babies, and some my age."

"But how wonderful for you. You'll have a marvelous time."

"Yes, and this year I have my mother, too, like them."

David cleared his throat. "Speaking of Stowcroft, I think it's time we were returning."

"Oh, Papa, now?"

"So soon, David?" Tess said, rising, with the fluid grace he remembered so well. "But you just got here."

"You'll have a chance to visit again. Besides, I don't like the looks of that sky."

Tess glanced outside. "No snow yet," she said,

with the assurance of a lifelong Yorkshire resident. "Perhaps tonight."

"Oh, do you think so?" Jennie exclaimed, her face brightening.

"If it does, poppet, our guests will have a hard time getting through."

"Oh." Jennie's face fell. "I forgot about them."

"Well, never mind." Tess laid a motherly hand on Jennie's shoulder, and Jennie gave her that radiant smile again. "There'll be plenty of chances before you leave. And we'll visit together again tomorrow."

"Promise?"

Tess looked challengingly at David, her chin up. "I promise."

"With Nurse, of course," David put in.

"Of course, Stowe." Tess's voice was cool. "I quite understand your requirements."

"Good." He held her gaze for a moment, and then turned away. "Come, poppet. Let's go home."

"How did you happen to find her in London?" he hissed when they stood in the hall and Jennie's nurse was helping her into her coat.

"It wasn't hard. Of course I knew where you lived. From there it was easy to find out where Jennie was taken when she was brought out every day for her airing."

"Good lord." He stared at her. "You spied on us?"

"No. I waited for a chance to see my daughter."

For a moment, David held Tess's gaze with his, and then, not trusting himself to be civil if he spoke, turned sharply away. Outside, he took a moment, ostensibly to pull on his gloves, but in reality bracing himself for Jennie's inevitable onslaught of questions. He raised his eyes, and there were the moors, rising against the sky. Oh, he remembered those hills. It was there that, in spite of the cold, he'd taken long, rambling walks with Tess, talking and laughing and holding hands, when they were so newly acquainted and so besotted with each other. There, they had first kissed; there, they had tentatively touched and caressed and kissed again. And, there, on an unusually warm day, they had lain together for the first time. He could still remember the wonder in Tess's eyes, her awe as she looked at him. The wedding had followed very soon afterward. He still sometimes suspected Jennie had been begun that first time on the moors, until the doubts crept in again.

The thought brought him back to the present as nothing else could. Abruptly he swung into the carriage, rapping his walking stick on the roof as he took his seat across from Jennie. She kept her gaze trained outside the window as they drove on, so quiet that he frowned. For her, that was unusual.

"Jennie?" he said, when they'd been riding for a few minutes.

Jennie glanced incuriously at him. "Yes, Papa?"

"Did you enjoy your visit?"

"Yes, Papa," she said, turning back to the window.

"Did seeing your mother upset you? You can tell me, you know."

"No, Papa."

"Because, if it did, you don't have to see her again."

"But I want to!" she burst out. "She's so pretty and nice and—she's my angel lady, Papa."

"I see." He sat back against the leather squabs, cold bleakness settling in the pit of his stomach. Tess was winning her over, and the battle was barely joined. Battle? Nonsense. When all was said and done, Jennie would remain with him. *Two weeks,* he reminded himself. *It's only for two weeks.*

It was hard to remember that, though, when Jennie

addressed not another word to him the remainder of the ride; harder still, when she ran inside once they reached Stowcroft, and pounded up to her room. He stood at the bottom of the stairs, helplessly watching her go, and then turned away. Damnation. This was all Tess's fault.

Handing his greatcoat to a footman, he stalked into his study in the old part of the house and poured himself a measure of brandy, tossing it off at one gulp. Everything that had happened in his life, all the bad things, was due to Tess. Well, no, that wasn't completely true. He couldn't blame her for his own mother's actions. For hers, though, and for what had followed, yes, he could indeed blame her. Had he never met her, his life would have been much better. Even Jennie, much as he loved her, much as he would fight with every fiber of his being to keep her, had been at one time nothing but another problem caused by Tess. And all because, once, just once, he had acted impetuously, and had paid the consequences.

Sitting in his favorite leather chair, his crystal tumbler refilled, he gazed reflectively into the fire, remembering that long ago winter. Remembering, and aching in a way he'd thought long behind him. So lost in his thoughts was he that it took him a moment to realize that someone was knocking at his door. "Come in," he called, and the Duke of Bainbridge strolled in, bringing David to his feet. "Oliver." He held out his hand, smiling. "Did you just arrive?"

"Some time ago." He looked at David inquiringly. "Please, sit. Would you care for some brandy?"

"Thank you, no," he said, joining David before the fire, and David looked at his crystal tumbler, realizing that he'd risen more than once to refill it.

No more. He needed a clear head to deal with Tess. "You were still from home."

David's face darkened. "Yes. I took Jennie to visit her mother."

Oliver's eyebrow rose. "Oh. Did it not go well?"

"She has been meeting Jennie in the park," he bit out. "Knowing quite well that she's not supposed to."

"You still bear her a great deal of ill will, after all these years."

"Oh, yes. I expect I always will." He was aware of Oliver looking at him questioningly. *Oh, the devil take it,* he thought, and looked at the other man. "I never told you what happened," he said, his normally strict control loosened by the drink he had consumed.

"No, you did not." Oliver looked at the tumbler, and then at him. "If you'd rather not now—"

"No. No. I think I would like to. No one has ever understood why I acted as I did, ruining my career. I think I'd like someone to know."

"Go on, then. You know you can trust my discretion."

"Thank you." David looked ahead, seeing a time long, long ago. "It was just after my father died. I missed him like the devil, you know, he'd died so unexpectedly, and I felt odd being the marquess. Well." He took a deep breath. "I decided to tour my estates. Stowcroft was the last one. I nearly left it to the spring, you know. I wasn't sure I wanted to chance winter in Yorkshire."

Oliver glanced out the diamond-paned windows, glazed with thick, heavy glass. "I cannot say I blame you."

"I knew everything was well run here, but I had to see for myself. It was the family seat at one time, you know, until my grandfather built a house closer to town."

"Yes, I know."

"Tess and I met by chance, in the village. I don't think she even knew who I was at first, and still she smiled at me. She was alive, incandescent, spontaneous, all the things I knew I wasn't and never would be. And beautiful, Oliver. The most beautiful girl I'd ever seen, all dark curls and huge blue eyes. God help me, she still is." He looked up. "You know what London is like, Oliver. The Marriage Mart."

Oliver shuddered. "Lord, yes."

"All those overbred, spoiled beauties and debutantes who had never given me a second look clustered around me once I became Stowe. If truth be told, they were part of the reason I wanted to leave London for a time. But, Tess." He smiled, slightly. "I've tried being cynical, tried telling myself that she wasn't about to let a marquess escape her, but it's not so. I don't think she ever cared a jot about the title. She liked me, for myself. And I was captivated by her. Well." Another deep breath. "We fell in love, and married so quickly that her brother didn't have a chance to return from Leeds. He'd gone there on business. I don't think he even knew what happened until he did return. We had a wonderful few weeks together. The happiest of my life."

"What happened, then?"

David's brow furrowed. "I still don't know. She turned cool. I couldn't find out why, until she finally told me." He stopped for a moment. "I'll never forget it. I'll never forget what she said, her exact words. We'd made a mistake, marrying so quickly. She was really too young, she said, even if she was of age, and she had found that she didn't want to settle down so soon. She had her life to live. She didn't want to be a matron, before she'd had a chance to be a young woman. But we loved each other, I said." David stopped abruptly.

"And?" Oliver prompted, when the pause had gone on for a while.

"And? Oh. Yes. Seven years ago." He gave Oliver the parody of a smile. "Do you know what she did? She laughed. Love? What was that? Said she'd been dazzled by a handsome face—which is absurd, I've never been handsome, not now and not then—and, she'd admit it, by my title. But love? No, she never had loved me. She would, however, do one thing for me. She would go quietly away, with no demands upon me. It was Christmastime."

"Oh, lord."

"Yes." All the pain of that long ago time had flooded back. It was the nightmare of what had happened with his mother, only so much worse this time. "I was furious. Hurt, as well, of course. I returned to London and proceeded to take up with an older widow—thus the crim-cons, Oliver—and then I informed my wife"—he bit the words off—"through my solicitor that now she had grounds for divorce. It didn't matter that she protested that it wasn't what she wanted. I wanted to be free of her, the sooner, the better, and hang the scandal. I didn't care that I was destroying my career. I wanted never to see Tess again. Except." He looked at Oliver. "Except that she sent me a note a few weeks later to tell me that she was expecting a child. It wasn't what I wanted, I didn't want any link with her, but I wasn't going to let any child of mine be raised by her. I was in Yorkshire when Jennie was born, to take her away. When the divorce finally went through in Parliament, Tess had no right to anything of mine.

Not my name, my title, and certainly not my daughter."

"I remember," Oliver said quietly. "I tried to convince you not to go through with it."

David shook his head. "I had to. Thank God I came to love Jennie as I do." His Jennie, in spite of his doubts.

A log cracked and fell in the fireplace, and David started, brought rudely back to the present. "It was long ago. I thought it was all past. Oh, I knew Jennie would ask about her mother someday, but I never expected this. Oliver, I might lose her." And all because of Tess. *Damn her,* he thought, tossing off the remainder of his drink. Damn her for interfering between them, for not doing as he had decreed. "I should have known she'd do something like she did," he said bitterly. "She knew I didn't want her to see Jennie. But she had to go to London. I should have known."

Oliver's fingers were steepled. "There's something you're not thinking about."

David looked up. "What?"

"You've worked hard these six years past, to undo the damage of the divorce. People are starting to listen to you. You don't wish to risk losing their respect again."

"I can't consider that now." David's voice was clipped. "I've a more immediate concern. I cannot let Tess come between Jennie and me more than she has."

"However, apparently you can't keep them apart."

"I'm aware of that. But I will not let Tess charm her the way she did me." His jaw hardened. "She is not going to take Jennie away from me."

Oliver shook his head. "She can do nothing legally."

"Not legally, no. But she can gain Jennie's sympathy, and turn her against me. What better revenge could she have?"

"What will you do, then?"

"The only thing I can. Make sure Tess is never alone with Jennie." He raised his glass and stared at it in perplexed surprise when he realized it was empty. "Good lord, I've had too much to drink this afternoon."

"Not a good idea."

"No. I need a clear head to deal with Tess. And I don't know what I'm going to say to Jennie." At this very moment, she was probably putting all the facts together in her logical way, not yet knowing that some things defied logic. Lord knew what she'd decided about the separation between him and Tess. "I don't know how to explain to her that what I've done has been for her own good. I can't tell her that I didn't want her to be exposed to an unsuitable mother."

"Why not?"

David shook his head. "It will undermine Tess. I might despise her, but if I do that, I'll hurt Jennie." And he couldn't explain that he'd been something of a coward, that he'd hoped to put off for as long as possible her realization that he was the one who kept her mother from seeing her, because he hadn't wanted to see that look of disillusionment in her eyes that he had seen today. "Well." He set the glass down on a table that stood between the two chairs, and rose. "I shall have to talk to her. If you'll excuse me, Oliver?"

"Certainly," Oliver said.

David smiled slightly and left the room. The smile faded, however, once he was in the hall. What was he going to say to Jennie? Whatever he told her, he thought, climbing the stairs heavily, he knew he'd lost stature in her eyes. Nothing would ever be quite the same between them after today.

Carriage by carriage, cavalcade by cavalcade, the guests for the house party at Stowcroft began to arrive. The village of Stowfield was abustle as it had not been in a very long time, not since the marquess had made his initial visit seven years ago. No one quite knew what had happened between the marquess and Miss Tess, though there were those who said they'd of course known it wouldn't last. He was a stranger from London, wasn't he, no matter how long his family had owned the Hall? And look how quickly he'd found another woman. Happens he'd kept several mistresses during his brief marriage, and poor Miss Tess just hadn't known. No, depend upon it, they'd been well shut of him.

"And, depend upon it, there'll be scandalous doings at the Hall again, Mr. Frakes," the squire's wife said to her husband, the day after David's arrival at Stowcroft.

Mr. Frakes peered at her over his copy of *The London Times*. "With his daughter there? I hardly think that's likely," he said mildly.

"Of course not. Orgies and drunken sprees are quite in the ordinary way of things. I daresay you wouldn't find them in the least scandalous."

Mr. Frakes had returned to his newspaper. "Very likely not, my dear."

"Of course not. Of course you are not listening to me, but that's to be expected."

"Certainly I'm listening, my love." He looked at her again. "Orgies and drunken sprees at the Hall? Wherever did you hear of such things?"

"There, I knew you weren't listening." She returned to her tapestry work, a self-satisfied smile upon her face. "I had it from Mrs. Naseby. She is from—"

"London. I know, and if she even knows what an orgy is, I'd be very much surprised."

"She is the vicar's wife, Mr. Frakes. Do you think that spares her any knowledge of sin?" Mrs. Frakes managed to look scandalized. "Rather the opposite, I'd think. Vicars must hear any number of things from their flocks."

"And likely they don't share them with their wives. Really, Lobelia, you are being melodramatic about this."

"I hardly think it melodramatic to worry about the morals of this neighborhood. When I think of Miss Harwood—and why she is called miss again, when everyone knows she was married, is beyond my understanding—living among us every day—"

"You cannot blame her for what happened."

"Oh, can I not? A man does not divorce his wife without cause."

"As I recall, she was the one with reason. And it seems to me," he sat back, his newspaper forgotten upon his lap, "that she's never been quite the same since."

"You've always been too kind to her, Mr. Frakes. Too taken in by her eyes, I think."

"No, my dear, not a bit of it," Mr. Frakes protested.

"And now we have the *ton* about to descend upon us. Depend upon it, Mr. Frakes, they will be up to all manner of things. Why, Mrs. Naseby was telling me just the other day of what it was like to live in London."

"And if Jane Naseby ever moved in *ton* circles

I'll eat my hat," Mr. Frakes snorted. "Really, my dear, you refine upon this far too much."

"I don't believe so. And I hope, Mr. Frakes, that you will not expect us to be social to such people, because that I am quite unable to do."

Very much to Mrs. Frakes's surprise, her husband began to chuckle. "Oh, I think you are, my dear. I don't believe you'd miss this for the world."

"Mr. Frakes! What a thing to say!"

"Admit it, Lobelia. You would give your eyeteeth to see how Miss Harwood and the marquess behave toward each other."

"Well! Of all the shabby things to say! I might have expected such levity from you," she said, though she was already wondering if it would be so very bad to accept just one invitation, just to see for herself, of course.

"Yes, my dear, you might have." He rose, folding his newspaper. "You might expect this from me, as well." His gaze was no longer quite so humorous. "Whatever happens, once the marquess leaves, Miss Harwood has to live in this neighborhood. I hope you'll remember that, and try to make life easier for her."

"Of all things! When she has been nothing but a common—"

"Lobelia," he said warningly.

"Oh, very well," she subsided with bad grace, determining at that moment that they would accept any and every invitation to the Hall, no matter what protests her husband might raise. She, for one, would do all she could to safeguard the morals of the neighborhood. Nor would she be alone in such a crusade. Mrs. Lansdale wouldn't take such a deplorably humorous, or sympathetic, view of the situation. . . .

* * *

"Poor Tess," Miss Emery sighed, pouring tea into a cup so thin it was nearly transparent, and handing it to her visitor. "How she must be feeling, to have to face the marquess again."

"Well, I, for one, think he should never have returned," Mrs. Lansdale returned darkly. "I never did trust him. I do hope he shows no interest in my Sophia this time."

Miss Emery looked up quickly. Since the marquess hadn't shown the least jot of interest in poor, plain Sophia Lansdale during his first visit, it wasn't likely he'd do so now, either. Not with Tess, still beautiful in spite of a certain dampened spirit, present to give anyone competition. Though Miss Emery, like everyone in the neighborhood, wondered what had brought him back after all this time. "Perhaps he thought it was time to show his daughter the Hall."

"Oh, yes, poor little thing. Have you seen her? She is a very plain child. Her life can't be very easy," Mrs. Lansdale said, thus summarily dismissing Jennie from her thoughts. "How is poor Miss Harwood taking all this? Do you know?"

"Tess only smiles," Miss Emery said. Not for anything would she disclose to Mrs. Lansdale her suspicion that Tess was quite overset at the prospect of seeing her former husband again. Mrs. Lansdale was a neighbor, but Tess was a friend.

"Poor Miss Harwood is very brave. I am persuaded I would not be so calm were I in her shoes."

Miss Emery smiled, much as she had just described Tess doing. Mrs. Lansdale liked to think she knew all that was happening in the neighborhood, whether she did or not. As for Tess—well, no one knew quite what she was thinking. All Miss Emery was concerned about was that her friend not be badly hurt again. " 'Tis only to be a brief visit," she said, reaching for the teapot again. "Tess will bear up under it."

"Oh, of course. But we who are her friends must support her in this time." Mrs. Lansdale sipped at her tea, frowning. "I wonder if we should refuse, if we're invited to any entertainments at the Hall."

Miss Emery lowered her teacup, genuinely startled. "You're not seriously thinking of doing so?"

"I might. Let that man know what we all think of him."

"Well, I intend to go."

"Anne!" Mrs. Lansdale stared at her. "You wouldn't."

"Of course I would. Tess needs her friends around her at such a time."

"Of course." Mrs. Lansdale frowned. "And I mustn't deny Sophia her chance, should there be any eligible men among the party."

"Oh, no," Miss Emery murmured.

"Still, you must admit 'tis all very awkward. Poor Miss Harwood." She sighed. "If only she could have married again, but with what happened."

"We all know it wasn't her fault."

"Yes, of course, that man gave her cause quickly enough! But I confess, I do wish I knew just what went wrong."

"I don't know, Fanny, so 'tis no good asking me."

"Oh, I wouldn't, of course, even if Miss Harwood had confided in you?"

Miss Emery smiled slightly, raising her cup again. No, she had no idea what had happened to estrange Tess from the man she had so quickly wed, nor had she ever asked. It wasn't any of her affair. "Well."

She set her cup down on the piecrust table, gleaming from years of loving care. "I intend to give Tess whatever support she needs while the marquess is here."

"Oh, so do I. Nearly everyone will, I imagine." Her brow puckered. "I do wonder what Mrs. Reeves thinks of all this. . . ."

But as Mrs. Reeves was the wife of the only linen draper in the village, and as she had a son to educate and three daughters to marry off creditably, she could be excused for going to sleep that evening thinking only of the extra profit the guests to the neighborhood would bring.

Tess's thoughts weren't quite so turbulent as her neighbors speculated. True, having David so near unnerved her, unsettled her, but she was coming to accept it as a necessary evil. Really, he'd taken the news that she'd broken the edict of the divorce decree and had managed to see Jennie remarkably well, all things considered. Perhaps Jennie had talked to him about it; she seemed, after all, to have him wrapped about her little finger. Or perhaps he had simply decided to call a truce for this time, for Jennie's sake. Two precious days of the visit had already slipped by. After today, there would be only twelve remaining to her.

Thus she was determined to enjoy every moment spent with her daughter, even with the constraining, and sometimes daunting, presence of a chaperon. For Nurse, whom she had seen immediately was wholly devoted to Jennie, she had always a smile; for David, nothing more than politeness. How Jennie took that, she didn't know. Her logical child was self-possessed far beyond her years.

For all her maturity, though, Jennie was as artless as any child, chattering about the houseguests and the way they seemed to warm the old timbers of the Hall. Two viscounts, and even a duke. Tess would have been less than human if she didn't feel at least a twinge of envy at not being included in the festivities. Such could have been hers, if only . . .

But she had promised herself not to have regrets, she reminded herself, sitting straighter, aware that Nurse, for all that she appeared busy with her knitting, was actually a diligent guardian. Tess had no doubt that the woman reported back to David all that was said and done, as well she should, she reluctantly concluded. Were the situation reversed, she would want to ensure that her child was protected. Useless to protest to David that no harm would come to Jennie through her. He had ample cause not to believe her.

Still, had she not been punished enough? Her brief, constrained meetings with her daughter seemed hardly enough, especially when Jennie spoke enthusiastically of having other children around at Christmastime. Belatedly, Tess had discovered one of the pleasures of parenthood still denied to her: the company of other mothers, with whom to discuss the joys and trials children brought. Other mothers must, she hoped, feel the occasional exasperation her daughter raised in her, when she stubbornly refused to do as she was asked, for example, or when she asked questions that Tess just couldn't answer. What a relief it would be to admit to this. Yet, as matters now stood, she was as alone as ever she had been. She had yet to be introduced to any of the guests, and doubted she ever would be.

A fire was crackling cozily on the hearth in Harcourt Manor's morning room. Richard sat at a table across from Jennie, patiently teaching her the intricacies of piquet, his easygoing smile revealing that he was as entranced by his niece as Tess was. Outside the sky was lowering. There'd be snow by and by, but not yet, Tess's experienced eye told her.

"I do hope it snows," Jennie said at that moment, in an eerie echo of Tess's thoughts.

"Happens you'll get your wish soon enough," Tess said, eyeing the discard Jennie had just made. "Are you sure you want to do that?"

"Quite sure." Jennie sat very still, so like David it made Tess's heart break. "You're long on hearts, I think, but not so long on clubs," she said to Richard. "A decent club could beat you."

"Well, there you're out, infant," Richard said, laying out his cards and taking the trick. "Good observation, though. Play a little longer and you've the makings of a regular cardsharper."

Tess looked up from her mending, smiling. "Richard. Are you corrupting my daughter?"

"Not a bit of it," he protested. "Quite the opposite."

"Hmph. I rather doubt that." Tess bit off the thread she had been using. It would have been so easy to begrudge Jennie this contact with her uncle in favor of herself, but it was so obvious she craved family, in the way her eyes took everything in, in the way she sometimes looked, as if she were memorizing everything. Tess wondered if she, too, were aware of the passing of time. Only twelve more days. "Tell me. Who is at the Hall already?"

"The Duke and Duchess of Bainbridge. I like them," Jennie confided. "The duke frightens me, rather, he's so much, well—a duke! But the duchess comes from America, and she's very nice. Imagine, she says there are red Indians where she lived! Vis-

count Sherbourne comes today. He and the viscount-
ess have a daughter who's a year younger than I.
And Lord Walcott should arrive, too. His father's the
Earl of Braintree."

"Goodness! Such elevated company!"

"I suppose. Mama?"

"Yes, dear?"

"Will you come to the Hall sometime? Because
no one's ever seen me with you, you know," she
rushed on. "I don't think anyone even knows I have
a mother, and I'd so like—"

"Of course I will," Tess said impulsively, stretch-
ing her hand out to Jennie, and then, on second
thought, glancing at Nurse. Nurse might be warm-
hearted, but it was David who paid her salary. Uneasily she wondered if Nurse would return to the
Hall and repeat all that had been said here today.
Well, let her! Tess thought defiantly. She was not
going to lose this chance to be close to her daughter.
Lord knew if, once they'd left, she'd ever have another. "If your father approves."

"Oh, good! Because sometimes it gets lonely, you
know, when I see my friends with their mothers."

Tess reached out her hand again. "Oh, Jennie—"

"But a lot of them have parents who live apart,
too, so that's all right."

It wasn't, but there wasn't much Tess could do to
change things for her child. "So everyone will be
here, then."

"Yes. Except for Lord and Lady Burnet and their
baby, and Mr. and Mrs. Fosdyck, he's something in
government, and Mrs. Granfield. They're supposed
to come tomorrow."

"Who is Mrs. Granfield?" Tess asked absently, remembering again David's political ambitions, and
how her own well-meant behavior had ruined them.

"Oh." Jennie blinked, for the first time shifting in her seat and playing with the cards that lay on the table. "I thought you knew."

"No. Who is she, dear?"

"I'm not sure, but I think Papa wants to marry her."

Four

Over Jennie's head, Richard's gaze met Tess's, though she was oblivious. She sat very still, seeing nothing, feeling nothing. The numbness was not unfamiliar to her; she'd suffered it during other severe shocks. Soon it would wear off and she would be prey to a host of emotions she didn't even want to consider just now. For now, though, she had the blessed feeling of being wrapped around with cotton wool. "Oh. I'd no idea," she said inadequately. "He said nothing to me."

Jennie shrugged with a child's apparent lack of curiosity over such mysterious adult matters. "Maybe he will. Mama." She cleared her throat and looked up. "Why don't you and Papa live together?"

That one Tess felt like a blow to the stomach, so unexpected was it after the last revelation. "We found we weren't suited to each other. We were very young when we married."

"How old were you?"

"I was twenty-one."

"But that's grown up!" Jennie stared at her, as well she might. It was, Tess admitted to herself, an inadequate answer at best.

"Yes, but I'd seen nothing of the world, Jennie,

when I met your father. We'd known each other only a few weeks when we married."

"But I still don't understand."

"We married too soon," Tess explained. "We rushed into it. If we'd taken the time to think about it, we would have realized we shouldn't do it."

"Oh." Jennie's eyes were alert, making Tess dread what she would say next. Yet, she almost welcomed this discussion. As long as it lasted, she would be spared the exquisite pain of knowing that David planned to marry again. "Then it's not because of me that you stayed away?"

"Oh, Jennie, no!" Tess exclaimed, kneeling by her chair, reaching for her. "Whatever gave you such an idea?"

"I don't know." Jennie stared at her cards, though she was close against Tess. "I thought I'd done something that made you mad at me, that maybe if I was a very good girl—"

"Now, listen to me, Jennifer Mary Ann," Tess said sternly, holding her by both shoulders and looking down into her face. "I don't want to hear any such nonsense from you again. Do you understand?"

Jennie gazed solemnly back at her, and then suddenly smiled. It transformed her face from plainness to something approaching beauty. Heavens, but she would be striking someday, Tess thought in surprise, appraising her daughter through new eyes. Not a classic beauty, perhaps, but with her deep hazel eyes and those strong cheekbones she would be hard to overlook. "Yes, Mama." Jennie nestled her head confidingly against Tess's shoulder. "I understand."

I've missed this, Tess thought, rocking her child against her. *I've missed so much.* Soon, too, Jennie would have a new mother. Another mother, she amended. That hurt in a way she didn't want to consider. "What is Mrs. Granfield like?" she asked casually.

"She's nice."

Tess's eyes widened just a trifle at the decided lack of enthusiasm in Jennie's voice. "Do you like her?"

"Yes," she said again, with that same inflection.

Hm. Something odd was going on here. "And is she nice to you?"

"Oh, yes."

"Tell me about her," she invited, all the time knowing it was shameless of her to use Jennie for information on her enemy. No, she mustn't think like that. Not if the woman was going to be Jennie's stepmother.

"She does a lot of needlework."

"Does she talk to you?"

"She asks me if I'm behaving."

Oh, dear. "And is that all? Does she talk about what you and she will do together when she's your stepmama?"

"No."

"Has she asked you what you like to do?"

"No."

This time, exasperated by Jennie's brief answers, Tess did meet Richard's gaze, reading there the same belief she herself had. The woman didn't care two pins for Jennie. "Well. Perhaps that will change, once she knows you better." Curiosity got the better of her. "Is she pretty?"

Jennie shifted a bit. "Not as pretty as you, Mama."

"Well." Tess couldn't help being gratified by that. Not that it helped. "I imagine things will work out."

"I suppose."

"Of course they will. Your father loves you, Jennie." Tess drew away enough to see Jennie's face. "I'm sure of that."

"Yes."

"He wants only the best for you."

Against her shoulder Jennie nodded, and then was still. "Mama?" she said presently.

"Yes, angel?"

"Couldn't I stay with you?"

Tess's heart clenched. "No, angel, I'm afraid not."

Jennie wrenched away. "Then you don't want me!"

"Oh, Jennie, I do—"

"If you did, you'd want me to stay with you."

"I do want you! It's your father . . ." She stopped, appalled at what she had said.

"Doesn't he want me, either?" Jennie asked in a small voice.

"No, angel, that's not what I meant." She looked up to the ceiling, as if searching for guidance, aware all the time of both Richard, sardonic and yet sympathetic, and Nurse, an unknown quantity, listening. "Your father and I agreed, a long time ago," she began, choosing her words carefully, "that it would be best if you stayed with him. I rarely leave Yorkshire, you know," she went on, to forestall Jennie's protest. "We decided that in London you'd be able to see so much, and to meet other people."

"But it isn't fair!"

Tess smiled at this, a child's eternal protest, though it made her ache. It *wasn't* fair. It was, however, how things were. She'd come to accept that, if reluctantly. "All will be well, Jennie. I promise you that."

The clock in the hall struck the hour. Nurse cleared her throat. "Excuse me, ma'am, but . . ."

"I know." Tess rose, laying her hand on Jennie's head. " 'Tis time for you to go."

"I don't want to," Jennie said.

"I know you don't, angel, but we'll have tomorrow." Only twelve more days, she thought again.

"Why can't I stay?" Jennie asked again, a logical child baffled and battered by adults' illogic.

"Because." Tess kept her voice light. "That's why. Nurse will be wanting her tea, among other things."

"Come along, then, Lady Jennie." Nurse was all stolid practicality as she helped Jennie don her outer garments. "Time we were going."

Tess followed them into the hall, feeling bereft, forlorn. The hours until she could see her child again stretched out barren and empty. "Tomorrow, angel."

Jennie nodded, her head down. It was Nurse who stopped, Nurse who looked up at her, as though to speak. "Yes, Nurse?" Tess said encouragingly. "What is it?"

Nurse glanced quickly at Jennie, who had gone ahead with Richard and was smiling at something he'd said. "If I could be forgiven for speaking, ma'am?"

"By all means."

"She'll be taken care of. I'll see to it."

Tess smiled. "Thank you, Nurse. I appreciate it." She bent to receive one last hug from Jennie, who had waited for them to catch up with her, and then watched as the door closed behind the two, her stomach going hollow. Dear God. David was marrying again.

"There's trouble there," Richard said, standing beside her.

Tess spun on him. "And he accuses me of being selfish!"

Richard backed up a pace. "Easy," he said, startled. "Happens we might be all wrong about this."

"And happens we might not," she retorted. "What then?"

"Unfortunately, that's up to Stowe."

"No, it isn't. It's up to me."

Silence fell between them. "Are you saying you're going to fight this Granfield woman?"

"No, of course not." She gestured impatiently with her hand. "What will that serve, but to anger David? No. But I am going to fight him about Jennie."

He stared at her. "You never did before."

"I was a fool." She bit off her words. "Oh, aye, I didn't think so. I thought it was a losing battle. It still may be, for all I know. But if I don't try . . ."

"He's giving Jennie a stepmother."

"She needs her own mother!" she said in swift, instinctive denial. "I don't give two pins for what David does. It's how it affects Jennie that I care about."

He stared at her. "How will you do it? All the power is on his side."

Tess's chin was outthrust in a way David would have recognized in Jennie. "I don't know. I'll find a way," she promised. She had to. It was easier than considering the other, awful thing she had learned this afternoon. David was marrying again.

The promised snow had fallen, although only a dusting covered the landscape and it wasn't enough to impede travel. Now it was looking proper Christmaslike, people told each other. Cold enough, too, Tess thought, pulling her fur-lined cloak more closely around her as she walked through the High Street in Stowfield, with its shops on one side and cottages on the other, the following morning. The night had brought her little counsel as to how to fight David. She had learned, to her cost, that he could be stubborn, and so an honest, frontal assault was likely not the best approach. Instead, she would have to use more devious means. The problem was, the last time she'd done that, it had ended disastrously. During the long hours of the night, when she had been unable to sleep and had made sketch after sketch of new frocks, only to discard most of them, she had planned her strategy. This time she would have to think everything through, and take it step by careful step, if she were to have any chance of success. This time she must win, for Jennie's sake.

As for her own—well, that was best not thought of. The numbness that Jennie's news had brought her had begun to wear off, but Tess still didn't want to contemplate the welter of painful emotions within her. She would have to eventually, but not yet. Not yet.

Instead, she passed a pleasant time in the shops, looking at fabrics and matching them in her mind with the sketches she hadn't discarded last night. Though Jennie was here, she couldn't ignore her work. When her daughter left, Tess would still be designing clothes which Jeanette, the modiste who was her partner in London, would make up and sell under her own name. Even now, after having been in trade for all these years, Tess acknowledged wryly that it was an odd thing for her to be doing. It was a lifesaver, though, in its own way. It had helped her to find Jennie in London, and it was a marvelous distraction when things went wrong. It was going to be very, very hard to let Jennie, and David, go.

Fortunately, she had enough done that she could concentrate on her Christmas gift for Jennie, something that had occurred to her just after David had written to her, telling of his planned visit. It had

kept her busy planning and stitching for many a long
hour. The joy that this year she'd actually be able to
present her daughter with her gift sang within her.
No matter what else happened, she would see Jennie
this Christmas, she thought, stepping out of the linen
draper's, and stopped. Just down the High Street a
carriage with a crest upon the door had pulled up,
and elegantly dressed ladies were being helped out.
Oh, no. It had to be the party from the Hall.

Almost Tess turned and fled, so strong was her
aversion to meeting them under such circumstances.
At that moment, however, someone stepped before
her. She looked up into the bluff, comforting countenance of Adrian Rawley.

"Tess," Adrian said, beaming down at her as he
took her hand, and she relaxed. Here was someone
who demanded little of her, except for one thing.
She could rely on him. Facing the members of the
house party would be difficult, but at least she
wouldn't have to suffer the ordeal alone. "I was hoping to see you. I planned to come to the Manor this
afternoon."

"Oh, please do," she said, with more enthusiasm
than she usually showed, and saw his eyes light up.
Oh, no. Another problem to be dealt with. Now he
would think she was encouraging him, when that was
the farthest thing from her mind. Right now, she
couldn't think about that, though, not with the guests
from the house party so near. Some of them were
looking into the shops, she noticed, her fingers resting lightly on Adrian's arm. Others, the men in particular, were glancing about the High Street for other
sights, and she saw more than one look longingly at
the inn. "Did your business in town go well?"

"Aye, that it did. I found a new estate manager.
He seems better nor the last one. At least, he knows

about sheep," he said, and launched into a discussion of farming techniques that allowed Tess's mind to roam free. How fashionably the ladies were dressed, she noted, and how expensively, with a simplicity of design that only a skilled modiste could achieve. More than one, she noted with amusement, wore something that she knew could have come only from Madame Jeanette's shop. She'd have to tell Richard that.

For all his bluff, North Country ways, Adrian wasn't unobservant. He broke off his discourse on raising sheep long enough to follow her gaze. "They seem friendly enough."

"I wonder if they would be, if they knew who I am," she said. No one had seemed to notice her. She was just beginning to feel relief at that when David stepped from behind the carriage, a woman on either arm. Tess scanned them quickly. One was a petite, pretty blonde, dressed stylishly in a high-crowned bonnet made of beaver and a coat of blue wool with beautifully shaped princess lines, trimmed at collar, wrists, and hem with fur. The color exactly suited her, and its lines told Tess where it had come from. She turned her head to hide her smile. What would these fine London ladies think if they knew she had designed that coat?

The woman on David's other side wasn't quite so fashionable. She was older, and her three-quarter-length coat was more boxy in shape, disguising a figure that Tess suspected had settled with age. It was in a serviceable shade of green that, while not particularly unsuitable for her, did nothing to enhance her appearance. Nor did her bonnet, which had a coal scuttle look to it. Tess would almost have believed her to be someone's companion, except that, for all their dullness, the clothes were made well, with good materials. Nor would David be escorting a companion. "Who are they?" she whispered to Adrian.

"I'm not certain," he said, his voice as low as hers. "I believe the younger woman is the Duchess of Bainbridge."

"Goodness! She doesn't look at all as I'd expect. She's quite young, is she not?"

"Yes. The other lady . . ." He frowned. "Nay, I'm not sure who she is, though I've seen her."

"Adrian, you have moved in *ton* circles when you've been in London, have you not?"

"Summat, because of my relations. Why are you so concerned?"

"I don't know. I think knowing as much as I can will help me be prepared."

He shot her a look, but, as the others were approaching them, had no chance to answer. It seemed for a moment as if David would have gone by them if he could, cutting them altogether, and the insult of that nearly took Tess's breath away. At the last moment, however, he paused. "Rawley, Miss Harwood. I'm told that the ruins you can see at the top of that hill are of an old monastery," he added to his companions, preparing to go on again.

"Stowe," Adrian put in. "Eh, 'tis good to see tha back here. I'd be fain to meet your charming companions, think on."

Tess glanced quickly at Adrian, startled at this lapse into broad Yorkshire speech, which apparently served its purpose. David stopped. "How rude of me," he said, pleasantly enough. "Your Grace, Mrs. Granfield, may I introduce to you Mr. Rawley and Miss Harwood. My, er, former wife."

So that was David's intended! The shock of meeting her cushioned Tess from the insult implied in his introduction of her. Why had he chosen her, of all people? She was short, plump, and unfashionable. In short, she was everything Tess was not, and older, to boot. Older, of all things!

Sudden anger shot through Tess. How could David do this, after being married to her? How could he choose a creature whose features resembled that of a particularly contented cow? Without vanity, Tess knew that she, herself, was considered attractive. If she sometimes appeared frivolous, with her love of fine clothing, she knew she was not. It was an insult of the highest order that David should prefer someone like Mrs. Granfield to herself.

"Eh, I'm reet happy to meet tha," Adrian was saying, and Tess came back to herself. She couldn't very well show her anger, not here. Not in front of David. "Have I meet thee in London?" he added to Mrs. Granfield, and Tess watched in astonishment as he somehow managed to detach the woman from David's arm and engage her in conversation, leaving the other two to her. She had no desire to speak to David, however. Not just now.

"That is a lovely coat you are wearing," she said to the duchess.

"Why, thank you," the duchess answered. "Do you ever get to London, Miss Harwood?"

Tess shook her head. "Only rarely."

"Oh. And yet I could swear your cloak came from a London modiste."

Tess smiled in secret amusement. Jeanette did indeed sell cloaks of this design. "York isn't so very far distant. There are some fine dressmakers there, you know."

"Oh, of course. I didn't mean any insult, Miss Harwood. I do hope you realize that."

Tess took one look at the anxiety in the other

woman's eyes, and smiled again. "Yes, of course I do. Actually, your comment was flattering."

"Well, thank goodness! My husband keeps hoping I'll gain some town bronze, but I fear I'll always be hopelessly provincial. If you could see the village where I grew up! A tiny place, with only miles of forest between us and the next settlement."

"My daughter mentioned that you are from America."

"Yes." She leaned toward Tess. "Please don't tell anyone, but part of me wanted to cheer when I heard of the outcome of the battle at New Orleans."

Tess laughed outright. "I'll keep your secret, Your Grace."

"Oh, please do call me Sabrina."

"Thank you. My name is Tess."

"Miss Harwood," David's voice broke in, very cool, and her smile faded. So. He was acknowledging her at last. "Please share the jest."

" 'Twas nothing, Stowe." She looked at him with her chin up. "Something only two women would understand."

"Indeed?"

"Indeed," she answered, warily. Mrs. Granfield, distracted for the moment from whatever it was Adrian had been telling her, was studying her critically, making all of her defenses rise. " 'Tis a pity, in a way, that your guests are not here in the summer. There are some places hereabouts worthy of a visit."

"I am capable of entertaining my guests."

"Of course you are. Castle Howard is nearby," she went on. " 'Tis an astonishing sight. Unfortunately, the family is in residence just now for Christmas, so they would not welcome visitors. And that is, indeed, a ruined monastery atop that hill." She turned to look at it for a moment. "Only we call it a moor here, even though the real moors are farther north."

"Yes, your village is quite charming," Mrs. Granfield said, with just enough of a pause before her last word that Tess's wariness grew.

"We believe so. Stowfield may be small, but 'tis pleasant." She eyed Mrs. Granfield as the other woman had surveyed her. "Are you enjoying your stay here?"

"Oh, yes," Mrs. Granfield said, smiling placidly. "I've heard a great deal about you from Jennie."

"Have you," Tess said, relaxing in spite of herself at the mention of her daughter's name.

"Yes. She's a good girl."

Tess gave her a quick look. "Good" was not the word she would use to describe Jennie. "Yes, she's mentioned you to me, too."

"If you will excuse us, I believe the ladies would like to visit the shops," David put in quickly.

Tess stifled an urge to let out a hysterical giggle. It was almost farcical, David and his soon to be fiancée, facing his estranged spouse. No wonder if David were so uncomfortable. It served him right for bringing Mrs. Granfield here, Tess thought, and, as she did so, began to have the glimmer of an idea. "Of course—" she began.

"Eh, ladies, have tha seen our church?" Adrian put in. " 'Tis held to be a fine specimen of Gothic architecture, if a trifle small. Happens I'm something of an expert on it. If you'd care to tour it, I'd be reet happy to show you."

"Thank you, sir, I'd like that," Sabrina said, giving Mrs. Granfield no choice but to go along, too. She laid her hand on Adrian's proffered arm, and they strolled away, leaving Tess and David at last alone.

"Stowe, I wanted to ask you—"

"Was that your idea?" he demanded

"What? What Adrian did? No." She eyed him for a moment, seeing only hostility. "Stowe, about Jennie—"

"Are you going to marry Rawley?"

"And what if I am?" she said airily. "You gave up any say in what I do six years ago."

"As did you," he shot back. "But when it involves my daughter, I make it my concern."

"My daughter, too, or had you forgotten?"

"You also gave up rights to her six years ago."

"I had no choice! And I carried her for nine months. That makes me her mother—"

"In name only," he bit out.

She stared at him incredulously. So much anger, after so long a time. She wondered if she could get past it before Jennie's stay in Yorkshire was through; she wondered if he would ever relent against her. One thing she knew, though. A direct assault on Mrs. Granfield, gratifying though it might be, would only defeat her purpose. "I love Jennie as only a mother can," she said quietly. "That's something that will never change."

"Really," he said, his voice cold in spite of the anger boiling inside him. No matter her clandestine trips to London, to visit Jennie—and the thought of them still made his blood boil—Tess would never be, in his mind, Jennie's mother. It was one thing to see a child for an hour or two in the park, or to entertain her for an afternoon here in Stowfield. It was quite another to be with that child day in, day out, to see that she was adequately fed and clothed and had proper care, to listen to her talk, to hold her when she was sick and hurt. All that had been his responsibility, and his joy, for six years. He it was who had watched Jennie grow, who had guided her first steps, who answered her questions. Not Tess. There was more to being a mother than giving birth to a child. She needed to learn that, and soon.

"You put her up to that yesterday, didn't you?" he demanded.

Tess blinked. "Put her up to what?"

"She wants to stay with you."

"Oh, no. She didn't ask you that, did she?"

"She did. Your idea, I presume."

"No! In fact, quite the opposite. Stowe, I told her it couldn't happen—"

"Ha."

"—but you know how she is once she has an idea." Her smile was rueful. "She's a stubborn little girl."

"You've no right to encourage her in this."

"Stowe, I didn't!"

"I won't countenance it, you realize. To have her come here and be influenced by you and your paramour—"

"What!" she exclaimed, blinking.

"Rawley. I saw you hanging onto him. And the way he acted, as if he'd the right."

Tess had gone very white. "If what you're saying weren't so absurd, I think I'd slap your face for that."

"Why? Because I speak the truth?"

"We decided, did we not, that we have no say in each other's lives?"

"And I told you that where Jennie is concerned, I have the final word."

"I'll do what I wish, David," she said, forgetting in her anger to use his title. "I may even marry Adrian."

"Then you might as well resign yourself to never seeing Jennie again." His voice was quiet enough for him to hear her draw her breath inward. "Don't think, either, that you can come to London to see her in the park. Nurse has her instructions about that."

"Oh, I just imagine she does. You are a fool, David."

"Oh, am I."

"Yes. But then, you always were."

"Yes, I was, wasn't I?" he said, quiet again. "I married you."

This time, Tess looked away. Almost he regretted his words. Almost, except he knew them to be the truth. The only good thing to come out of his marriage to Tess was Jennie. "You never used to be this way, David. You never used to be so unkind."

"Times have changed, Tess. So have I."

"So you have. Poor Jennie."

"Do you imagine I'm like this with her?" he shot back, stung.

"I certainly hope not. And what of Mrs. Granfield?"

"We will leave her out of this, thank you."

"Why? You brought Adrian into it."

"He is not a person I want anywhere near my child."

"Adrian? Why, he wouldn't hurt a fly."

"Nevertheless. I don't trust him."

"You're jealous!" She stared at him. "That's it, isn't it?"

"Don't be ridiculous," he snapped, more annoyed than her comment warranted. "What has he to recommend him, a Yorkshire farmer—"

"While you're the grand marquess of Stowe."

He held onto his temper by a great effort. "It matters little to me what you do, Tess. Marry your farmer. Marry a shepherd, for all I care. You may laugh," he said at her reaction, "but I want better things for my daughter."

That stopped her. Tess's laughter died as abruptly as it had begun. "We've made a mull of it, haven't we, David?"

"I don't know what you mean."

"I think you do."

He looked down at her. "Why did you act as you did, the other day?"

"When?"

"When Jennie asked about the divorce. One word from you, Tess, would have destroyed anything that's between her and me."

She stared at him. "I'd never use Jennie as a weapon against you, if that's what you're thinking."

"Wouldn't you?"

"No. I couldn't hurt her that way." Pushing a strand of hair away from her face with a careless gesture, she looked away. "They're coming back."

David glanced past her to see Adrian returning from the church with the two women. "Then I will leave you," he said, and, bowing curtly, stalked away.

Adrian joined Tess as she watched David go. "What did you learn?"

"Learn?" he said. "Don't know what you mean, Tess."

"When you start using Yorkshire speech, I don't trust you, Adrian. I also know you wouldn't have left me alone with Stowe without a reason."

He smiled. "True." He turned with her, and they walked back toward her waiting carriage. "I wanted to find out if Stowe is serious about marrying Mrs. Granfield. If he's leaving the field open, that is. Her name is Emily, by the way."

"Adrian, for heaven's sake. No one is in competition for me, including you."

He turned the smile on her. "I can but try."

"Adrian—"

"Happens we'll discuss it at another time."

Tess let her breath out in a gusty sigh and shook her head. Anyone more persistent than Adrian, she had yet to meet. Except for Jennie, of course. "Well? Did you learn anything?"

"No." He stopped walking. "She's like a mirror."

"What do you mean?"

"Seems to be made of glass, but all she does is reflect back what she wants one to see."

"She didn't tell you?"

"No. Each time I so much as hinted, she asked another question about the church." He looked morose. "Never knew there was so much of interest in the place."

"Poor Adrian," she said, though she smiled.

"Aye. And what of you and Stowe?"

She shook her head. "Not so very much." Not for the world would she tell him he'd been the focus of their talk. "I must go, Adrian. It must surely be near time for luncheon."

Adrian consulted his watch. "So it is. Is there a chance I might be invited?"

"No," she said firmly. "I've presents to see to, among other things, and of course Jennie will visit this afternoon."

"I can but try," he said again, and she laughed.

Any amusement fled, though, as she headed toward her carriage, no longer enthused about the various tasks which had brought her to the village. All she wanted now was to return home and seek solace in solitude. Her emotions had coalesced into a hard little knot inside her. She knew what they were now: shock, certainly anger, and, above all else, pain.

David was marrying again. She didn't know how she would bear it.

There was one thing she did know, though, she thought, signaling to the footman who had accompanied her to carry her parcels. She was more determined than ever not to lose touch with Jennie. After all she had heard and seen today, that was imperative. Somehow, she would find the means to fight. Somehow, she thought, climbing into her carriage, she would win.

Five

It snowed again the next night, this time in earnest. Jennie awoke to a white world, made more magical by the hills and folds of the country, so different from London. With a shawl hugged tightly around her thin frame, she knelt on the window seat and stared with wonder through the frosty glass at the whirling, swirling flakes. Oh, this was just what she had hoped for, just what she had dreamed of. Snow for Christmas. She only hoped she could share it with her mother.

"Papa, I was thinking," she said, sliding into her seat at the polished oak table in the dining room, to have her breakfast. In general children took their meals in the nursery, but Papa had always relaxed the rules for her, so long as she behaved. He seemed to enjoy her presence at the table, and he never talked to her as other grown-ups did, about such silly things as how tall she'd grown, or her schoolwork. Papa took her seriously and treated her concerns seriously. So, come to think of it, did Mama. She was, she realized, very lucky in her parents.

"About what, poppet?" Papa answered, not turning from the sideboard, where he was filling his plate from pans kept warm by candles.

"About Mama. Will I be able to see her, with the snow?"

There was an odd look on Papa's face as he sat at the head of the table, his plate filled with eggs, bacon, and kippers. "I don't know. With the snow still coming down, I don't think we'll be able to go anywhere, even in a sleigh."

"Ahem." Williams, the butler, leaned over to pour Papa's coffee. "If I may say something, sir?"

Papa looked up. "Go on, Williams."

"They are saying in the servants' room that the snow will end before noon. You may be able to get out in the sleigh."

"And you consider this to be reliable, Williams?"

"I've found, sir, that these Yorkshire people generally know what will happen with the weather."

"Hm. Thank you. That is good to know."

"Oh, good!" Jennie bounced in her chair. "It's beyond wonderful."

"Good morning, Stowe, Jennie," a musical voice said in the doorway, and in came the Duchess of Bainbridge, trailed by the duke. He looked bemused, as Jennie had noticed he sometimes did with his wife. She didn't quite understand that, as she found the duke to be rather a forbidding man, tall and dark and given to making pronouncements, but the duchess didn't seem to be overawed by him at all. "What is your wonderful news?"

"Williams has just told us the snow should end by noontime and we can go in the sleigh to Harcourt."

The duke, sitting near to Papa, sent him a look Jennie didn't quite understand. The duchess, however, was smiling. "But that is good news. It also means that the rest of us can go out in the snow. Is the pond frozen yet, do you know, Stowe?"

"I believe it is," Papa said, taking a sip of coffee. "As soon as the snow ends I'll have it cleared for skating. There's also a hill for sledding."

"Good morning." Several more voices came from the doorway, and Mrs. Granfield walked in, with Lord and Lady Sherbourne walking behind. Mrs. Granfield sat beside Papa, smiling impartially at everyone. She always asked about one's schoolwork, Jennie thought.

"Did I hear someone mention sledding?" Lady Sherbourne said. She, too, was sitting down, and like Mrs. Granfield was contenting herself with only a slice of toast from the rack upon the table and a cup of tea.

"I hope so." Lord Sherbourne returned to the table, his plate as full as Papa's. "Pamela has been beside herself all morning, wanting to go out." He cocked his head toward his wife. "I can't imagine where she gets her energy from."

"But it will be fun," the viscountess said. "You and she will be able to play together, Jennie."

"Oh." For the first time, Jennie's spirits fell. "But I am supposed to visit my mother."

"Oh, dear." The viscountess gazed sympathetically at her. "That is a problem."

"Surely you can miss one day, dear?" Mrs. Granfield said.

Jennie didn't even look at her. "Papa," she said, suppressed excitement in her voice at the idea that had just come to her. "Why can't we bring Mama here?"

That same strange look passed over Papa's face. "I'm not sure that's a good idea, Jennie."

"Why not? She'd enjoy it, Papa, I know she would."

"Perhaps she would feel uncomfortable, dear," Mrs. Granfield said, and silence fell over the room.

"Why?" Jennie asked, directly challenging her.

Mrs. Granfield didn't look at her, though Papa, Jennie noticed, was frowning. "I only meant that I wonder if she feels the cold."

"Of course," Lady Sherbourne said. "We all rather thought that was what you meant."

"Ariel," Lord Sherbourne warned, in the kind of voice Papa used when he was about to scold.

"Mama's not such a poor honey," Jennie said scornfully, ignoring the adults. "She grew up here. She's used to snow."

"Of course she is," the duchess said in unexpected support. "You miss your mother, don't you, Jennie?"

An unwanted lump caught at Jennie's throat. "Yes, Your Grace, I do."

"Sabrina," the duke murmured, though Jennie didn't know why.

"Well, 'tis only natural, Oliver." The duchess looked at her husband. "And I do think that being out of doors will be enjoyable, for us and the children."

"If I go to Harcourt, Papa, I imagine we'll go out, too. Only I won't have Pamela to play with, or anyone else." And no one would see that she did, indeed, have a mother. Nothing had been said about inviting Mama to Stowcroft, not even for the Christmas ball Papa was planning. It wasn't what Jennie had expected when she'd learned, not only that she'd be seeing her mother, but that there'd be a house party with other children. Oh, she visited Mama, yes, but Mama wasn't there in the morning, to kiss her and greet her, or to run to during the day, or to tuck her into bed at night. Mama was, Jennie thought, that lump forming in her throat again, still too far away from her. "Papa." She turned to him for one last appeal. "Please let's bring Mama here. Please?"

Papa glanced at her, and then about the table. "Oh, very well," he said finally, making Jennie again bounce in her chair with happiness. "If the roads are passable enough for the sleigh, we'll send for her."

After breakfast, the guests moved out into the hall, each to go to their various activities. "Jennie, dear," Emily called, and Jennie turned. "I fear I owe you an apology."

Jennie looked up at the people ascending the stairs, some going about the drawing room, others to the nursery to be with their children. She was supposed to play with Pamela this morning, not with Mrs. Granfield, whom she hadn't trusted since she'd overheard that remark about her looks. Courtesy and politeness, however, ingrained in her since birth, made her turn back, no matter how much she wanted to go. "Yes, Mrs. Granfield?"

"About what I said about your mother, dear."

"Mama?" Jennie looked up in puzzlement. "That doesn't bother me."

"I am so glad." Mrs. Granfield smiled, making Jennie tense. For some reason, she was more uneasy when this woman smiled. "You care a great deal about your mother, don't you?"

"Oh, I do," Jennie said earnestly, and then risked a look up at the woman. "Do you mind?"

"Oh, gracious, no, child," she said, her face still wearing that pleasant smile, though Jennie didn't relax. She didn't like being called "child" in that way, but what could she do about it? "I expect 'tis only natural."

"But you and Papa . . ." She stuttered to a stop,

and began again. "But if you become my stepmama, won't you mind then?"

"I shall try very hard not to." Her smile broadened, and Jennie tensed even more. "I realize her importance to you. That is why I was so afraid you'd taken offense just now. Especially with what she did."

Jennie frowned. "What did Mama do?"

"Oh, dear. Don't you know?"

"What?"

"That she divorced your father, of course."

It hit Jennie like a thunderbolt. "My parents divorced each other. Papa told me."

"Oh, dear." Mrs. Granfield looked disturbed, her brows puckered. There was, however, an odd note in her voice. "I have put my foot into it. I thought you knew."

"What?" Jennie demanded. "Tell me."

"Oh, dear," Mrs. Granfield said yet again, glancing away for a moment. "I thought you knew that when a couple divorces, it's because one person has asked for it."

"No!" Jennie exclaimed involuntarily. "My mother wouldn't do such a thing."

"Jennie, dear." Mrs. Granfield rested her hand on Jennie's head, and Jennie pulled away. "I am so sorry to have been the one to tell you. Do but ask your father. He'll explain."

"But Mama wouldn't do that to me."

"I'm sorry, Jennie," she said, but, even through her distress, Jennie heard that odd note in her voice again. She wasn't sorry at all, she thought, and at that moment, decided she didn't like Mrs. Granfield.

"I will talk to my papa about it," she said, and, back straight, turned and walked to the stairs without even asking to be excused. Not for anything would she let Mrs. Granfield know how upset she was. She wouldn't believe what she'd just been told until she'd talked to her father. He was the one person she could be absolutely sure of in her life.

As for Mrs. Granfield becoming her step-mama. . . . Jennie's stomach sank. How was she going to bear it? Something would have to be done. Just now, though, she had no idea what.

That afternoon, most of the guests went out to enjoy the snow. Only Emily had elected to stay within by the fire, this time with some knitting. David, leaning against a tree, watched the scene with some detachment. Some of the children were too young to be out in such conditions, but Sherbourne and his daughter were busily engaged building a snowman, aided by Master Nigel Walcott. To one side, the Duchess of Bainbridge held her baby son, so well wrapped against the cold that he resembled a little round ball. Earlier the duke had scraped up snow for the baby to touch, and now the child surveyed everything through wide, wondering blue eyes, including the startling sight of his usually dignified father caroming down the hill on a sled. Few other adults had chosen sledding, but were instead on the lake, some skating in pairs, others showing off fancy, stylistic moves. And, closer to him, Tess frolicked in the snow with Jennie.

The sight made him frown. Earlier, Jennie had seemed preoccupied about something, but now she was as carefree as a child should be. He had to admit that Tess was good with the child. She brought Jennie out, made her laugh in a way that he himself could rarely do. It didn't seem fair. He'd had the care of Jennie for six years, and almost overnight it seemed she'd transferred her allegiance to this un-known woman. Laughter wasn't necessarily so important, though. Anyone could entertain a child for a few hours. It was another matter altogether to bring that child up.

Just now the two of them were throwing snowballs at each other, stumbling over hidden hollows and laughing breathlessly in their efforts to escape having snow go in their faces or down their backs. It was nothing so organized as a fight; neither was taking the time to pack snow together or to aim with any accuracy. Rather, they were just enjoying the moment.

One of the others called to David, making him turn away. The next moment, snow landed on his head, falling uncomfortably chill onto his neck and melting down his back beneath his shirt. Startled, he twisted back to see Tess standing still, her mittened hands covering her mouth but her eyes, above, sparkling. "Stowe, I'm sorry," she called. "I truly didn't mean that to hit you. I was aiming at Jennie."

David didn't answer. Instead, seized by an impulse toward mischief such as he hadn't felt in years, he bent down and scooped up some snow, packing the soft, powdery stuff as well as he could into a small, compact missile.

Tess eyed him with misgiving. "What are you doing—no, don't!" This as he strode toward her with as much dignity as calf-high snow would allow him. She turned and began clumsily to run, laughing, and he found himself grinning, for the first time enjoying the snow quite as much as his guests.

"You deserve it," he called. It wasn't going to be much of a contest; the snow might hamper everyone, but Tess was further impeded by her skirts and by the fact that his legs were longer than hers. Within a few paces, he could have thrown the snowball at her with deadly accuracy, but that wouldn't do. He wouldn't be satisfied until she, too, felt cold wetness trickling down her back.

Tess twisted around to see how close he was, and at that moment stumbled on something covered by the snow, a branch, perhaps, or a rock. Instinctively he reached out to grab her, to break her fall, but it was too late. Already her forward momentum was unstoppable. Before David quite realized what was happening, he, too was falling, his arms about Tess's waist, her hair uncomfortably close to his face. What happened next was, perhaps, inevitable. They landed on the ground with him partially atop her. Tess had a growing awareness in her eyes, and suddenly he was struck by memory. The last time this had happened, seven years ago, he had kissed her, again and again, right there in the snow, and he wanted to do so again. Oh, how he wished to. God help him. After all that had happened, despite all he knew of her, he was still attracted to this woman.

A few feet away Jennie bent double, convulsed with laughter. Oh, this was wonderful! She'd never seen her father like this, so playful, so free. And Mama—Mama looked so pretty, with her cheeks pink from the cold and her eyes bright. Mrs. Granfield couldn't be right in what she'd said. Mama and Papa looked so right, so perfect together, that it was harder than ever for her to understand just why they were separated. It was hard to understand why they weren't still married.

Maybe they didn't realize it themselves, Jennie thought, watching them. Maybe they needed help in doing so, help that she could give. Thus it was that the wondrous idea came to her, making her go utterly still. Somehow, some way, she would bring her parents back together.

* * *

Tess, lying in the snow, blinked up at David. "Stowe?" she said uncertainly. There was a look in his eyes she hadn't seen there in many a year. It startled her. It also put her on her guard.

"My apologies." David sounded surprisingly normal as he levered himself upright. "I meant to save you from a fall, not make matters worse."

"You didn't." She was strangely composed, all things considered. Oh, she might be short of breath and uncomfortably damp, but she was elated in a way she hadn't been since—when? Since she had reluctantly and impulsively told David she didn't love him, she thought in astonishment. "I—thank you for trying."

He nodded, releasing her at last and stepping back. Already his expression was more remote, but she was certain she hadn't imagined it, that look in his eyes, that awareness. *Goodness!* She dusted herself off quite as if nothing of moment had happened, not looking at him. "You're quite welcome. Now, if you will excuse me, I need to see to my guests' comfort, for when they return to the Hall."

"Of course," she said, watching him go, feeling her heartbeat return to normal. It had been an exhilarating moment, but of course that was all it could ever be. Just a moment. David no longer had any affection for her. She would do well to remember that.

Jennie now stood beside her, dancing under her hand, unusual in her normally self-contained daughter. "Oh, that was beyond all things grand!"

"Was it, Jennie?" she asked absently.

"Yes! When I saw you and Papa falling—Mama, I never saw him act like that before."

"He used to." Tess focused on her. "Is he always so serious, then?"

"Yes, most of the time."

"Oh, dear." She had done that to him, she realized. It was another of the long list of sins for which she needed to atone. It didn't make matters easier for her. Still, she thought, suddenly falling back into the snow to show Jennie how to make a snow angel, she would not give up her fight. For Jennie's sake, she couldn't.

Amid much laughter and more throwing of snowballs, the guests had trooped their way back to the Hall and were going inside. Clearly this was the time for her to leave, Tess thought, and was glancing around for a footman to call for the sleigh, when a small hand caught hers. "Come inside, Mama, and see my room," Jennie said, her eyes sparkling, her cheeks pink with the cold and exertion.

"Oh, Jennie, I can't," Tess said, and just like that saw the sparkle drain out of her child. "I must return home."

"But I want you to." She looked up, her gaze clear and innocent. "Will Uncle Richard mind?"

"No, but your father might."

"Not if I ask him. Papa." Jennie grasped David's sleeve as he started to walk by her. "You don't mind if Mama comes to see my room, do you? Because it would only be for a moment. It isn't as if she's staying for tea."

Tess looked up at David, and for a moment rueful acknowledgment of their daughter's logical mind, and the problems it could pose, passed between them. "If you'd rather I didn't—" she began.

"No, come in," he interrupted, and turned away. "It will only be for a moment."

"There!" The sparkle was back in Jennie's face. "I told you, Mama."

"So you did." Her mouth quirking in wry amusement, Tess took Jennie's hand again, nodded at a startled Williams, and stepped once again into Stowcroft Hall.

It seemed so very long since she had lived here, and yet it also seemed like yesterday, so clear were her memories of that long ago Christmas. She glanced with fondness at the burnished paneled walls and the low-beamed plaster ceilings, and then determinedly looked away. The past was past.

Upon the flagstone floor, guests were already being divested of their damp outer garments. Tess turned to let a maid help her out of her cloak, and, after a moment, the morning room door opened. Into the hall stepped Emily Granfield.

For one startled moment silence lay between them, until Jennie spoke, drawing near to Tess as she did so. "Mrs. Granfield." Her voice was unnaturally high, Tess thought, and frowned. "This is my Mama, and she's coming up to see my room."

"Why, how nice, Jennie," Emily said. "I do hope you straightened it this morning?"

Cat, Tess thought, bristling both at Emily's arch tone and what she had said. She obviously did not know what mattered to a child. How could she possibly be a mother to Jennie?

"Yes." Jennie, already pounding up the stairs, said carelessly over her shoulder, "Mama, will you stay for tea afterward?"

"Now, Jennie, enough." Time to be firm, she thought. In her effort to make up all the lost years to her child, she had been rather lax, she supposed.

"You know that won't be possible unless your father invites me."

"This is all so very awkward," Emily murmured, bringing Tess's gaze back to her in surprise. "For you as well as for me, I suppose, being in this house again."

"Yes, it is, rather," Tess said, aware that there were others nearby to overhear this conversation, aware that there was so little she knew of her rival. Rival? For Jennie's affections, of course. David, she had lost long ago.

"Still, I shall do all I can to make you comfortable."

Why, the nerve of her! She talked as if she were already the mistress of the house, when that had once been Tess's role. Yet, she likely soon would be, and might even do her job well. Her expression was warm, her bearing resembled nothing so much as a pouter pigeon. Why, she was matronly, almost motherly, Tess realized for the first time. Not at all who she would have expected David to choose, judging by prior experience, but what he apparently wanted. Again, she felt insulted. "Thank you."

"I suppose you do not often come to London."

"Actually, I do occasionally," she said, and had the guilty pleasure of seeing Emily's rather shallow blue eyes cloud over. *Good.* She would also continue to travel there, no matter what David thought. She might never be allowed to see Jennie as freely as she had in the past, but perhaps something could be arranged about visits. She would have to keep meeting with Jeanette occasionally, as well. Nothing would keep her from that, not when it might be all she had left.

"I've met Mama in the park," Jennie had returned

downstairs and now clung to Tess's hand, uniting them against the interloper.

"Have you, indeed," Emily said.

Ah. Another reason for Jennie not to care for Mrs. Granfield. The woman clearly was not that interested in what she had to say, judging by her reaction; surprised though she obviously was, it was Tess at whom Mrs. Granfield looked, not Jennie. This was not good. Tess's dislike of the woman grew. Something would have to be done about this.

Jennie's tug on her hand brought Tess back to a sense of her surroundings, and the knowledge that the pause since Emily had spoken had been overlong. "Yes. If you'll excuse me, I really should see Jennie up to Nurse."

"Jennie is quite a big girl. I am persuaded she can reach her room alone. Do join us."

Join them, indeed! As if Emily had the right to invite her. "I must claim a prior engagement. Remember, I did promise Jennie I'd see her room." She smiled down at her daughter. "I wonder if I could share your tea, Jennie?"

Jennie's rare, radiant smile burst upon her face. "Oh, yes! That is, if Nurse doesn't mind."

"Of course."

"Of course," Emily chimed in. "Do enjoy yourself."

"Thank you, we shall," Tess said, and turned with Jennie to the stairs at last.

In the hallway, as aware of the others about her as Tess had been, Emily watched her rival climb the stairs, the face that she knew was too round for real beauty still wearing a calm expression. So. She now knew more about the woman David had once preferred, and it was daunting. Emily had heard tales of her beauty, but they were nothing against the truth of huge blue eyes and dark, dancing curls, with a porcelain complexion that just now had been rosy from the cold. She herself was only too aware of the defects of her own appearance; life had seen to that. She was too short, too plump, and her face perpetually wore a docile look that only she knew hid her real nature. Always she had been relieved, and just a little chagrined, that her family had not seen fit to give her a season, instead arranging a marriage for her when she was just out of the schoolroom, to a man vastly older than she. George had been estimable, that was certain, and a decent enough husband, but he had far preferred his horses and his hounds and his port to a young wife who, appearances to the contrary, would have liked to dance the soles out of thin satin slippers every night; to a woman who would have given all her love to him, and that passionately, had he only taken the time to notice her.

Granfield's death had, on first appearances, freed her, until she had learned both that she had less of an inheritance than she had supposed, and that life in London was far more expensive than in the country. Not for her, then, the gay round of parties and assemblies and balls. She was lucky if she were invited to the occasional dinner or soirée. It was vastly frustrating. She might as well have stayed in the country.

Then, one evening, she had somehow been seated next to Stowe at dinner, a prize indeed, and one she was persuaded had fallen into her lap by chance. Since she had been brought up in a political atmosphere, in a large, contentious family that was never shy about airing its opinions, she had been able to talk with him, enjoying his attention as few other women did that evening. It had been heady, wonderful, and for a few brief moments she had felt beautiful.

Since then, Stowe had come to visit her at the small, comfortable house she had taken in Upper Brook Street—at least there she had managed a fashionable address—to pour out his opinions and the doings of his life. Gradually the attachment between them grew, until there was an understanding between them that one day they would marry. If she sometimes wondered if he viewed her as motherly, based on the way he brought her his triumphs and disappointments, she never once let on. Passion was no longer something she cared so very much about, but she intended to enjoy her life in London as Stowe's wife very much. She would be a brilliant political hostess, and take pleasure in every moment of it. In return, she was apparently giving him something that he needed. That was quite enough.

Now this. Nothing had really changed, she knew. Here in Stowe's country house, she was his unofficial hostess, she thought as she glided into the drawing room to be certain that all was ready for tea. Tess was out of his life, her only connection to him their daughter. And yet— And yet Emily couldn't help remembering that once he had loved Tess, once he had been so devastated by whatever it was she had done that he had taken the nearly unprecedented step of divorce. Oh, Tess might have been the one to instigate it, but not until David had given her cause. No, David had wanted the divorce, and she still didn't know why. That was dangerous. Tess was dangerous, living so near, being so very beautiful. For the first time in her life Emily had within her grasp something she truly desired. She would do what she had to, to keep it.

The other guests began to drift into the room: the

duke and duchess, Viscount Sherbourne and his wife;
Mr. and Mrs. Fosdyck. The chatter was light, infor-
mal, about the pleasant time all had spent outdoors,
the very thought of which made Emily shudder.
When she married Stowe, she would see to it that
they spent little time here.

"I must admit to being a trifle surprised to see
Miss Harwood here." Mrs. Fosdyck said, and Emily
became alert. "I didn't think Stowe would invite
her."

"It was her daughter's idea," the viscountess said
quietly. "She does seem to be good with the child."

"Oh, doubtless. Still, I do wonder what happened."

"For God's—heaven's sake," Mr. Fosdyck said between his teeth. "We're in the man's house. We
should speak of something more suitable."

"I found her to be very nice," the duchess put in.

"She would never be received in London. No one
in politics would have anything to do with her."

"Of course, it did cause a dreadful scandal,"
Emily said, placidly going on with her knitting.

Outside in the hall, Tess, about to be shown into
the drawing room by Williams, who apparently had
his own ideas on loyalty, froze. Of course it had
caused a great scandal, her well-meaning, bumbling
separation from David. Had she thought things
through so long ago, she would have stayed with
him and helped him brave the lesser scandal that
would erupt when it became generally known that
he had married her. That she could hold her head
up here was due only to the kindness of neighbors
who had known her all her life, and their instinctive
Yorkshire distrust of an outsider. In fashionable circles, however, it must have been fodder for many a
conversation. Even she, isolated though she was, had

realized that, she thought, with a little gesture to Williams as she turned from the drawing room door. She could no longer stay here, an unwilling eavesdropper, an unwanted interloper.

Well wrapped in warm rugs, and with a hot brick at her feet, Tess set off for Harcourt in the sleigh, the passing scenery an icy blur. Once she had intended to salvage David's political career from the mistake he had made in marrying her; instead, in her ignorance, she had ruined it. Unfortunately, David had made not even a pretense of listening to her reasons when, too late, she'd tried to explain them to him. Nor, she thought glumly, as the sleigh pulled up before Harcourt, did she think he would believe her now. Likely he never would. After seeing David and Jennie again, after feeling again that painful rush of emotions, she wasn't certain she would handle losing them a second time. She would have to do something about it, she thought, stepping out of the sleigh. The question was, what?

Six

"There's a visitor here for you, miss," Bailey said, taking her cloak as she walked inside.

"Who is it?" she asked, without much interest.

"Mr. Rawley."

"Again?" she exclaimed involuntarily. "Oh, bother. Can you not tell him—no, I suppose he must have heard the sleigh pull up."

"I told him you were from home, but he insisted he would wait," the butler said apologetically.

"It isn't your fault, Bailey. I suppose I shall have to see him." She sighed. "Where is he?"

"In the morning room, with Mr. Richard."

She nodded. "Thank you, Bailey," she said, and went to face her fate.

In the morning room, Adrian rose from the sofa to greet her. "I came as soon as I heard."

"Did you? Is there tea?" she asked Richard, who raised an ironic eyebrow at her.

"I'll ring for some."

"Thank you. As soon as you heard what, Adrian?"

"That you had been invited to Stowcroft."

That stunned her for a moment. What was she to say to it? Only Adrian, she reflected, would blunder so as to come here at such a time, when he must know that her feelings were rubbed raw. He did not usually behave so, she thought, and instantly became alert. Depend upon it, he had his reasons. "Oh?"

"Yes. I can't believe Stowe's nerve."

"I think I'll see what's keeping the tea," Richard said, and went out, though Tess glared at him.

"It was my daughter's idea, Adrian."

"Might be, but he didn't have to follow through on it." He paced in front of the fireplace. "Happens I don't like to think of you in that place."

"As you can see, I survived it. Besides," she went on, pouring the tea, which had come in on the tray with no sign of her brother following, "I cannot see what concern it is of yours."

"Cannot see!" He stared at her. "It would be my concern, if only you would say the word."

Oh, no, she thought, steeling herself for what was to come. "Adrian—"

"Marry me, Tess. I'd make you a good husband. You know that."

"Yes, but—"

"Better than Stowe has. I wouldn't let you go, Tess."

His words made her shudder inwardly. Yes, David had left her, but no one could have been a better husband. Of that she was certain. "Adrian, we've been through this before." She forced herself to sip her tea, forced herself to think and act calmly. "Marriage to me would ruin you."

"I don't care," he said stubbornly. "What other people think has never mattered to me."

"Perhaps it matters to me. Adrian, we are friends." She gazed up at him, hoping to be properly persuasive. "I would not want to bring any harm to you."

"That is up to me to decide, isn't it, Tess? I believe 'tis still my life."

"Yes, but I'd have to live with it. Frankly, Adrian, I don't wish to be ostracized." She set down her cup with more of a clatter than she had intended. Foolishly, part of her wondered about accepting Adrian's offer, wondered how it would feel to have someone to share the burden with her, wondered how David would react. The look on his face might almost be worth it. "What I have to face this time is hard enough."

"But you wouldn't be alone," he said, echoing her thoughts. "You would have me. I may not be a marquess, but at least I can offer you a name."

That hurt. She had lost so much when she had lost David. This man standing before her, no matter what he might feel, could not change that. "No, Adrian. I'm sorry, but there it is."

"I suppose 'tis that I don't belong to the company you kept today."

"Adrian!" She stared at him in shock. "You know that's not so. You belong there as much as anyone in the neighborhood."

"What, a great lout like me, hobnobbing with the *ton?*"

"As I recall, you have hobnobbed with the *ton.* Your grandfather was an earl."

"My father was a third son, think on, and I'm a farmer. Besides, happens Stowe thinks of me as a rival."

"You're not," she protested.

"Happens I am."

"No. Not the way he thinks."

He took a sip of tea before answering, looking reflectively into the fire. "No. But I am, all the same."

"Adrian—"

"The offer stands, Tess."

"Oh, Adrian." She put her fingers to her forehead, which now ached in earnest. "If I were half as impetuous as I once was, I just might accept."

"Then do it, Tess." He leaned forward, face intent. "Think of yourself for once."

"I can't." She lowered her hand and faced him directly. "I've my child to think of, especially since . . ."

"What?" he prompted, when she didn't go on.

"David is going to marry again."

"As I thought." He settled back in his chair. "And all the more reason. 'Tis time for you to find some happiness, Tess."

She looked away. How could she ever hope to explain that her happiness lay, as it always had, with David and Jennie? Her dreams might be hopeless, but they were all she had. " 'Tis enough for me that you stand my friend, Adrian. There's many a person in this neighborhood who would have cut me had you not."

"Happens I think friendship could make a marriage work. And you'd have my name, Tess."

There it was again, the reminder of what her long-ago disastrous actions had caused. "My good name is gone." She gazed into the fire. "Nothing can change that."

"People will forget."

"People have long memories." She held out her hand to him. "Cry peace, Adrian. This is one argument you'll never win."

"Aye, I know you're stubborn. Happens I am, too." He rose. "Happens I just might mention this to you again."

"Maybe you will," she retorted, though she smiled. "And my answer will be the same."

"Someday, Tess." He smiled down at her. "Someday, maybe not." He bowed over her hand, and then, smiling in a way that told her this wasn't over yet, left.

Richard came back into the room a little while later and poured tea for himself into a substantial mug, not waiting for her to do so. "He's gone?"

"Yes." Tess turned from gazing out at the eternal moors, snow-covered though they now were, and looked crossly at him. "Craven of you not to stay."

"I knew what he wanted to talk to you about."

"And you could not have spared me?"

"He's a good man, Tess. You could do worse."

"Do you think I don't know that?" she snapped, dropping into her chair and pushing her fingers into her curls. "He's too good a man to have his life ruined, and that's what I'd be doing to him."

"Would you? I think you underrate yourself, Tess."

"Oh, for heaven's sake." She rose again, to pace in front of the fire. " 'Tis beside the point, anyway. I don't intend to marry again. Especially . . ."

"What?"

"Nothing." *Now,* she'd nearly said, but had stopped herself in time. Oh, she was learning, if slowly, to control herself. Pity, in some ways, that she hadn't learned the lesson earlier.

"Someday you'll need to take a chance again, Tess. I know it frightens you—"

"Is that what you think?" she interrupted, turning to him.

"Isn't it?"

"No."

He watched her closely. "You forget. I know you, Tess."

"Maybe not as well as you think." She tugged at

her curls again, and then gave him her most winning smile. "Must we brangle? It's been a tiresome day."

"I wasn't aware we were." He rose, too. "But you are looking rather tired, so I won't go on." Lightly he kissed her forehead. "I don't want to add to your troubles."

"Believe me, Richard, you aren't." She smiled, but the smile faded as she turned away, walking out and heading to her room. If Richard only knew. But then, it was possible he did. It never had been easy for her to hide anything from him. Had he not been away from home during those vital weeks nearly seven years ago, matters might have turned out far differently than they had. But then, she thought, looking out at the moors from her window and remembering that enchanted Christmas, they might not have.

No use now, though, to dwell on the past, or what might have been, she reminded herself as she turned away. Not when there was Jennie to think of. Her future was what mattered. Tess could live with the mistakes she'd made; Jennie shouldn't have to. No matter what she had to do, Jennie would be happy. She would see to it.

It was Christmas Eve day, and at last it was time to gather the greens with which to decorate Stowcroft for Christmas. Jennie, looking very earnest and serious, slid into her chair at breakfast. "We have a lot to do today," she announced to the table at large, and David noted that more than one person looked away, presumably to hide a smile. "We have to pick the Christmas greens. We couldn't do so before, 'tis bad luck to bring them inside any earlier than today. I don't really understand why." She wrinkled her nose at the illogic of that. "But there's plenty of holly on the grounds and anyone can pick that. We just have to remember that the points of the leaves are sharp. Do the little ones know they're not to eat the berries?"

"We'll watch them carefully, Jennie," Lady Sherbourne assured her.

"Good. Mistletoe berries shouldn't be eaten, either. They're for the kissing bough. I don't understand that, either."

"It's customary, Jennie," David said, as gravely as she, lest he betray himself by laughing.

"Oh. You'll have to find the Yule log, Papa. Will I really be able to light it tonight?"

"Stowe, I think that's dangerous for a child," Mrs. Granfield said, frowning.

"We'll help her," David said. "I understand that in some families 'tis the custom for the eldest girl to light the log. I saved a piece of kindling from last year's log for the purpose. And"—he looked at Jennie—"I think I know just where a good log might be found."

"Oh, Papa, do you?" she said, bouncing in her seat, more a child now than the miniature adult she had appeared.

"Yes. Of course, I'll need all the gentlemen to help me bring it in."

"Do you mean we have to work, too?" Lord Burnet complained, looking sleepy, as he always did, with his heavy-lidded eyes.

"If I have to, you do as well," David said, rising from the table.

"And there'll still be more to do once we come in," Jennie said. "We'll have to make laurel into ropes, and put the holly on the mantels, and make the kissing boughs. Do we have apples and oranges for the main one, Papa?"

"You intend us to have more than one, poppet?" David said, glancing at Emily to share his amusement. Somewhat to his surprise, she was still frowning. Odd.

"Yes. One in the drawing room, of course, that's the main one, and others—oh, we'll likely find places."

"Likely we will." He put his hand on her shoulder as they walked out of the drawing room. "You're excited about this, aren't you, poppet?"

"Oh, yes! Last year we bought the greens. Remember?"

"Yes."

" 'Tis wonderful to go out and get our own, and to decorate them. Mama gave me scarlet ribbon for everything."

"Did she."

"Yes. It's ever so pretty. Papa." She looked up at him, awe and wonder in her face. "It's almost Christmas."

"So it is, poppet." He smiled down at her, and for the first time in a very long time he was glad of it. "So it is."

Jennie's wonder seemed to have infected his guests as well, David thought later, standing in the hall and pulling on his gloves before going out to collect the greens. Yesterday everyone had insisted on trooping down to the kitchen to stir the Christmas pudding for luck, and more than one of them had hinted to Cook about which trinkets they hoped to find in their slice. At night, standing about the spinet, they had sung carols, and then had sat before the fire to tell stories of Christmas past. All agreed that the Duchess of Bainbridge, who had grown up in America, had the best stories, of her mother's Dutch family and their traditions, and of the fur traders and natives who had come to her little village on the banks of the broad Hudson River, which no one could quite imagine.

"Papa?" Jennie said beside him, bringing him back to the present.

He looked down at her. "I thought you'd be with the other children, poppet," he said, noting how very serious she looked. From time to time over the past days, she had worn the same preoccupied air he'd noted the day everyone had gone out into the snow. It bothered him.

"Yes. May I ask you something?"

"Of course you can."

"Not here." She glanced around, nervously, he thought, making him frown. Something was definitely wrong.

"Very well. My study."

"Yes, Papa."

"Stowe?" one of the guests called to him.

"In a moment," he answered. Jennie, and whatever was bothering her, was more important.

Inside the study, Jennie sat fidgeting in the chair before his desk, which he leaned against, facing her, rather than sitting behind it. "Now, poppet. What is bothering you?"

Jennie looked down at her hands. "I like Mama," she said, apparently at random.

"Yes, I know you do." He waited. Jennie would tell him the problem in her own good time, he knew from the few times she had come to him in the past. Those problems had been childish ones. If this one had to do with Tess, though, it was of far more import.

"Papa?" She looked up at him. "Why did you and Mama divorce?"

"I told you, poppet. There were reasons."

"But can't you tell me what those reasons were?"

"No, Jennie, I can't."

"Oh." She looked back down at her hands. "Did Mama divorce you?"

"Who told you that?" he exclaimed in surprise. "Your mother?"

"No. Did she?"

Good God. How was he to handle this? "Yes, Jennie," he said, finally. "She did."

"But why?" It was a howl of pain. "Why did she do such a thing?"

"I can't tell you."

"Didn't she want me?"

"Oh, poppet." He went down on one knee so that he'd be at her level. "We both wanted you. But Parliament said I was the one who was to have you."

"I hate Parliament."

He suppressed a smile. "Yes, I imagine you do. Jennie, your mother managed to see you, even though she wasn't supposed to. You know that."

"Yes."

"Doesn't that say anything to you? She wanted to be with you. She still does." *Good God,* he thought again. *Listen to him.* He was actually pleading Tess's case. "Don't blame her for what happened. Sometimes, Jennie, things just go wrong. And no, before you say it, it isn't fair."

She looked up. "Did you want the divorce, too?"

Oh, lord, another hard question. "Yes."

She frowned. "Then why did she . . ."

"It was the best way to do it."

"I don't understand, Papa."

"No, I know you don't. Someday I'll explain it to you."

"I know. I'm too young for it now," she said, too

bitterly for someone her age. What were they doing to this child? he wondered. "I hate being young. I want to be a grown-up."

"All in good time, Jennie. Don't rush things." He leaned forward to hug her. She didn't come into her his arms as quickly as she usually did. "I love you, Jennie. You know that."

"I love you too, Papa," she said, and pulled away, an oddly adult child who was facing something she shouldn't even have to know about.

"Why don't we go outside now?"

"All right."

"Wait. One more thing, Jennie, before we do."

She turned back from the door. "What?"

"Who told you about this?"

"Mrs. Granfield," she said, after a moment.

"Emily?" He frowned. "When?"

"The day it snowed."

"Oh," he said blankly. "I'm glad you asked me about it."

She nodded and turned away. At the door, though, she stopped. "Papa?"

"What is it?"

"Can't you and Mama live together again?"

"No, poppet. I'm afraid not."

"Oh." She looked disconsolate as she turned to the door. "I wish you could."

"It's not possible." He forced a smile to his face. "Go along, poppet. I'll be there in a moment."

Good God, he thought as he stood on the steps of the Hall, watching his guests, who had gathered in the drive and were chattering together, apparently ready and eager to begin the search. All but Emily, who apparently felt the cold. Why had she done such a thing? he wondered. She must have known it would hurt Jennie. She must have known he'd hear of it, as well. What did she think he'd do? Thank her for putting Jennie's mother at a disadvantage? Oh, no. No matter what his feelings were about Tess, he had no desire to use Jennie as a weapon against her. Not when doing so would hurt his child. On that, he and Tess were in agreement.

Thank God for Tess, he thought, watching as Jennie ran to her mother, who had just arrived from Harcourt in a sleigh. It was the last thing he'd thought he'd ever feel, yet now he was grateful that Jennie had someone to run to. As recently as an hour ago, he hadn't felt this way. Nor had he wanted Tess there. It was Jennie's doing, of course. He'd known the previous evening, when the children had come down from the nursery wing to bid their parents good night and Jennie had moved unerringly toward him, a martial light in her eyes, that he was for it. In a tone of voice which was becoming all too familiar, she'd demanded that Tess be allowed to accompany them today, and to return to the Hall to help in decorating and partake of luncheon. With his guests watching him, and with Jennie's chin thrust out at a particularly stubborn angle, he'd realized quickly that refusing her request would only be a losing battle. Difficult though it had been for him, he had agreed, to be rewarded by the rare, radiant smile which changed her face from plainness to something approaching beauty. Tess, it seemed, would be a part of his life while he was here in Yorkshire, whether he wished her to be or not.

So it was that, this clear, frosty morning, he watched with mixed feelings as Tess set off, Jennie's hand tucked securely in hers and the Duchess of Bainbridge at her side, looking quite unruffled and calm. "Remarkable, really," the Duke of Bainbridge said in a low voice.

"What is?" he answered absently. Jennie was giving Tess the same wide smile she previously had only gifted him with. The sight made him tighten his lips.

"I don't believe I've ever seen you change your mind once you decide something. Yet one word from Jennie, and you do something completely opposite from what you planned." The duke sent him a look. "Or am I correct in assuming that you had no intention of inviting Miss Harwood today?"

For a moment David considered telling Bainbridge to go to the devil, but then stopped himself just in time. "Jennie should see her mother as much as she can."

"Granted, especially as she won't once you remove to London." David could feel that penetrating gaze on him again. "Or will she?"

"No," David said, more strongly than he had intended. When he left Yorkshire, he would leave Tess behind. Again. He would not have her disrupting his life in London, as well.

"Good." Bainbridge nodded. "I need hardly tell you what effect she could have on your career."

Not for the first time, David regretted his impulsive actions of several years previous, though whether he referred to his brief marriage, or to his equally hasty divorce, he couldn't always say. "No, you do not."

"Good. I know you cannot do the work you wished to do," Bainbridge went on as they strolled away from the Hall. "But you are an extremely valuable man to the party. We'd hate to lose you."

David didn't answer right away. For a very long time, he had lived for only two things: his daughter and his career. Now he wondered if the latter were worth the sacrifices he'd made for it. "No," he said.

Bainbridge followed David's gaze, to where Tess was talking with Sabrina. What had they found for conversation, David wondered? "She wouldn't have been a suitable political wife, anyway. Not with her background."

David looked at him sharply. "What background?"

The duke raised one eyebrow in surprise. "I merely meant her country origins. Although it does seem that I heard something about the family, once . . ."

"From what I understand, 'tis a very old one," David said, at last annoyed with this line of conversation. "Nor would she be the first from her family to serve the country."

"Doubtless. But a man in your position needs the proper wife."

David snorted. "Yet your wife's from America."

"So she is," the duke said mildly.

"My apologies, Bainbridge," David said after a moment. "I meant no offense by that."

The duke waved his hand. "None taken."

"Good." David again looked at Tess and the duchess. Much as he didn't care to admit it, Bainbridge was right. If he were to marry again, he did need a wife of spotless reputation. Emily certainly had that. Yet why had she behaved as she had? *Thank God for Tess,* he thought again, and shook his head. For Jennie's sake, of course. He would give a great deal, however, to know just what Tess and the duchess were discussing with such absorption.

"I do like that cloak," Sabrina was saying. " 'Tis very dashing."

"Thank you." Tess was rather proud of the cloak, if she did say so herself. Of cherry red velvet lined with fur, its epaulets and frog closures made with gold braid gave it a distinctly military air. Even her hat, high-crowned and made of velvet to match, was trimmed with gold braid, giving it a martial look. Jeanette had recently written to tell her that this one was selling briskly, though the war on the Continent had been over for months. They both knew they had taken a risk with this design. "I think it turned out well."

Sabrina stood back a pace. "Never tell me you made it!"

Tess flushed. "My maid did most of the sewing."

"But you designed it? How marvelous! I could swear I saw something similar at Madame Jeanette's salon. She's a modiste in London."

"Really?" Tess said, hoping she looked merely interested, and not alarmed. If David knew of her other reason for going to town, she would never be allowed to see Jennie again.

"Yes."

"Yes, well, please don't tell anyone. I don't want people thinking I'm totally provincial."

"Oh, I am persuaded they don't. But, as for that, do you not ever come down to town?"

"I met Mama in town," Jennie interjected.

"Hush, Jennie," Tess said, flushing again. Jennie might not look like her, but she did apparently have her mother's unruly, impulsive tongue. "I have been there, occasionally."

"But you must come to call, next you are there."

Which would not likely be soon. Nor would she likely be welcome, in spite of the duchess's obvious sincerity. Americans were apparently not quite so aware of the proprieties as most people. The duke, however, she felt certain, was. "Thank you. That is much too good of you."

"Not at all. I'll send you an invitation." She

glanced back. "I believe I just heard my husband call me. If you'll excuse me?"

"Of course," Tess said, watching as the duchess returned to the duke, who tucked her hand into the crook of his arm. What must it feel like, she wondered, blinking back sudden tears, to be so secure in her husband's regard? She herself had lost all hope of that long ago.

"Oh, look, Mama." Jennie interrupted that languorous line of thought as she pointed high at a tree. "I see some mistletoe. I want to climb up to it."

"For heaven's sake, no," Tess said, alarmed.

"Uncle Richard said you did, once."

She would have something to say to Richard about that, when she returned to Harcourt. "And did he tell you that I fell and broke my arm?"

Jennie waved that off. "I'll be careful. Please, Mama?"

"No." Tess kept her face stern. "I think your father would agree with me on this."

"On what?" a voice said behind them, and Tess turned to see David, only a few paces back.

"Climbing a tree to pick mistletoe. I've tried telling her that's not something for little girls to do, but—"

"It's not so very high, Papa, and I've climbed higher."

He bent her a stern look. "Oh, have you."

"But not often," she hurried on. "See? If you look up, you can just see it, near those two branches. In fact"—she looked from one to the other and broke out into a smile—"it's just over your heads." She caught at their hands, tugging Tess off balance, so that she almost fell against David's chest. "Mama, Papa, you've been caught beneath it, and it's not even part of the kissing bough yet. You do know what that means."

"Oh, Jennie—"

"Don't be foolish," David said at the same time.

"It's the rule," Jennie said, linking their hands together. "You have to kiss."

Seven

For what seemed like a very long time, the three of them stood in tableau, silhouetted against the bleak winter woods. Then David pulled away. "If it's not part of a kissing bough, then it's not official," he said firmly.

"That's right," Tess quickly agreed. "Perhaps if it happens again, inside—"

"It won't." Jennie turned away, her shoulders slumped. "I know it won't."

David took a deep breath. "Jennie, I made you no promises when I agreed to come here for Christmas."

Jennie's gaze was fixed to the ground. "I know."

"Your father and I are friends, Jennie," Tess added. "That's all."

"Friends kiss sometimes," Jennie argued.

"Yes, but . . ." Helplessly she met David's eyes, to find them impenetrable. Not for the first time, it occurred to her how unbending he had become. It would only be a brief kiss, after all, for Jennie's sake. It didn't have to mean anything, though she knew quite well that it would. "You're right, though. Friends do kiss, occasionally."

"Tess," David warned.

"You refine too much upon it," she said, and, before she could stop herself, reached up on her toes to kiss him on his cheek. Something happened, though. Perhaps he turned to protest; perhaps he was more willing than he appeared. Whatever the reason, at the last moment he turned his head, so that the brief, impersonal kiss she had intended landed on his mouth instead. And that was something very different, indeed. For if his lips were cold from the weather, still there was fire there, so well remembered from their brief interlude, long in the past now. Her hand came up as if to clutch at his lapel, while her other one itched to twine into his hair. Perhaps they might have done so, too, except at that moment Master Nigel Walcott, son of Lord Walcott, came bounding up.

"Mistletoe!" he said breathlessly, holding a sprig up. "We found some and I climbed up to get it!"

Tess looked up at David a moment longer, and then, slightly disoriented, smiled down at the boy. "All by yourself?"

"Well, my father helped," he confessed. "Is it enough for the kissing bough, do you think?"

"Oh, more than enough."

"Unless we have more than one," Jennie put in. Her cheeks were unusually pink, and there was a light in her eyes Tess had never seen there before, making her heart sink. Oh, no. She prayed she and David hadn't raised Jennie's hopes by their impulsive behavior just now.

"I think perhaps we should," David said gravely, not looking at Tess, and then, before anyone could guess at his intentions, hoisted Jennie into the air. "Well, poppet? Are we going to let a mere boy best us?"

"No! Look, Mama!" Jennie grabbed hold of one

of the lower branches of the tree. "Papa is going to help me get the mistletoe."

"Yes, I see," Tess said faintly, watching as the two people who meant the most to her in the world climbed ever higher. How, she wondered, had her mother survived her childhood? Foolish question, she thought almost immediately. She knew the answer to that all too well.

"Jennie!" Nigel bellowed as soon as Jennie neared the ground again, a sprig of mistletoe clutched triumphantly in her mittened hand and a smile on her face that brought beauty to it. "I found the most capital holly tree!"

"Did you?" Jennie asked, and bounded off after him into the woods.

"Don't get lost," Tess called after them, though she knew her words were likely to go unheeded. Jennie was enjoying this brief time with another child, and why shouldn't she? Soon she'd be back in London, living all too adult a life. With her would go David.

Tess's gaze met David's at that thought, to see him looking both sheepish and thoughtful. "You do realize what she's thinking, don't you?" she said.

"That you and I will reconcile? Hm. I wonder who set her to thinking it?"

The patent unfairness of that took her breath away. "I never did!"

"Then who did?"

Tess started to answer, but then bit off her impetuous words, glancing off instead into the woods, where gleeful, childish shouts gave testimony to the wonder of the holly tree. David held the power in this situation. She would do well not to cross him. "She isn't stupid, David. She's capable of coming up with ideas on her own."

"That's true." He, too, looked into the woods. "She's happy here. I suppose it's natural for her to think such a thing."

"I wouldn't be surprised if she thought it in London."

He looked at her swiftly. "Then she did know who you were."

Tess held up her hand. "No! I swear I never told her that. You saw for yourself her surprise when she arrived at Harcourt."

His lips tightened, but he nodded. "I've also seen how she tries to include you in every activity, no matter what I say."

"I think that's natural, David. Please, try to understand. I'm her mother. She's been without me since she was very small. 'Tis not surprising she wants to see me as much as she can." She sighed. "I still miss my mother sometimes, and I'm a woman grown."

"How old were you when you lost her?"

Tess's lips tightened this time. "Old enough. David, please, we shouldn't argue about this. Not when there's Jennie to consider."

"I wondered when you'd start trying to use her."

"That's unfair!"

"Is it?" His eyes met hers, opaque and unyielding. Had she put that expression there? She remembered, oh, so well, when he had looked at her with such warmth and admiration. Would he forgive her if she told him about her mother? She opened her mouth to speak.

"Papa!" Jennie cried, running up. "Nigel really has found a wonderful holly tree. Do you have the shears?"

David looked away, and Tess breathed in relief. She had come so close. What good would it serve now to tell him, when she'd kept quiet all these years? "Someone does," he answered vaguely. "I believe Nurse might."

"I'll ask." She dashed off again, leaving an awkward silence between her parents.

David broke it first, clearing his throat and turning to Tess, his gaze clearer, more like the young man she remembered. "We do have a problem."

Tess sighed again. Would it be so terrible—but, yes, for him, it would. And her sacrifice would go for naught. "Yes, I suppose we do. But what can we do about it?"

"Ignore it, I suppose."

"We can't, David," she said, and neither seemed to notice she hadn't used his title. "Not if she thinks it's something she can really make happen. She may be intelligent, but she is just a child. She doesn't think the way you or I do. She may really believe she can make it come about."

"Then we'll have to keep on our guard, I suppose."

"And hope it goes away? It won't, you know." She turned, and they fell into step together, walking under bare-branched trees toward the laughter and noise of children thoroughly enjoying themselves. Children truly were amazing. One moment they could be plotting their parents' downfall, and the next immersing themselves in whatever activity was at hand. "We'll have to do something."

"There's not a chance in—excuse me. There's no chance she'll get what she wants."

"Of course not, David, I realize that." Tess stopped, reluctant to reach the others just yet and end this rare moment of togetherness. It didn't matter what she and David were discussing. At least they weren't quarreling. "But I don't want her to be hurt."

He nodded. "We'll have to tell her. In fact"—he frowned—"I did so, this morning."

"Why?" she asked, startled.

He looked away. "She asked."

"Did she understand?"

"No." He turned to face her. "I don't see any way around it, Tess. She's bound to be hurt."

"Poor child." She began walking again, and he followed suit. "I never thought . . ."

"That's the problem, Tess. You don't think. Not then, not now."

"I've grown up since we were married," she said, stung by the accusation. "Sometimes, yes, it is true I speak before thinking. But I think I've learned how my actions affect others." She let out her breath. "I learned the hard way."

"Excuse me? You learned the hard way? How do you think I felt, Tess, hearing the wife I adored telling me she had never loved me and we had made a mistake?"

"David—"

"Oh, yes, I learned, too. Learned enough to stay away from you, and women like you."

Ah. So that was why he was marrying Mrs. Granfield. At least, one of the reasons. But that wasn't something to pursue today. "It's past, David."

"Is it? With Jennie thinking we'll be together, a happy family?"

She winced at his sardonic tone. "I see no need for us to behave this way, do you? If you can't think of your daughter, at least think of your guests."

"Ha. You're a fine one to talk. You didn't have to deal with the scandal."

"I'm sorry, David! I thought—"

"What?" he said, sounding almost reluctant, when she didn't go on.

"Nothing." He wouldn't believe her if she told him she'd truly thought she was rescuing him from a greater scandal than what he'd actually suffered. Not now. "I love Jennie, David," she said quietly. "No matter what else you think of me, please believe that."

He was quiet a moment. "I believe you do."

"David," she began hesitantly. "Will Mrs. Granfield be a good mother to Jennie?"

"Of course," he said coolly. "Why shouldn't she be?"

"I don't want to intrude, but I've noticed her with Jennie, and she doesn't seem to know how to act."

"Tess, you know nothing of the matter!" He spoke with more force than she thought her comment warranted, making her blink in surprise.

"I do not mean to come between you and her, David."

"Oh, don't you."

"No." She looked away. The children's voices were getting louder. "David, I wonder if—"

"What?" he prompted again.

"Nothing." Oh, her unruly tongue. She nearly had said something truly impulsive, and truly disastrous. If, she had wanted to say, it really would be so bad if they reconciled. If, once again, they were husband and wife, parents and child. But matters had proceeded far beyond the point where that was possible. She was foolish to even consider it. "We'll have to sit down with her and tell her, David," she said, echoing his words.

"I suppose we will." His voice was heavy as he stopped to look at her. "Let's leave it to the end of the holiday, though, shall we?"

She frowned. "Do you think that's wise?"

He indicated the children, still not visible, with a

jerk of his head. "I don't want to ruin her pleasure. I've never seen her like this."

"True. But we don't know what she'll try next. She's a bright child."

"We're adults, Tess. I think we're a match for her."

"I hope so." It wasn't what she really wanted, though, she thought, as they rounded a slight bend and at last saw the children, helping Lady Sherbourne cut bunches of holly from a large, round bush and place them in a basket. Watching as David went forward to join them, she knew that what she really longed for was foolish, and far beyond her reach. She wished David would love her again.

The house party arrived back at Stowcroft, pink-cheeked and ravenous for luncheon. As they entered the hall, Jennie throwing off her mittens and hat, Emily stepped out from the morning room, hands folded contemplatively before her. "Oh, Mrs. Granfield!" Jennie exclaimed, throwing herself at her, having apparently forgotten what Emily had told her, in her excitement. "You should have come. We got ever so many greens! And enough mistletoe to make three kissing boughs."

"Really." Emily disentangled herself from Jennie's clinging arms. "How nice for you."

"Yes, and I brought back some holly, just for you."

Emily reared back from the prickly leaves. "Jennie, really, you'll stab me with that."

David frowned at that. "Surely there was no harm done, Emily?"

"No, not this time."

"Really," he said, echoing her earlier reaction,

though his tone was noticeably cooler. He was beginning to learn things about Emily he'd never known before, things he didn't like. "Then there is no need for a fuss, is there?"

"It is the principle of the thing. Suppose it had scratched me in the eye? It would have been uncomfortable, at the least."

His frown deepened as he looked at her. "But it didn't."

"It could have," she repeated. "I do think I am owed an apology, at the least."

Jennie looked up, her expression both baffled and mutinous. "It was a present," she muttered.

"Still, a truly polite little girl would apologize."

David placed his hand on Jennie's shoulder. All this fuss, and for what? Tess would have hugged the little girl and then exclaimed over the offering, had she stayed for luncheon instead of tactfully crying off. Tess was quite good with Jennie, he admitted to himself, no matter what else he might think of her. Better than he had expected her to be. "Well, poppet?"

Jennie's head was bent. "I'm sorry."

She didn't sound it in the least, but he thought it the wisest course not to pursue it. "There. Your apology and your holly, Mrs. Granfield."

Emily held the holly gingerly. "Thank you," she said, and her gratefulness held the same lack of sincerity as Jennie's apology. Tess's concerns about Emily came back to him, and ruthlessly he pushed them away.

"Now, poppet." David squeezed her shoulder, smiling at her when she looked up. "Run up to the nursery. It's my guess Nurse has hot chocolate ready for you."

Jennie's face cleared. "Yes, Papa." She rose up on

her toes to kiss his cheek before bounding up the stairs to the nursery, her heavy outdoor boots echoing noisily in the hall.

"Really, Stowe." Emily was frowning openly now. "The way the child behaves—"

"Yes?" he said coolly, before she could go on.

"There, now, I suppose it can't be helped, here in the wilds. I'm sure her manners will improve once she's in town again."

"Are you implying there is something wrong with my daughter?"

"Of course not, Stowe, I'd never say such a thing. I truly do not mean to offend you. But you must admit she needs discipline."

"I admit nothing of the sort." If his voice had been cool before, now it was positively arctic. "She is well brought-up and behaved when she needs to be, and spirited when she needs to be."

"But—"

"Emily." He spoke through his teeth, glad that his other guests had had the discretion to withdraw and leave the hall to the two of them. "Jennie's upbringing is my concern."

"And mine, if I am to be her stepmama."

"As you say, madam. If you are."

It hung heavily in the air, the implication that they would not marry. For the first time, a look of dismay appeared in Emily's eyes. "Stowe, I did not in any way mean to imply that the child is naughty."

He inclined his head. "As you say. Now. Shall we join the others?"

"In a moment." Emily stepped back from his hand. "I'll just fetch my knitting from the morning room."

He nodded. "Tea will be coming in soon."

"Yes, Stowe," she said, and watched as he climbed

the stairs toward the drawing room, taking a deep breath for the first time since the confrontation between them began. Make no mistake about it, she told herself, entering the now-deserted morning room in search of her workbag, seething within, though on the outside she schooled her face to calmness. It had been a confrontation, for all that their voices had been kept low and civilized. It did not bode well for the future, not if Stowe would not allow her any influence over the child. Heaven knew, too, the child needed her guidance. Being raised as she had been, without any feminine influence, had been bad for her; coming here to Yorkshire and being in the company of her undisciplined mother had only worsened matters.

It was all the fault of that wretched woman. Thank heaven she herself had had the good sense to come to this house party, uncomfortable though it was at times. For if Stowe were occasionally in his former wife's presence—and she was lovelier than Emily had expected, making her feel dowdy—still he seemed not to show any preference for her. That was all to the good. Now, if Emily could manage to point out, tactfully, of course, that any fault of Jennie's behavior was surely due to her mother, it would go a long way toward mending any damage that had been done this morning. Yes, of course, that was what she must do. Make Stowe realize who was really in the wrong here. *Yes.* She nodded, well satisfied with her plans. Do that, and she would have success over that woman once more, she thought, and headed toward the drawing room at last.

"Happy Christmas, angel," Tess sang as she swept into the nursery at Stowcroft, her arms laden with packages. Behind her trailed her maid, burdened with yet more parcels.

"Mama!" Jennie jumped up from the stool before the dressing table, where Nurse was plaiting her hair into its usual heavy braids, and ran to her. "All the children will be allowed down to Christmas dinner. Papa said so. And he gave me a crystal angel."

Tess held up the angel of exquisitely cut crystal which Jennie had carefully placed in her hand. "How lovely. Is that where you got your other angels?"

"Yes." Jennie set the ornament down beside a row of other angel figurines, some of porcelain trimmed with gold, others carefully carved of wood and gilded. "He gives me one each Christmas."

This year Tess would be able to give Jennie her present, instead of keeping it aside. The thought made her heart well with a mixture of emotions. "And did Mrs. Granfield have something for you?"

Jennie's nose wrinkled. "Yes, a book about a brother and sister. She told me it is a moral tale."

"Oh. Well, I'm sure it's quite worthy," she said blankly, after a moment. She gave her a sidelong look. "I've something for you."

"Do you?" Jennie bounced about her in excitement. "Oh, what? What?"

"Well, let us see." She made her way to the bed, where the parcels had been deposited with great care. "Which one shall we open first?"

"That one." Jennie pointed unerringly at a large box.

"Hm. Are you sure? Oh, very well." She stepped back and watched as Jennie tore into the wrapping and opened the box, revealing a porcelain doll. Every detail of it had been perfectly executed, from its golden ringlets to its white satin gown and slippers. "Happy Christmas, angel," Tess said again, smiling.

Jennie gazed first at the doll, her eyes filled with wonder, and then back at Tess. "For me?"

"Well, of course for you, silly. Who else? I think Nurse might be a little old for dolls, and Mrs. Granfield might not appreciate it."

That made Jennie giggle. "You're silly."

"Yes, well, it's Christmas." She paused. "I bought that two years ago."

Jennie had finally taken the doll from its protective wrapping of tissue paper, and so that took a moment to sink in. "Two years ago? When I was four?" she said, looking up at Tess.

"Yes."

"You thought of me then?"

"Jennie, I've never stopped thinking about you."

"Then when I saw you in London, you knew who I was."

"Yes, angel. I knew very well who you were."

Jennie looked at the doll again, and then ran to Tess, grabbing her about the waist. Tess's eyes squeezed shut as she rocked her daughter back and forth. If there were only some way to keep her—but there wasn't. She must always remember that. "I'll keep it with me forever and ever."

"I'm glad, angel, but that might prove a trifle inconvenient when you make your come-out and attend your first ball."

Jennie giggled again, as Tess had intended. "Mrs. Granfield wouldn't like that."

Tess laughed outright. No, Mrs. Granfield likely wouldn't like that at all, nor any of Tess's other presents. Far too frivolous for her tastes. "Open the others, angel."

Jennie needed no urging. Soon her bed was covered with a silver-backed hairbrush engraved with Jennie's initials, with comb to match, from when she was two; a book with the alphabet illustrated in beautifully illuminated letters, from when she was three; and a skillfully constructed telescope, which Tess had bought last year after learning that Jennie and David liked to study the night sky together. Still, though, there were parcels left. At Jennie's curious, longing look, Tess moved over to the bed. "Well, now, and let's see what's in these," she said.

Jennie moved to her side, her eyes widening as Tess untied the string on one package to reveal a frock of emerald green, its merino wool almost as soft as silk. "For me?" she said again.

"Of course for you, silly, it wouldn't fit Nurse. Jewel colors for you, angel," she went on as Jennie, garbed unfortunately in stark white muslin, with a pale green satin sash as a concession to the season, turned her back to have her dress unbuttoned. "Ruby, sapphire, and creamy white. And do not ever allow anyone to force you to wear pastels when you make your come-out." The dress pooled around Jennie's feet, and she stepped out of it. "Peach, apple green, light turquoise, perhaps. No light blue, and by no means, no pink, unless it's a deep shade. There." She stepped back, surveying the effect of her handiwork. Just as she had thought, the rich shade of the frock brought color to Jennie's ordinarily pale cheeks and made her eyes sparkle. "And your coiffure is of utmost importance."

"Braids are the only way I can manage Lady Jennie's hair, 'tis so thick," Nurse said defensively.

"Um-hm." Tess was running her fingers through Jennie's curly, light brown locks. "It must be very difficult to wash."

"Oh, indeed, and to comb."

"I know you do your best, Nurse. I'll speak with the marquess about having a coiffeuse see to Jennie's hair when you return to London, shall I? But for now," she tied a velvet ribbon of the same shade as the frock about Jennie's head, "I think leaving it loose with this ribbon to hold it back will do."

Nurse was quiet for a long moment. "You're right, of course, miss."

"There." Tess stepped back, well pleased with her handiwork. When she had planned this ensemble, she had thought it would flatter Jennie's appearance, but even she hadn't realized how much. "Well, angel? Would you like to take a look?"

"Oh, may I?" Jennie approached the long pier glass with some trepidation, and then stood there for a moment, her fingers to her lips. "I'm pretty," she whispered. "I look pretty."

"Of course you do, angel. I didn't have the slightest doubt."

"But I never was before." She stared at herself for a moment longer, turning this way and that to gain the full effect, and then whirling around, flung herself at Tess. "Oh, thank you, Mama! 'Tis the best Christmas gift ever!"

Tess laughed for sheer joy and swung her around. "You're welcome, angel." *Treasure this,* she told herself fiercely. *Treasure her while you can.* "Let us open the rest of the packages and then go down to dinner to show you off, shall we?"

When Tess and Jennie entered the drawing room together, it was to find it already filled with all the members of the house party. Nigel, excited because it was Christmas, but on his best behavior because of being allowed the rare treat of eating with adults, nevertheless bounded up to Jennie to show off his new present, a toy soldier. Emily, smiling as she always did, looked on critically as Jennie chattered about receiving a doll and books and a telescope, of all things. A most unsuitable present for a child, she thought, studying Jennie's frock and hair. What had the child's nurse been thinking of, to allow her to wear her hair loose? It would become tangled in no time. And she certainly had never worn anything like that frock before. Emily wasn't altogether certain she approved. Although its high neckline was modest enough, surely its cut was too adult for someone of Jennie's tender years. Emily nearly frowned. Clearly Jennie needed to be taken in hand. It was not something Emily had anticipated, when she had become involved with Stowe.

"And I have more frocks, lots and lots of them, and hair ribbons, and a new cloak and everything!" Jennie was chattering to her father. "And Mama says I must see a coiffeuse when we return to town. That's someone who styles hair."

"Does she?" David looked at Tess. "It's quite a present, Miss Harwood."

"Thank you, Stowe."

"Did you send to London for everything?"

"No. I made them."

"Why, you're quite the seamstress," Emily said, and an awkward silence fell.

"You do lovely work," Lady Sherbourne said. "Your own gown is beautiful."

"Thank you."

"She designs her own clothes," the Duchess of Bainbridge put in. "I think they're lovely."

"Oh, certainly. You could almost be a London modiste, Miss Harwood," Emily said, and again there was a moment of silence. "Jennie, surely your hair should be braided?"

"It was Mama's idea to do it like this," Jennie

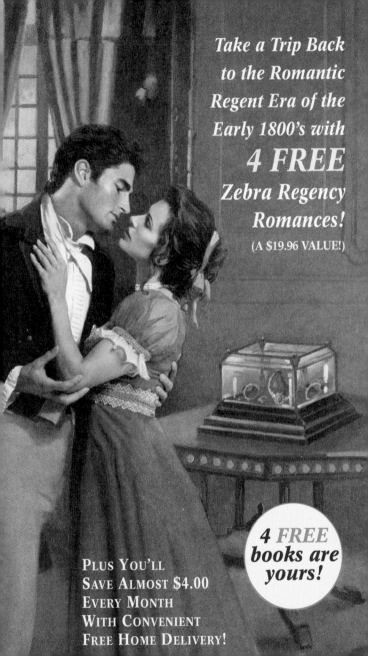

We'd Like to Invite You to Subscribe to Zebra's Regency Romance Book Club and Give You a Gift of 4 Free Books as Your Introduction! *(Worth $19.96!)*

If you're a Regency lover, imagine the joy of getting 4 FREE Zebra Regency Romances and then the chance to have the lovely stories delivered to your home each month at the lowest prices available! Well, that's our offer to you and here's how you benefit by becoming a Zebra Home Subscription Service subscriber:

- **4 FREE** Introductory Regency Romances are delivered to your doorst
- 4 BRAND NEW Regencies are then delivered each month (usually befor they're available in bookstores)
- Subscribers save almost $4.00 every month
- Home delivery is always **FREE**
- You also receive a **FREE** monthly newsletter, *Zebra/ Pinnacle Roman News* which features author profiles, contests, subscriber benefits, bo previews and more
- No risks or obligations...in other words you can cancel whenever you wish with no questions asked

Join the thousands of readers who enjoy the savings and convenience offered to Regency Romance subscribers. After your initial introductory shipment, you receive 4 brand-new Zebra Regency Romances each month to examine for 10 days. Then, if you decide to keep the books, you'll pay the preferred subscriber's price of just $4.00 per title. That's only $16.00 for all 4 books and there's never an extra charge for shipping and handling.

It's a no-lose proposition, so return the FREE BOOK CERTIFICATE today!

Check out our website at www.kensingtonbooks.com.

Say Yes to 4 Free Books!
Complete and return the order card to receive this $19.96 value, ABSOLUTELY FREE!

(If the certificate is missing below, write to:)
Zebra Home Subscription Service, Inc.,
120 Brighton Road, P.O. Box 5214, Clifton, New Jersey 07015-5214
or call TOLL-FREE 1-888-345-BOOK

FREE BOOK CERTIFICATE

YES! Please rush me 4 Zebra Regency Romances without cost or obligation. I understand that each month thereafter I will be able to preview 4 brand-new Regency Romances FREE for 10 days. Then, if I should decide to keep them, I will pay the money-saving preferred subscriber's price of just $16.00 for all 4...that's a savings of almost $4 off the publisher's price with no additional charge for shipping and handling. I may return any shipment within 10 days and owe nothing, and I may cancel this subscription at any time. My 4 FREE books will be mine to keep in any case.

Name _____

Address_____ Apt. _____

City_____ State_____ Zip_____

Telephone ( ) _____

Signature _____
(If under 18, parent or guardian must sign.)   RN119A

Terms and prices subject to change. Orders subject to acceptance by Zebra Home Subscription Service, Inc.
Offer valid in U.S. only.

said, with just that touch of defiance Emily had noted before. Oh, yes, the child needed to be taken in hand.

David was frowning a little. "You look pretty, poppet," he said to Jennie, making her smile radiantly before she dashed off with Nigel to demonstrate her telescope. "Miss Harwood, it's an extraordinary gift."

"I was glad to do it," Tess said, from her seat between the duchess and the viscountess.

Emily looked up from her embroidery hoop. "You must have worked your fingers to the bone, to have it done in time. I do needlework myself, but—"

"I like pretty clothes," Tess retorted lightly, and for the first time today Emily decided to retreat in the undeclared battle between them. She was sitting alone in a chair some long ago ancestress of Stowe had stitched in crewel; Miss Harwood was chatting animatedly to other members of the house party, quite as if she had never been in any sort of disgrace. Not only that, but her dark, glossy curls shone with brushing, and she wore a gown of cherry red velvet. Together she and Jennie looked like the very embodiment of Christmas. Emily had chosen an ensemble of forest green bombazine, which, though sedate and practical, she had considered to be festive enough. It wasn't fair that Miss Harwood should outshine her when she herself was Stowe's chosen, but there it was. Emily's only comfort was that Stowe had rejected Miss Harwood once. She would have to make certain he did so again.

Tess did not enjoy Christmas dinner, though the food was sumptuous and delicious. It began with a soup course, consisting of, among others, a rich pea soup and mock turtle soup. This was followed by a fish course that included a filet of sole in a fine

lobster sauce, poached turbot, and trout. Then, at
last, the main course, a magnificent roast goose, was
carried in, along with potatoes and salads and other
vegetables. Finally, the traditional plum pudding
came in, all aflame, and the children in particular
singed their fingers trying to pluck out the trinkets
Cook had placed in the pudding.

Tess cut into her slice of pudding, and almost immediately hit something hard. Eyebrows raised just
a bit, she used the fork to pull out the trinket, and
held up, to her dismay, a wedding ring. "Oh!" she
said involuntarily, and quickly drew the ring toward
her. Not in time, however. Lady Walcott, sitting
across from Tess, had looked up at her reaction.

"Why, you found the wedding ring," she said,
smiling. "You'll be married within the year, Miss
Harwood."

David pulled back in his chair, and for the first
time his gaze met Tess's. It seemed to her for a moment that silence descended upon the room, that no
one else was there but the two of them, until Jennie
tugged at her sleeve. "Mama, let me see."

Tess came back to herself, a little dazed. " 'Tis
only a trinket, Jennie. What did you find?"

Jennie shrugged. "Nothing."

"That doesn't seem fair. Here, you may have this,"
she said, and handed her the ring with careless
aplomb.

Jennie smiled. "Thank you, Mama," she said, and
dashed back to her chair.

David cleared his throat. "Shall we adjourn to the
drawing room?" he said, and everyone rose, to Tess's
relief. She could, she thought, wait a suitable time
and then make her escape. After all, she was here
only because Jennie had invited her, and, like David,
she was not proof against Jennie's persuasions. Seven

days were all that were left to her. That was all. Just seven days.

Jennie, of course, gravitated to her side, and she couldn't resist stroking the child's thick, springy hair as she leaned against her, a warm, comforting weight. More surprising was that most of the women of the party gathered near her as well, though she had chosen a chair in a corner of the drawing room, sheltered by the mantel. Only Mrs. Granfield sat apart, doing her eternal needlework in apparent peace. Tess had her measure now, though. She wondered if David did.

"I wouldn't say no to a hand of cards," Viscount Sherbourne said. The viscountess, who had been discussing the latest fashions with her and had, to Tess's amusement, mentioned that she sometimes patronized Madame Jeanette's salon for her clothing, looked up and smiled. It was just the sort of smile she and David had shared once, a smile that spoke of shared secrets and happiness, and suddenly she had had too much. Though tables were already being set up for cards, she rose.

"I must take my leave," she said, smiling impartially at the gathering.

"But the afternoon's barely begun," the viscountess protested.

Jennie looked up at her. "Mama, must you?"

"Yes, angel, I fear so." She rested her hand on her daughter's curls for a moment. "Your uncle Richard is spending rather a lonely day."

"Oh. We should have invited him, too.

"I imagine he's had some visitors."

"Rawley, I suppose," David drawled, the first time he'd addressed her directly in some time.

"I wouldn't know," she answered coolly, glancing quickly at the Duke of Bainbridge, who had, she was aware, been regarding her throughout the day with a speculative expression in his eyes. At David's mention of Adrian, his gaze had sharpened. She wondered why.

"I shall see you out, then."

"There's no need, really."

"But there is."

"Will I see you tomorrow?" Jennie asked, hugging her around the waist.

Tess smiled down at her. "Of course you will, angel. You'll be at the Manor in the afternoon."

"And the Christmas ball is the day after tomorrow."

Tess's smile faded a bit. "So it is." Thanks to Jennie's persuasions, she had at last been invited to the ball, a mixed blessing at best.

"Will I see you there?"

"Yes. I promise." Tess bent to kiss her. "Tomorrow, angel."

"Yes, Mama."

"I'll see you out," David said again, and though Tess wanted to protest, his grip on her elbow was too strong. Making her good-byes to the rest of the guests, she at last took her leave.

To her surprise, David pulled her into the morning room when they reached the hall, rather than calling for her cloak. Freeing herself from his hold on her, Tess turned to look up at him. "David?"

"I want a word in private with you, madam."

"Of course." She let out a gusty sigh. "We never see each other but that we must brangle."

"I don't intend to argue with you, madam. But I do want to know whom you plan to marry."

"Stowe, surely you don't believe in that superstition?" she said in astonishment.

"Is it Rawley?"

"No! I've told you that before. When will you believe me?"

He raised his eyebrows at her. "You need ask?"

She let out her breath. "If this is all you wish to say, then I would like to leave."

"No. Don't." He reached out to catch her wrist, and she looked down in surprise. The contact of his hand on her skin was as warm, and as electric, as ever it had been. "There's something else I'd like to discuss with you."

"Which is?"

"Your present to Jennie."

"Oh." She relaxed. "That."

"Yes. That."

"I know I should have asked your permission before I did anything with her appearance, but—"

"So you should have," he broke in. "You forget yourself sometimes, madam."

"She's my daughter. No matter what your wishes might be, nothing's going to change that. And as her mother, I can't just stand by and see her looking as she did. David, she's so much happier now," she went on, pleading with him, trying to make him see. "I know you've never been a—a man-milliner, so concerned with clothing and your appearance, so perhaps you don't understand how important such things are to women."

"Some women." He eyed her gown. "My wager is that that ensemble cost you a pretty penny."

"Not so much as you might think. I made it, David. I design and make most of my clothing."

"Even so, what you gave Jennie was lavish. I know what your income is, Tess. I provide it."

"What I gave Jennie is what any mother would give to her daughter," she said quietly. "My time and my concern. I remember my mother brushing my hair, braiding it at night for me when I was Jennie's age, trying out different styles. Oh, we used to laugh at some of the things she thought of."

"You miss her." David's voice had softened.

"Very much. That's why I know how important this is to Jennie. David, I know I have no say in anything concerning her anymore. But please, when you return to London, remember that. Find her a governess who can help her with these things, if Mrs. Granfield won't."

He frowned. "What are you saying about Mrs. Granfield?"

"Nothing, David. Only that she's not particularly stylish, is she?"

"Not very important, is it?"

"It will be when Jennie makes her come-out."

"That's in the future, Tess, and it's my concern."

Tess very briefly closed her eyes. It always came down to that. Jennie was not hers. "I must go," she said, stepping away.

"I must say, your influence over Jennie has been better than I expected," he said, as if she hadn't said anything, hadn't moved.

"It cheers me immensely to know that."

"There is no need to be sarcastic. I was paying you a compliment." He glanced away. "Perhaps we can do naught but brangle when we're together."

Oh, but once they had done more than that. Perhaps that was at the root of their arguing, a little voice whispered in her head. She forced her mind away from the thought. "Have you said all you wish, Stowe? Richard really will be waiting for me."

He nodded and stepped back, glancing up as he did so. And then he stopped, his gaze returning upward. "Well."

Tess looked up as well and saw a kissing bough.

It was beautifully made, of evergreens decorated with velvet ribbons of scarlet and green, making the mistletoe berries that descended from it glisten that much whiter. In fact, she realized, the entire room was decorated, much as the drawing room had been, with pine boughs that gave off a strong, clean scent, and more ribbons. She wondered how she had missed that before. She wondered how she would remove herself from this situation. "The decorations are beautiful," she babbled, stepping back, as he had, only to be brought up short when he caught her hand. "Stowe—"

"I fear there's no help for it, Tess." For the first time since his return to Yorkshire, she saw the old gleam in his eye, the one that had attracted her so, seven long years ago. "We seem to be under the kissing bough." And with that, to her immense surprise, he bent his head to hers.

Eight

He hadn't kissed Tess in years, David thought, as his lips met her soft, startled ones. Ah, but it was exactly as he remembered, though until this moment he would have said he'd completely forgotten what kissing her was like. Her lips, pliant, warm; her body, more womanly with age and with childbearing, yet still slender; her hands, small, white, coming up to clutch his sleeves. Then, suddenly, she was kissing him back, pressing against him, twining her fingers into her hair, and he was utterly lost. Tess, ah, Tess. He'd missed her. Not even to himself had he ever admitted that, but it was true. He'd missed her warmth, her laughter, her mischievousness and impulsiveness. He'd missed her in his bed. And she was right. A child needed a mother.

That awoke him to his danger. Yet it was Tess who broke the kiss, Tess who pulled back, swaying a little bit. "Well, Stowe," she said, her voice thready, but with an edge to it. "You once said you'd be damned if you ever did that again."

He blinked, still dazed. Dear God, what was he doing? If he kept on this way, he'd be enslaved again, and that would never do. Not with Jennie to think of. Not with—lord help him—Emily, as well.

"I have no doubt you meant for it to happen," he said, stiffly.

She stared at him. "I'm not the one who brought us in here!"

"So this was my idea? Oh, no, Tess. Remember, I know you too well."

"Ooh!" Tess paced away from him, her fists clenched. "As if I'd wish to kiss you again, after all the grief you've caused me."

"I've caused you!" Now it was his turn to stare. "My life was ruined because of you."

"And mine wasn't? I'm forced to stay here in Yorkshire—"

"You're no prisoner, not if you've managed to go to town to see Jennie. Against our agreement, I might add."

"I never agreed to it."

"Perhaps I should have said against my express command."

"Yes." Her hands gripped the back of a chair. "It would have been better had I seen this side of you before we married."

"So it would. And it would have been well for you to think of the consequences before you made your decision."

"Before you took Jennie away, you mean."

His breathing had quieted, but there was a strange ache in his heart. "So it was true, what you said. You never did care for me."

"I said I made a mistake." She briefly closed her eyes. "Please believe me, Stowe. I truly never meant for all that happened, to happen."

He didn't answer for a moment. "You believe that, don't you?"

" 'Tis true. I didn't want you to be hurt. Nor Jennie."

"I am glad of that. Pray remember, madam, that I will do all I have to do to protect her."

"Which means?"

"It means I am here only because she wishes me to be."

Tess narrowed her eyes. "You're jealous, aren't you?"

"Good God, no. Why should I be?"

"Because I can do things for her, as her mother, that you cannot." Tess's voice was quiet, with no hint of triumph. "Because, in spite of everything, she loves me."

God help him, but it was true. "God help you if she's hurt because of it."

"What have I done to hurt her, Stowe?"

"You are raising her expectations."

"In what way?"

"That you will be there in her life in some way. Those clothes, Tess—"

"My Christmas present to her."

"The attention you shower on her—"

"Which your fiancée does not."

"We will leave Mrs. Granfield out of this, thank you," he said, deeply irritated and not liking the feeling.

"Has she gone under the mistletoe with you yet?" she taunted him.

"Be very careful in what you say, Miss Harwood."

"She will not be a good mother to Jennie. She doesn't love her."

"Love is not enough."

"But it matters a great deal."

"So does constancy."

She opened her mouth, and then closed it again. "So it does."

"So, madam. What next do you plan to do?"

"What do I plan to do?" She frowned. "I don't exactly know what you mean, Stowe."

"I think you do." He faced her coolly. Coming to Yorkshire had been a mistake, no matter what Jennie had wanted. "I think you have been using Jennie to insinuate yourself back with me."

Tess lifted her chin. She was a game one, he'd say that for her. Always had been. "That sounds almost as if you would like to be involved with me again."

"Good God, no!" Agitated, he took a turn around the room. "That would be pure folly."

"Yes, we all know what a villainess I am."

"I didn't say that, Tess." He braced his hands on the back of a chair. Now that the firestorm of emotion between them had passed, he was shaking. God help him, but that kiss had affected him. "But if I didn't have guests, I'd . . ."

"What?"

"Pack up Jennie and return to London."

"Oh, no!" She hurtled toward him, her hands outstretched. In spite of himself, he took them. "You can't do that, not yet. I still have seven more days."

"I cannot trust you, Tess."

"Oh? Is it me you don't trust, or yourself?"

"What do you want with us, Tess?" he asked, after a few moments had passed in silence.

"I love Jennie. Is that so hard to believe?"

"Coming from you? Yes."

"Oh, really, Stowe! As if I'd use a child."

"I'd not be surprised if you did."

She turned away. "This does us no good. 'Tis past time I was returning to Harcourt."

"So it is. And perhaps 'tis better if you do not return."

"Oh?" She looked back at him. "Can you imagine the comments from the neighbors if I am not here for the ball, especially since Jennie has told everyone I will be?"

"Can you imagine them if you are?"

"I don't care, really." She moved toward the door. " 'Tis Jennie I care about. David, she wants me here. And I have yet to manage to refuse her, when she really wants something."

"Neither have I." For a moment they shared a wry smile, and then he sobered. "Very well, then. I suppose there's no way we can avoid your being here for the ball."

"No. But I promise not to inflict myself on you very often, Stowe." Her arm was stiff on his as he escorted her toward the hall. "I know how you feel about me."

Conscious of the presence of his butler and several footmen, David only nodded. If she knew how he felt, that was more than he did just now. He'd never been more confused in his life. "Then I shall see you in two days."

"Yes." Wrapped in her cloak of red velvet and looking more than ever like Christmas personified, she walked out the door, her head held high. "At the ball."

In two days, David thought, and all the days after, until he and Jennie could return to London. It seemed like an eternity; it seemed as if the days were speeding by. How he would survive them, he didn't know.

"My lord?" Williams, his butler, cleared his throat, and David returned to a sense of himself. "Is there anything you need?"

"No, Williams." David began to climb the stairs. "I shall be in the drawing room, with the other guests."

"Very good, sir."

David continued up the stairs, his tread heavy. No matter what happened, there was one thing he knew. He had never been so confused in his life.

The invitations to the Christmas ball at Stowcroft, with dinner before, had gone out, and the neighborhood was predictably aflutter with excitement. Such doings as they hadn't seen in ages! Why, the London folk, when they came into the village, appeared to be quite nice, and very condescending. True, the duke appeared to be a starchy sort of person, but then, one wouldn't expect less of such an august personage. And to think they would all be hobnobbing with such a set!

"Two viscounts, a duke, and the marquess, of course," Mrs. Frakes counted on her fingers. She was in alt at having received one of the coveted invitations, though she wouldn't admit it. "I daresay they behave differently at the Hall than they have in the village, or at church."

"Um," said her husband, a presence visible only by the stream of smoke rising from behind *The London Times*.

"I do expect to see some goings-on there. Why, I wouldn't be surprised if at least one of them were conducting an *affaire.*"

"Um," Mr. Frakes said again, and, putting down the paper, reached for a lucifer match to relight his pipe. "What is this nonsense you are spouting now, Lobelia?"

"Why, nothing, Mr. Frakes. Simply that I cannot believe that the *ton* truly behave as we have seen them do, these past days."

"Why not? They are people, like anyone else."

"And there have been dark doings in the village,

from time to time, too. We haven't far to look to see not one scandal, but two."

"Now, Lobelia." Mr. Frakes's voice was mild, but it held a hint of steel, as befit the man who, being from a family long established in the area, administered judgment as a magistrate in the county. "That is in the past."

"Is it? Have you seen Lord Stowe with Mrs. Granfield? I've heard talk there's an agreement between them, but, mark my words, Miss Harwood will come between them somehow."

"Now, Lobelia, enough!" he said sharply. "I don't believe this visit is easy for her, considering the circumstances."

Mrs. Frakes sniffed. "It is as I have always said. You have been taken in by her eyes. I daresay Lord Stowe was, too. But he learned soon enough, poor man."

"I wish I had," he muttered, and returned to his paper.

"What is that you say, Mr. Frakes?"

"Um." The paper rattled, and soon the stream of smoke was rising from behind it again. Mrs. Frakes eyed it balefully, and returned to her gleeful thoughts of all the scandalous behavior she was likely to witness. She could hardly wait to discuss it with Mrs. Lansdale. . . .

"You are really going to the ball, Anne?" Mrs. Lansdale asked as Miss Emery poured out tea for both of them.

"Of course. And don't tell me you're not, Fanny, because I won't believe you."

"Anne!"

"You'll be there, if only for Sophia's sake."

Mrs. Lansdale's face brightened. "Yes, I do have a duty to her, do I not?" She took a sip of tea. "Is Miss Harwood going, do you know?" she asked, elaborately casual.

"Yes, I believe she is. Her daughter wants her there, of course."

"Poor Miss Harwood. How difficult this must all be for her."

Miss Emery smiled to herself. The one time she had spoken with Tess, her friend had been in good spirits. "She seems to be bearing up under it."

"Oh, Miss Harwood is very brave. I am sure, were I in her position, that I could not do what she is doing. I believe, don't you, that we should be there to support her?"

Miss Emery took a sip of her tea, to hide her smile. Mrs. Lansdale would not, she knew, miss this for the world. "Oh, certainly."

"I wonder," she said, setting down her teacup in its saucer, "if Mrs. Reeves will go."

Mrs. Reeves was, as it happened, in alt about the ball, though not simply because she, too, had received an invitation and would be attending. Everyone in Stowfield had come to her husband's shop for fabric for their ensembles. They had realized a tidy profit, and that, she thought, eyes gleaming as she again looked over the books she kept for her husband, was quite enough for her.

Two evenings later, Tess handed her cloak to a footman in the hall at Stowcroft and took a deep breath as she and Richard, her escort, prepared to climb the stairs to the ballroom. It was not only the ball she dreaded, with its necessary proximity to David; it was the fact that this would be the first time the neighborhood would see her here since her marriage had broken up. In the main, she thought as she climbed the stairs, holding the skirts of her spangled blue gauze ball gown so that they wouldn't trail, the neighbors had taken what was surely a scandalous event quite well. Of course, there had been those who'd wondered what she'd done to turn such a prime matrimonial catch away, primarily those with daughters of marriageable age, or who tended to be gossipy or malicious. Others had whispered far more hurtful words, so far as she had been concerned. Like mother, like daughter, they'd said. Fortunately, however, they were few and far between. All told, she had managed to scrape through rather well. The fact that she had since lived a blameless life likely had something to do with it. She wondered what people would say after tonight.

"You don't have to do this," Richard said abruptly at her side.

Tess didn't look at him. She needed all her strength to get through the night. "I absolutely do have to do this."

"He could have at least invited you to dinner."

"I'm pleased he didn't," she snapped, though she hadn't wanted Richard to see how much that deliberate cut had hurt. She knew quite well of the dinner David had hosted before the ball, with not only all his houseguests present, but most of the gentry of the neighborhood. Only she, Richard, and Adrian had not been invited. She thought that significant.

"Reason enough, I'd think, not to come to the ball."

"I have to. Jennie is expecting me, you see."

For the first time since they had arrived at Stowcroft, Richard's face softened. "It's all about her, isn't it?"

"Of course it is," she said, irritated, though she knew she was being less than truthful. It was about David, too, and herself, about the past and the future and a tangled morass of emotions. "Why else would I be here?"

"Why, indeed?" he agreed, with enough dryness to make her wonder if he suspected the truth.

Perhaps fortunately for her, they reached the top of the stairs at that moment, and the crowd of people made private conversation impossible. In spite of that, a draft seemed to touch her shoulders, making her shiver. Somehow she'd managed to forget how chilly it could be at Stowcroft in winter. Perhaps it was because that first winter spent here had begun so warmly, in David's arms.

Now, though, she only felt the cold. Not for the first time she regretted the impulse that had made her choose such a gown for tonight, no matter the shawl draped carefully about her. It was more suited for a London ballroom in the spring, as she had intended, rather than a Yorkshire winter. For another, it was much too revealing, too closely cut in the waist and hips, too low across her bosom. She wasn't sure why she had decided to wear it, unless it was in response to some undeclared gauntlet thrown down by David on Christmas Day, during their disagreement. Clearly, he regretted what he considered to be succumbing to her lures by kissing her; just as clearly, she hadn't thought her actions through when she had decided on this dress. Instead, she had given in to what she considered to be the worse side of her nature, she thought as she waited for them to be announced, the rash, impetuous side. It had got her into trouble more than once in the past. It had led to her marriage to David.

It could have been Tess's imagination, but she

thought there was a little hush when her name was called. Certainly Mrs. Frakes was staring at her and whispering to Mrs. Lansdale. But then, she had expected that. The London ladies, she couldn't help noticing, were dressed in the highest stare of fashion, while several people of the neighborhood had outfitted themselves creditably. Mrs. Frakes, however, was garbed in what she likely considered to be a flattering, stylish ensemble, a gown of purple moiré that wasn't kind either to her stout figure or to her coloring, and a Moorish turban, stylish two years ago, in purple shot with gold, upon her head. Sophia Lansdale, too tall, too thin, and, worst of all, too silly, was dressed unsuitably in pastel pink. And Mrs. Granfield again was dressed sedately, this time in a full cut gray satin gown. Seeing all this shouldn't have bolstered her, she knew, but it did.

Holding her head high, she advanced to greet David, and he bent, quite correctly, over her hand. Oh, unfair of him, to be dressed as he was, in a beautifully cut coat of black velvet worn with white satin knee breeches and a silver-and-burgundy striped vest. On another man, the effect might have been austere. On him, it was merely elegant.

David's eyes briefly met hers as she rose from her curtsy, and she collected herself. "Is Jennie about?" she asked.

As Richard's had earlier, David's face softened at the mention of his daughter's name. "Up there," he said, turning toward the minstrel gallery that looked over the ballroom. Tess smiled up at her and gave a little wave, and Jennie, garbed in nightrail and dressing gown and with her hair braided, broke into that rare smile that so briefly made her a beauty. The joy and warmth that Tess always felt when she saw her child flooded through her. If only . . . But wishes were rarely granted, she reminded herself. She would never have the opportunity to be with Jennie on a daily basis.

Nurse touched Jennie's shoulder lightly, and the two of them withdrew, Jennie throwing one last longing glance back at the ballroom. Holding back her sigh, Tess placed her hand on Richard's arm again and prepared herself to face the people gathered for the ball.

"We had a ball when I was here," she said wistfully. "To celebrate our marriage."

Her gaze went about the big room. Unlike the rest of the house, it wasn't decorated specifically for Christmas. Instead, its pale blue walls, huge chandeliers with their many crystal lusters, and gilt-framed mirrors had been festooned with white draperies and silver ribbon. The effect was that of a winter fairyland. "We had flowers everywhere, heather, like we have on the moors. I don't know how David managed that, but it was beautiful, all purple and white. I know it raised a few eyebrows, but we liked it." And they had had special meaning to her and David, something she would share with no one. "We even had a trellis with white roses growing up it, and a little arbor, like the one in the garden here. I know he must have sent to London for those. It was such a surprise to me. Do you remember?"

"I was still in Leeds then, Tess, trying to find a way to make Harcourt more profitable, with no idea of what you'd done," he said grimly. "Do you remember that?"

"Yes," she said in a small voice. "But I hadn't thought about what I'd done. All I cared about was the way we felt then."

"I never did think the way you handled things was right—but that's in the past."

She stared at him. "What else could I do once you pointed out to me the damage I'd done to Stowe by marrying him?"

"You could have taken time to think about your plan and its consequences, instead of going ahead with it." He paused. "You could have told him."

Tess glanced away. She had been impetuous on that long ago day when David had begun to hate her, yet it had seemed at the time that she had little choice. "As you say, it's in the past."

"Yes. Oh, lord, look who's coming toward us."

Tess looked over to see Mrs. Frakes, the squire's wife, bearing down on them. "Oh, no. I don't suppose I can run away."

"We would be too obvious."

" 'We'?" She looked at him, fighting the urge to laugh. "I suppose we would be, at that. Mrs. Frakes," she said, greeting the woman with perfect composure.

"Miss Harwood. Mr. Harwood." Mrs. Frakes sounded breathless from her determined progress across the room. "Doesn't the ballroom look splendid? Oh, but I've forgotten. You've seen it at Christmas before. Though that was seven years ago."

Only the sudden pressure of Richard's hand on her arm kept Tess from blurting out some angry retort that would surely have led to a quarrel, and the kind of attention she didn't desire. "It does look lovely. If you'll excuse me, I hear the music starting."

"Yes, but—"

"We shall talk more later," Tess said and turned away, clutching Richard's arm. "That—that woman!"

"Bear up, Tess. Once everyone gets used to seeing you here, it won't matter."

"How utterly—vexed!—I am with her," Tess continued as if Richard hadn't spoken.

He laughed. "I suspect that's not what you were about to say."

"I should have pointed out that Stowcroft's been closed for six years."

"And then she would have been able to talk about the past. Give over, Tess. There's no satisfying Mrs. Frakes, and no good in trying."

"I know, but she makes me so angry." Tess glanced up at him. "I suppose you are right. If I could learn to keep a civil tongue in my head where she's concerned, I could deal with her."

Richard shook his head. "Tess, no one can deal with her."

"Who?" a voice said beside them, and they turned to see Adrian Rawley.

"Mrs. Frakes," Tess explained.

"Ah." Adrian nodded. "She can be difficult, but happens squire knows what to do."

Tess laughed suddenly. "Adrian, I do believe you missed your calling. You should have been a diplomat."

To her surprise, he turned a bright red. "Well, ah, happens I'd be tongue-tied and make a fool out of myself if I tried. I'm just a farmer."

"Nevertheless—"

"And I'd like to have this dance with you."

Tess, looking at the sets forming, saw David bending over Mrs. Granfield, smiling at her, and made her decision. "I'd like that," she said, and placed her hand on Adrian's arm.

Across the room, David, just taking the first steps in the quadrille, glanced up in time to see Tess smile up at Rawley. *Bloody hell,* he thought, and lost his footing, pulling the Duchess of Bainbridge, his partner for the dance, off balance for a moment. "Oh, dear," she said.

"I am sorry, Sabrina. My fault entirely."

She glanced across the room, as he had, and a small smile formed on her lips. "They're a handsome couple together, don't you think?" she said.

"No," he said tersely.

"And of course they have so much in common, both coming from the same neighborhood."

"All Rawley talks of is sheep."

"I suspect he's discussing other things besides wool," the duchess said, before the patterns of the dance separated them and then brought them together again. "It would do her a world of good to marry again, don't you think?"

"Sabrina, pray let us discuss other matters."

"Why, Stowe. One would think you still care about her."

David threw her a fulminating glance, and then, reluctantly, smiled. "I suspect Bainbridge has his hands full with you."

"Oh, he does. But then, you do, too," she said, and she smiled as once again they were separated by the dance.

What was that supposed to mean? he wondered, his brow wrinkled. Emily hardly gave him a moment's concern. Why, even now she sat on one of the chairs for chaperons and matrons set against the wall and calmly watching the dancers. It was frustrating that she had refused his request for the first dance, though he reluctantly understood why. After all, she had definitely promised him the supper dance, and she felt that for him to stand up with her twice would be to pay her attention that could only be interpreted one way. Surely, though, that wasn't so very bad? After all, everyone knew how matters stood between them, or nearly everyone. Those that didn't were of the neighborhood, and he suspected it wouldn't take them long to learn how matters stood. Nor did it concern him. Emily was his fiancèe, if not officially. Why shouldn't they dance more than once?

Tess chose that moment to smile radiantly at Rawley, and raw, hot anger twisted David's stomach. What *were* they talking about? he wondered, just as he had always wondered about Rawley's place in Tess's life. Lord knew what she saw in him. He was solid, rather than handsome; stolid, rather than dashing. God knew, he could be unutterably dull when he prosed on about his farm or his sheep. Someone had told David once that Rawley had once aspired to go to school and then to university. Looking at the man now, it was hard to credit it.

"Stowe." A tug on his hand made him look down at Sabrina. Belatedly he realized that the music had ended. "She's not in love with him."

"How can you tell?" he demanded.

"All you need do is watch her with him."

He raised his head, aware, suddenly, of what he had just revealed. "And why should I?"

Her smile was slight and mysterious as she stepped back. "Why, indeed? Oliver." She smiled at her husband. "We were just discussing how well Miss Harwood looks."

"Yes," Bainbridge said, though his gaze didn't leave his wife. "Criminal of you, Stowe, to lead my wife out for the first dance."

Stowe smiled, the lazy smile of one old friend to another. "Am I to expect a challenge?"

"Not this time. Come, minx." He took his wife's arm. "I've no doubt this was your fault."

David smiled as they moved away, but it faded quickly. Once he and Tess had been that close, secure enough with each other to tease and to trust. Once, long, long ago.

He shook the thought off. The past was the past and could not be brought back, even if he wanted it. Which he didn't.

On impulse, he picked up two crystal flutes of champagne from a silver tray held out to him by a bewigged footman, and crossed the polished oak floor to Emily. "Are you enjoying yourself?" he asked, smiling at her as he sat beside her.

"Very much so, Stowe," she said, making a little face at her first sip of champagne. "The musicians are nearly as good as any in London."

"You sound surprised. York is a fine city, you know."

"Oh, I don't doubt it. But it is all very provincial here, is it not?"

David sipped from his own glass, eyeing her over the rim with a slight frown. "I've always thought that was part of its charm."

"Oh, yes, of course. Though you have only been here twice."

His smile had completely faded. "Quite true. Emily." The same impulse that had caused him to reach for the champagne now made him place his hand on hers. He was surprised when, after a moment, she pulled hers away. Did the woman never laugh, did she never sing or wish to wear pretty clothes and dance the night away? Not that he wanted all those things in a bride, he reminded himself, uneasily aware that he had just described Tess. Or, not her as she was now. Rather, the Tess he had once known. It would be well, though, if she could balance her serenity with liveliness. "Stand up with me for the next dance."

"Oh, that wouldn't be wise. I am glad, Stowe,"

she went on, "that you didn't include a waltz tonight. Such a shocking dance. Though I imagine this entertainment will have the neighborhood buzzing for weeks. I'm persuaded they have never before seen the like."

"Only when Tess and I were first married," some imp of mischief goaded him to say. For a moment Emily's eyes widened, and he saw a flash of what he could swear was anger in them. Then she looked back down at her glass.

"Of course," she said, still calmly. "But that was long ago." She looked around the room. "The decorations are lovely, Stowe. They must have come quite dear."

Again his smile faded. "They're worth it, I believe."

"Oh, indeed. But was it seemly to allow Jennie to appear in the minstrel's gallery like that?"

He stiffened. "Yes. Quite," he said, and rose. "The music will be starting for the next set, and I imagine I am promised to someone, if you will not dance. Will you excuse me, Emily?"

"Oh, yes, of course."

David's mood was black as he stalked across the floor. For someone who appeared so calm and restful, Emily had the ability to make one angry and uneasy. He'd never noticed that before coming to Stowcroft. But then, he'd never thought that she had enough malice to tell Jennie what she had. He would have to ask her about that.

"Yes, Miss Harwood is on her best behavior tonight," he heard someone say. The squire's wife, he would guess, and paused. "Of course, she can't help what she is, though. Like mother, like daughter."

"You know that isn't true, Lobelia," someone answered, and he moved on, frowning. In his brief time at Stowcroft, both now and six years ago, he had learned to discount much of what Mrs. Frakes said. Still, there was often a kernel of truth in such comments. Troubled, he let his gaze seek Tess. Like mother, like daughter. Why? He'd never heard a word against Tess's mother before now. If there were something, though, it worried him. Had some fatal tendency in Tess been passed to Jennie? If so, he would have to guard his daughter against her mother's influence even more diligently than he had planned.

He reached for another goblet of champagne and stood surveying his guests. "A fine gathering, my lord," a voice said beside him, and he looked over to see Reverend Naseby, the vicar. His wife was something of a gossip, too, but the man himself was sound, David thought. "You've given Stowfield much to discuss in the future. Yes, much to discuss."

Oddly enough, it was the perfect opening for the question that nagged at David, yet he didn't want to ask it. "Reverend, you've been in the neighborhood for some years, have you not?"

"Indeed, I have. It was your father who gave me the living."

David nodded. "He made a wise choice, I believe."

"Thank you, my lord. I try my best."

"I'm sure you do. Vicar." His concern made his voice abrupt. "Did you happen to know Mrs. Harwood?"

The vicar's eyes were wary. "Yes, my lord, I did."

"I heard something tonight—well, never mind. Tell me, vicar, if you will. How did she die?"

The vicar's eyebrows rose. "Don't you know?"

"No. Miss Harwood has never told me."

"Oh, dear." He glanced off into the distance. "This is unexpected. Quite unexpected, indeed."

David tensed. So his instincts were right. There *was* something. "Why?"

"I can see, yes, why Miss Harwood didn't tell you. I remember you both as you were—"

"Yes, yes." David slashed through the air impatiently with his hand. "How did she die?"

"Oh, but she didn't. Die, that is, my lord."

Stupefied, not quite understanding, David looked at him. "I beg your pardon?"

"Miss Harwood's father engaged a painter from London to do a portrait of his wife. She was lovely, you know, much as Miss Harwood is. Though I think Miss Harwood's face is sweeter."

"Yes, yes. And?"

"They ah, eloped, I fear. Mrs. Harwood and the painter. To Italy, I think. So far as I know, they are still there."

David stood frozen. In his mind revolved two thoughts. "She never told me," he repeated.

"No, my lord," the vicar said, more gently now. "But you can hardly blame her. She—"

"I thought there was trust enough between us."

"She was young, my lord, as were you. Imagine how she felt, facing you with such knowledge. It caused the family terrible shame, and one might say it killed her father," he added.

"Yes." For the first time he understood why Tess had never had a season, not even in York or Harrogate. The scandal must have been terrible to face.

He glanced across the room to see Tess, her head thrown back in laughter as she stood with Lady Sherbourne and Rawley. Anger began to burn through the ice that had encased him. *Like mother, like daughter,* he thought, the second of the thoughts that had taken possession of his brain a few moments earlier. Rawley would not have her, though. Not if he had anything to say about it.

"Thank you, vicar," he said abruptly, and again stalked across the room, this time toward the musician's gallery. The conductor, about to raise his baton for the next set, looked startled when David spoke; even more startled when told what to play next. Then, nodding, he turned back to his musicians. David thus returned to the ball just as the strains of a waltz filled the room.

For a moment everyone stood still. Then people began to find partners, some with open pleasure, others with guilty delight at such a shocking dance. Still others, Mrs. Frakes among them, frowned mightily in disapproval. David glided across the floor and reached his intended partner just ahead of his competition, Adrian Rawley. "Miss Harwood. May I have the pleasure of this dance?"

Tess turned toward him, her lips parted in surprise. "Stowe, you can't be serious."

"But I am."

"Then I'm sorry, sir, but I must decline. I'm promised to someone for this set."

David turned and bent on Adrian a look of such ferocity that that man, hampered by the glass of lemonade in his hand, went still. "I am sure he won't mind this once."

Adrian stepped forward. "On the contrary, Stowe—"

"Good," David said, and swept Tess onto the dance floor. God help him, but he was glad he'd done this. He was glad he had Tess in his arms again.

Nine

"David!" Tess stared up at him, though her arms had gone into the proper position for a waltz and her steps matched his. "Whatever has possessed you?"

"Nothing. Oh, the devil take it." He looked down at her. "What happened to your mother?"

She blinked. "My mother?"

"Yes."

"Didn't I tell you?"

"You know very well you didn't."

"Well." She took a deep breath. "It was quite sad. When I was a young girl—"

"Oh, stubble it," he said wearily. "I know what happened, Tess."

Her eyes closed and she stumbled again, as she had when he first swept her up for the waltz. This time, though, he caught her by the waist, pulling her just that bit closer to him. She smelled of peaches, fresh and wholesome. How did she manage that, even in winter? "How did you find out?"

"I had it from the vicar, after I heard—well, never mind. Tess." He gazed down at her. "Why did you not tell me?"

She looked away. "I tried, David, several times,

but when it came to it, I couldn't. Don't you remember how it was?"

His teeth clenched. "I try very hard not to."

Tess briefly closed her eyes at that. "I was afraid of how you'd look at me, of what you'd think—David, please look at me."

"I am looking at you, madam."

"No. At *me,* the person you used to know."

"Ah, but that was the problem, wasn't it? You weren't who I thought you were."

"You won't listen." Her voice had gone lifeless. "I should have known. You wouldn't then, either."

"What is there for you to say, madam?"

"Nothing." She looked away. "Nothing."

For a time there was silence between them. Why in God's name had he requested a waltz? he wondered. Partly to spite Emily, he admitted, feeling just a little ashamed, just a little satisfied. Mostly, though, because it was the only way he could think of at the time to speak with any privacy to Tess. Now he was bound to her until the music ended. Now he was more and more aware of her, of his hand at her waist, still as slender as ever it had been; of her hair brushing against his chin; of the warmth of her body, though he held her, quite correctly, away from him. This had been a mistake.

"Was that why you called for a waltz?" she asked finally, and silence fell again, with the question in David's mind.

He looked down at her. Was it, if he were honest with himself? "Yes."

From the corner of his eye as he whirled Tess in the dance, he thought he saw someone beckon to him. Whoever it was was lost in a swirl of color and movement, until he turned and again found himself facing the doorway of the ballroom. "What the devil?" he exclaimed involuntarily.

"What?"

"Jennie's nurse."

Tess craned her head to see. "Where?"

"At the door."

"Whatever for?"

"I don't know. Tess, do you mind if I leave you?"

"If there's a problem with Jennie? Yes."

He had released her, but now he stared at her in surprise. "What?"

"If this concerns my daughter, I'm coming with you."

"Oh, no, you're not," he growled, as he worked his way through the dancers to the edge of the room.

"Oh, yes, I am," she answered, following him. "Or do you wish me to cause a scene?"

She would, too, he thought. "Oh, very well," he said, and struggled through the people, leaving Tess to find her own way. Jennie needed him. That was all that mattered.

A waltz. She'd never thought she'd see such a thing, Mrs. Frakes thought, watching from a chair near Mrs. Granfield. But then, she should have expected such fast behavior from London lords and ladies. She should also have expected Miss Harwood to stand up with Stowe. Some people had no morals, she thought, her indignation mixing with an odd kind of glee. Oh, she'd have this to ponder and discuss throughout the rest of the long, hard winter, along with everything else that had happened since the house party's arrival. It was quite a thrilling prospect.

A space cleared unexpectedly in the dancers before her, and she saw Stowe abruptly leave the floor, closely followed by Miss Harwood. *Well.* This was interesting. A quick glance showed her that Mrs. Granfield, who hadn't the same perspective, hadn't noticed. It was up to her, then, to learn what was happening.

Rising slowly, as if she were concerned about nothing more than obtaining a glass of punch, she peered over the bobbing, weaving heads to watch the progress of her quarry. They appeared to be heading out of the room, into the main part of the house. *Well,* she thought again, and, as Tess and David were doing, began to inch around the edge of the room. This bore investigation, she thought, if only for the sake of Lord Stowe's poor little daughter, or for Mrs. Granfield. Clearly it was her moral duty to discover what was about.

"I'm sorry, my lord," Nurse repeated, "but Lady Jennie is missing from her bed again."

David sucked in his breath. "Have you set other servants to searching?"

"Yes, my lord, but there's not a sign of her yet."

"Da—" David bit off the swear, and in spite of the situation, Tess held back a smile. Nurse looked so earnest and so upset, and he was, if nothing else, a gentleman. "Very well. I'll join you in searching."

"Oh, my lord, but I didn't mean for you to leave the ball," Nurse protested. "Nor Miss Harwood, neither."

"Do you think I'll stay here, dancing, while my daughter is missing? No."

"You did exactly right, Nurse," Tess said soothingly, following David as he stalked toward the main part of the house.

"Go back to the ball, Tess," David ordered, picking up a candle to light the way as he turned with one foot on the oak stairs that led to the family's private quarters.

She remembered a time once when David had swept her up in his arms and carried her up those stairs—but that was past. "I want to help you find her."

"You can't. You don't know the house."

"But I do. I lived here for some weeks."

He stopped. "So you did," he said in a toneless voice, and went on.

It was, she thought, a subject best left unexamined. "Where do you think she went?"

"Lord knows. She sleepwalks."

That really made her stop in surprise. "Often?"

David reached the top of the stairs and started for the nursery floor. "Often enough, but only since we came to Stowcroft."

"Oh." Since Jennie had met her. The mantel of guilt settled more heavily on Tess. She had done this to Jennie, the child she loved more than herself, the daughter whose well-being she would happily put above her own.

The sudden, sharp realization brought her to a dead halt on the stairs. "Why are you stopping?" David asked, impatiently tugging on her hand.

"I was just thinking." She started climbing again, though her mind was in turmoil. Six years ago, she had thought she was acting to save David from being touched by the scandal she'd had to live with for so long. She'd tried to save him from being hurt, or had she? In the brief moment when she had held Jennie after her birth, when she had looked down into the small red face, she had known she would do anything for her, she would give her up if that were best, she would die for her if she had to. Strong, dramatic thoughts, if true ones. Tess loved Jennie so much that she had realized, for the first time, that she had a higher loyalty, the duty to put someone else's well-being before her own.

She had thought she was doing that for David, but if she truly had been, she wouldn't have made such a grand, tragic gesture as she had. She would have told him the truth, borne his shock, and then let him deal with it. True, his career would have suffered, but not so much as it eventually had. Even had they simply separated, he would likely have been ruined. *Dear God.* Her intentions had not been so good after all, not if they were mixed with guilt and her own need to feel better. *Dear God,* she thought again. She had not, after all, acted in David's best interest.

"What is it now?" David asked, pulling at her hand, and she realized that she had again stopped.

"I'm sorry, I was trying to think," she said, with perfect, if inaccurate, truth. "Where does she usually go?"

"God knows. I've found her in the study, in my sitting room, even in the estate office. She could be anywhere."

"Why didn't Nurse keep an eye on her?"

"She fell asleep." His voice was terse. "God knows where Jennie could be," he repeated.

"We'll find her, David." She was breathless from the pace he set, and yet something he'd just said bothered her. The study, his sitting room . . . "David."

He looked back impatiently to where she had stopped in the dimly lit corridor. "What?"

"Jennie's logical."

"So?"

"She goes to places where it's logical she'd be safe. Your study, David. Your sitting room. Even your office."

His gaze held hers. "I hadn't thought of that."

"It's something I would have done, if I'd walked in my sleep as a child." If she'd had someplace safe to go to.

"Very well." He turned abruptly around. "I'll send someone to look in the study and the office. Come with me."

Instinctively she tried to pull back as his fingers closed around her wrist, but his grip was too strong. Nor did she really want him to let go, she admitted. David touched her so rarely. Never mind that he did so because of Jennie. For this brief time, they were united. "Where are we going?"

"To my room."

"David—"

" 'Tis a logical place, Tess. Even you have to admit that."

"Yes, but I surely don't belong there."

"If she isn't here, we'll leave." Candle held high, he opened the door to his room. For a moment it appeared deserted, and then they both heard it: the deep, even breathing of someone asleep.

Quietly they crossed the room, and there Jennie was, curled up in a ball on the big tester bed, fast asleep. "Oh, thank God," Tess said, her knees going weak with relief.

"Yes." For a moment they stood together, two parents looking at their child as she slept, and then the door creaked open farther.

"My lord?" a voice said tentatively.

David turned. "She's here, Nurse."

"Oh, thank heavens. I was that worried—"

"Yes, well, all is well now." He bent down and

carefully lifted the sleeping child. Jennie grumbled a little in her sleep as he cradled her.

"I'll just take her, my lord, and settle her in her bed again," Nurse said. "And I'll make sure she won't walk again tonight."

"Thank you, Nurse."

Tess stared after them. "But Jennie is surely too heavy for her," she protested.

"Shh, she'll hear you." He waited for a moment, until they could no longer hear Nurse's heavy tread. "Nurse feels guilty. She wants to do something to make up for what happened."

"Oh." She would never have credited David with such sensitivity. At least, not since their marriage had broken up. "Thank God we found her."

David stared at her as if he were seeing her for the first time. "You love Jennie," he said, in the tone of one experiencing a great revelation.

"Yes. That's what I've been trying to tell you."

"Good God." He turned away, toward the bed. "I'd never have credited it."

"I'm not heartless, David."

"No. I suppose you're not." He looked back at her. "Then why . . . ?"

"Please." She closed her eyes briefly. "For once, let's not talk of the past."

"It influences all we do."

She was silent for a moment. "I bear you no ill will."

He laughed mirthlessly. "Generous of you."

"I know." She stepped closer. "I know I hurt you."

"Hurt me!" He stared at her. "My God, Tess. You nearly destroyed me."

"We did some painful things to each other." She

held his gaze. "But we have a beautiful child. At least something good came of it."

"Yes." He turned away again. "We had some good times, didn't we?"

"The best." *Together on the moors,* she thought, and closed her eyes against the sweet pain of that memory. "David." Impulsively she laid her hand on his arm. "Don't keep Jennie from me. Don't keep us from each other. It's not fair to her." She paused, and then, as he frowned, rushed into speech. "I'll be discreet, I promise."

He grinned suddenly, the smile she hadn't seen in oh, so long, but which she remembered all too well. She had yearned for that smile, she realized now with some surprise. "You discreet, Tess? I'm not sure I believe that."

"You'd be surprised."

"Oh, yes." Still, though, he smiled. "But about Jennie. I agree."

She sucked in her breath. "You do? Oh, thank God," she said, as relieved as she had been when they'd found the missing child.

"I never knew how important you were to her, but I've seen the changes in her since we've come to Stowcroft. We'll work something out."

"But won't that be difficult, with Mrs. Granfield?"

His eyes clouded. "Jennie is still my daughter, Tess, and yours. She deserves to have her mother in her life."

"Thank you, David." She tightened her grip. "You don't know what it means to me."

"I think I do," he said, and, to her utter astonishment, pulled her into his arms.

For a moment, Tess rested her head against David's shoulder, reveling in his nearness. She had missed this so, this simple closeness. Yet it wasn't right, not now, and not in his bedchamber, of all places. She was usually the impetuous one, but this time she would have to be wise for both of them.

Determinedly, if reluctantly, she pulled away. "We must go back downstairs, David."

He sighed. "I suppose we must." A spark of deviltry lit his eyes. "Should I ask them to play another waltz?"

"Why did you do that?"

He pondered her question. "I was angry, I think, that you never told me about your mother. It explains a lot."

She stiffened. "Oh?"

"Yes. I daresay you didn't notice, but occasionally people give you pitying looks. I've often wondered why."

"I noticed," she said, feeling oddly relieved, oddly let down. She gathered up all her strength. It was long past time to leave. "We must go—"

"As for the waltz," he said, and she stopped at something in his voice. "Foolish of me, but I suppose I wanted to hold you again."

"David—"

"As much as, God help me, I want to hold you now."

She looked up at him, seeing reflected in his eyes the same confusion she felt, but also, more importantly, the same need, the same longing. It was enough. Without letting herself think, she went into his arms, as naturally as breathing. When he lowered his head, she raised hers for his kiss, as impetuously as she had ever done anything. As rashly, and as exultantly, as she had behaved on the moors, so many years ago. Who would know, after all, or see?

The kiss was more tender than passionate, more a reminder of days past, when they were young and newly in love, when they were tentatively learning to express that love, when passion was new to them both. Yet Tess gave herself up to it wholeheartedly, knowing that he might never hold her again. Knowing that she had to end this now, else the memory of this moment, sweet though it would be, would hurt beyond bearing.

With great effort, she pulled away. "We can't," she gasped, surprised to find herself more affected by the kiss than she had realized. By the glazed look in David's eyes and the heightened color in his cheeks, so was he.

"No. We can't, can we?" He sounded almost regretful. "Ah, but Tess. There was a time . . ."

"I know," she said, and suddenly, recklessly, went up on her toes to press her mouth against his. No tender caress this, as his arms clamped tight about her, as his mouth ravaged hers, as the kiss became hot and demanding and open mouthed. It could lead nowhere, she knew in some corner of her brain, but she didn't care. The future could go hang. This was what mattered, this moment now. She was in David's arms again, and that was all she cared about.

"Lord Stowe? Is all well?" a voice said from the doorway, breaking the bond between them and shattering it into a million shards. "I saw you leave the ballroom and I was wondering if something was wrong—oh!" Mrs. Frakes stood in the doorway, her hand to her mouth. "Oh, my goodness, I do apologize. I didn't realize you were here, Miss Harwood."

Oh, no, Tess thought, and her gaze met David's, grim and foreboding. They had been well and truly caught, and in the most compromising of circumstances, by the one person whom they could trust not to be discreet. Now they would have to face the consequences.

Ten

"I shall go into York for a special license," David said the following morning, in his study.

"Aye. See that you do," Richard answered. The two men were sitting in comfortable, wing-backed chairs upholstered in brown leather, but neither looked at ease. "I'll not have my sister's reputation blackened any further."

"Her reputation! If she hadn't persisted in following me—"

"You can return to London, with few people the wiser," Richard retorted. "Tess has to live here. Her reputation barely recovered the last time. My God, there are still people who whisper about what happened then. This time . . ."

"I know she'll suffer for this." David rose and paced the floor irritably. "And I know she only followed me out of concern for Jennie. But I cannot help being angry about this."

"You compromised her beyond repair."

"We compromised each other." He dropped down into the chair again. "It's a damnable situation."

Richard didn't answer right away. "So it is."

"I'll do right by her, of course. The marriage settlements will be generous."

"Tess never cared for that," Richard said quietly.

"No?" There was irony in David's voice. "That has not usually been my experience with women."

"What matters to me is that Tess isn't hurt." Richard leaned forward. "She was last time, badly."

David's face set into harder lines. He was not feeling kindly disposed toward Tess this morning, even though he knew, inside, that what had happened last night had been as much his fault as hers. Even if she had felt so damnably good in his arms. "This is not what I intended, Harwood."

"Aye, I know. You weren't officially betrothed to Mrs. Granfield, were you?"

"No." Oh, lord, Emily. He hadn't faced her yet. Even though he had begun to have doubts about her, she deserved an explanation. How he would find the courage to give her one, however, he didn't know.

"It's a mess, any way you look at it," Richard said frankly. "But there's no hope for it."

"I'm aware of that." David rose, and Richard rose with him. "I do not mean to be rude, but if I am to go to York and back I must leave soon."

"Of course." Richard seemed to hesitate, and then held out his hand. "Under other circumstances, I'd like having you as a brother-in-law."

Their hands clasped. "And I, you." He nodded at the other man as he turned and left the room, and then walked to his desk. He didn't sit down, though. Instead, he stood behind it, fingertips resting on the polished mahogany surface. It was a damnable coil. Tess, Jennie, Emily—so many peoples' lives were involved, including his own. Yet, as Harwood had pointed out, there was nothing for it. He had compromised Tess, and he would have to marry her.

He sat heavily behind the desk, fingers drumming on the desktop. He wanted to be angry at Tess. He really did. But if there one thing he had always been, it was honest, and he knew the truth. What blame there was was shared by him. It was he who had ordered the waltz; it was he who had not let Tess leave when she had pointed out the impropriety of being in his bedchamber. True, she had followed him—but he had wanted her there.

And therein lay the problem, he acknowledged, groaning a little as he sank his head into his hands. He had wanted her, not just last night, but from the first time he had seen her again. Even knowing her duplicity, knowing how she had hurt him in the past, he had wanted her, in his arms, his bed, even in his life. Now she would be there, and this time there would be no breaking free. Lord help him, it *was* a damnable coil, he thought again.

A commotion in the hall made him raise his head: the sound of his butler's voice, along with that of a woman. He also realized he had heard the rattle of carriage wheels on the drive without really paying attention to them. Frowning, he rose and went out into the hall, to see various trunks on the floor, with some in the process of being brought downstairs and others being carried outside. In the middle of the chaos stood Emily, her lips set in a thin line.

Impulsively he held out his hands to her, in a conciliatory gesture. "Emily, I am truly sorry about everything," he said, going to her, for once not caring about the servants nearby.

"I should think so!" Emily's eyes blazed. "I have never in my life been so humiliated as I was last night."

Startled, he almost took a step backward, to escape the fire in her eyes. This was most certainly not the calm, placid woman he thought he knew. "It wasn't something I planned."

"No? Admit it. You've been eyeing that woman from the beginning."

"Emily, for God's sake—"

"And do you really expect me to believe it was an accident that you left the ballroom together last night?"

"Of course it was. She was as concerned about Jennie as I was."

"Jennie!" She all but spat the name out. "And that's another thing. I believe she's all you really care about."

"I have to care about her. I'm her father."

"Most fathers don't. Especially not girls, and especially not in our circle."

"What would you have me do? Send her away to school?"

"Yes."

He went very still. No, he hadn't known this woman, in spite of the signs he'd seen, but Tess had. Tess had known Emily would not be a good mother. "I would not have done it."

"I should have guessed." Already garbed in her winter cloak, she now tied the ribbons of her bonnet with quick, savage motions. "There is one good thing that has come from all this," she said, pulling on her gloves in the same jerky way. "At least I won't have to look at her unbearably plain face any longer."

"You, madam, are a—"

"What?" she challenged, when he stopped

"I won't disgrace myself by saying." In counterpoint to Emily's fire, his eyes and voice were pure, sharp ice. "I'd wish you a good journey, madam, but I really don't care," he said, and, turning on his heel, strode back into his study.

Damn the woman! he thought, standing behind his

desk and staring at the papers there without seeing
them. He had had, he realized, a very lucky escape.
Bad enough what she had said about him and Tess,
but her attitude toward Jennie was unforgivable. And
Tess had known. All the time, she had known.

Once again, he sank down into the chair, resting
his elbows on the desk and putting his head in his
hands. It was truly a coil, and what would come of
it, he could not guess.

Something was wrong. Jennie stood at the nursery
window, looking below to where Mrs. Granfield was
getting into a carriage, with only her companion for
company. Jennie was not to have her for a mama
after all, she had gathered from the servants' whispers, though none of them had said why. At least,
not within her hearing. In any event, she could not
help being glad. She had not liked Mrs. Granfield,
she admitted now.

"Jennie?" she heard Papa say from the doorway,
the happiness she always felt in his presence cours-
ing through her. It burst into joy when she saw
Mama standing by his side. Something was wrong,
though, she thought again. They were smiling, yet
their faces were strained. Mama in particular seemed
tense; her smile quivered and her shoulders were just
a little bit hunched. Jennie was good at noticing
these things. She'd learned early in life that she had
to be. "May we come in?"

Impetuously she ran across the room and threw
her arms around him. His hand settled on her head,
and peace settled in her. Then, though, he held her
away. "May we talk to you?" he asked politely.

Uh-oh. Those words had marked the start of some
difficult conversations in the past, such as the time

when she had gone into his study in search of a new quill with which to practice her letters, and had accidentally spilled a bottle of ink all over some papers and onto herself. "What, Papa?"

"Come here." He crouched down while Mama sat in the rocker, her hands folded in her lap. Mama's knuckles were white, Jennie noted as Papa drew her nearer. "Your mother and I are going to be married again."

This was something she hadn't expected. Thunderstruck, not knowing what to say, she looked from one to the other. "Oh."

"You'll have a mama and a papa, Jennie," Mama said, her voice higher than normal. "What do you think of that?"

"I'm glad."

They glanced at each other. "Are you, poppet?" Papa asked gently.

"Yes."

"This must be quite a surprise." Mama again.

"Yes." She looked up, startled at what she had just realized. "Mama, the ring was right."

"What ring, angel?"

"The one you found in the Christmas pudding."

"Good heavens!" Mama looked at Papa. "So it was."

"But I didn't think . . ."

"What is it, Jennie?" Papa was watching her closely. For all that Mama loved her—and she didn't doubt that at all—it was Papa who knew her best. "What is bothering you?"

"Nothing."

"It's a shock to her, Stowe," Mama put in. "She'll need time to grow accustomed to the idea."

"Time is what we don't have." Papa rose, rubbing at his nose in the way he did when he was tired or upset or had a headache. Jennie felt so sorry for him suddenly, longed to make it all better for him, to make him smile again. For so long, Papa had been her whole world. "We'll be marrying tomorrow."

"Where?" she asked, curiosity stirring for the first time.

"At the church in the village. Would you like that?"

Jennie pondered that a moment. Papa usually did want her opinion when he asked questions like that, but this time she wondered why he bothered. They had decided already without consulting her, and would do as they pleased in any event. Sometimes Jennie couldn't wait to grow up and do whatever she wanted to, as adults did. "Will you wear a special gown, like the ladies in London do when they get married?"

A gleam appeared in Mama's eyes. "I daresay I can find something. And what of the royal blue silk for you?"

"Yes." She searched her father's face. "Papa?"

"Yes, poppet?"

"Will you and Mama live together again?"

Again they looked at each other. "There's much we still have to decide," he said. "This happened very quickly."

"Extremely quickly," Mama muttered, and Papa shot her a look.

"But where will I live?"

"Oh, angel." Mama suddenly went down on one knee and drew her close. "Here, of course. Nothing will change that much. The only difference is that I'll be here, too."

"And in London, too?"

"That's one of the things that needs to be decided. But don't worry, angel. We both love you and we both want the best for you. Whatever we decide, we'll be thinking of your good."

"My lord." A footman stood at the door, looking apologetic. "Viscount Sherbourne has asked for a moment of your time."

Papa nodded in acknowledgment. "You are happy about this, Jennie?" he asked, hand on her head.

"Yes, Papa," she replied docilely, because she knew he expected her to, and he'd feel bad if she didn't.

"Do you mind if we go?"

Her gaze sought her mother's. "Mama?"

"I must go pack," Mama said gently. "I've much to do, if I'm to remove to here tomorrow. Oh, Jennie." Mama caught her up suddenly in a tight, breath-stealing hug that Jennie returned in equal measure. " 'Twill all be well. You'll see."

"Yes, Mama," she said, and with Nurse beside her watched as her parents left the nursery. It was the happiest news, the best news in the world. Why, then, did she have this odd, hollow feeling inside her?

Nurse settled her to her mid-morning meal of bread and milk, which Jennie ate docilely. Something was wrong, she thought again. She didn't know what it was, and she suspected she wouldn't find out, either. It seemed to be something worthy of gossip, judging by the whispering and expressions of the servants, and that meant that it was a grown-up thing. And that meant that no one would tell her what it was. Certainly her parents wouldn't. She knew Papa well enough to predict that, and after this morning she doubted Mama would, either. Bother. She hated not knowing things. It wasn't that she enjoyed gossip, like her great-aunt Agnes, who was forever prattling on about this person or that, or Mrs.

Frakes, whom she already heartily disliked. It was more that she liked taking pieces of knowledge and putting them together, like pieces of a puzzle.

This time, she wouldn't be able to do that. Yet she had to do something. Her parents were unhappy, and that was dangerous. For if they stayed unhappy, they might one day decide to separate, and that she didn't think she could bear again.

Jennie pushed her bowl away with more than half left uneaten, so rare a circumstance for her that Nurse, clucking in dismay and concern, came across the room and placed a hand on her forehead. Someone was going to have to do something to make things right, and it looked as if that person was her. The only problem was, what?

"Poor Jennie," Tess said in the corridor, as she and David walked away from the nursery.

"Why? She'll have what she's probably always wanted, a mother and a father who are together."

"But it's all beyond her control." Her voice lowered. "We haven't decided where I'll live, or what happens when you have to return to London, or where Jennie will live, for that matter. She has no choice in any of it. For all she knows, we could decide to separate again, and how do you think that would make her feel?"

"She'd be upset, Tess, but—"

"She'll blame herself," Tess interrupted fiercely. "Do you think children don't do that when things like this happen between their parents? She'll wonder what she did wrong and what she can do to fix it. My God, David, she already does blame herself for the past."

David stopped walking and stared at her. "Good God. You feel the same way about your mother."

She shook her head. "No, not anymore, though it took me a long time to see it wasn't my fault. Not until you and I separated, as it happens."

"Good God," he repeated, walking again. "I never knew."

"No one did. How could I tell anyone? If they thought I was guilty, I didn't know how they'd punish me."

" 'They' meaning the adults in your life."

"Yes, and Richard, too. They might even have sent me away."

"Tess—"

"Oh, they wouldn't have, of course. But it was what I feared."

"How old were you?"

"Eleven. Old enough to know what was going on, but too young to understand it." She took a deep breath and looked up at him. "Jennie will feel the same way, and nothing we can do will change it."

"We can't let her be hurt like that, Tess," he said grimly, as they continued down the stairs to where Viscount and Viscountess Sherbourne, ready for their own long journey home, stood waiting in the hall. "We'll have to manage better this time."

"I don't know how," she muttered, still managing to paste a smile on her face. Now was not the time to talk of this, not with other people present. No matter what they did, though, they faced a difficult problem. They had to find a proper solution. She was not going to let her daughter be hurt. Not again.

Early that afternoon, a rider astride a fine black stallion came to a halt in front of Harcourt Manor.

A groom ran to hold the horse's head as the rider swung from the saddle. "Eh, sir, he's reet high-bred."

Only a raised eyebrow hinted at the rider's reaction to this bit of broad Yorkshire speech. "Yes. See that he's given proper care."

"Aye. I'll see t'him meself, sir."

The rider barely acknowledged the groom, though he did stop to survey the Manor. Just the slightest hint of decay was present in the old house, built of the same golden stone he'd noticed in many houses in the region. Some mortar loose here, a pillar in need of paint there, the sum of it making his lip curl. Then, his study completed, he swept up the stairs and into the house, holding out his card with unconscious arrogance. "I am Bainbridge," he announced. "Pray ask Miss Harwood if she will receive me."

"Certainly, Your Grace," the butler said. "If you would care to step into this receiving room?" the aged butler said.

Oliver nodded and stalked into the room just off the hall. Fortunately there was a fire lit here, and he went to warm his hands at it while he waited. Not that he expected to be kept standing long. Dukes rarely were.

The door opened again. "Your Grace." Tess Harwood, wearing a gown of sapphire blue in a wool so fine it could have been silk, and a paisley scarf about her shoulders, crossed the room to him. His gaze sharpened. No need to ask where the estate money went, which was oddly disappointing. He had observed Miss Harwood closely in the days past, and he'd received a far different impression of her than he had expected. "I am sorry Bailey put you in here, 'tis so dreary. I suspect he thought you were too important a guest to keep standing in the hall."

He inclined his head. "Miss Harwood. Then there is somewhere else where we can speak?"

"Oh, heavens, yes! My brother and I use the morning room," she said, leading him back out into the hall and along to a polished oak door. "The drawing room is too drafty in winter."

"Stone houses are often like that," he heard himself say inanely. "The family's original home was a stone house in a town not so far from here. Bainbridge. 'Tis where the title originated."

"I had wondered about that. There," she said as they entered the morning room. "This is better. Hush, Shep!" This to the ancient Border collie which had risen from the hearth, woofing once. The morning room had the same faint air of shabbiness as the rest of the house, in the faded chintzes and the slightly threadbare carpeting, but it was somehow a cheerful room, as if many generations had lived in this house and, for the most part, been happy. "I've rung for refreshments. Will tea do?"

"Tea will be fine." His gaze missed nothing as she sat across from him, not the artfully careless tumble of her curls, or the pink of her cheeks, or her rounded figure. Surely not all could be due to nature, could it? Sabrina tended to think they were, and she was usually a good judge of such things.

"Good." They both fell silent as the tea tray was brought in, and as she poured and handed him his cup. "I must say, 'tis a surprise to see you here today. I'd thought you might be with Stowe."

He frowned. "Why?"

"You seem to be the closest he has to a friend."

An apt way of putting it. Now that he thought about it, Stowe did tend to hold people at arm's length. "I did speak with him this morning, but he had no real need of me."

"Oh." She sipped her tea. "So to what, then, do I owe this visit?"

"I'll come to the point, shall I?"

"Certainly."

"What do you mean by this marriage?"

Her cup clattered in its saucer. "Wh-what?"

"It will be the ruin of him politically."

"Oh, no!" Her face was white. "When I went to such trouble—"

"Yes?" he said, when she didn't go on.

"It's of no import. Your Grace." She leaned forward, her face earnest. "Is there nothing I can do to salvage matters?"

Oliver sat back, fingers steepled, lips pursed. "He has worked in the shadows these six years past, and his advice has become respected. It may well be that he'll retain some credibility."

"But surely people will realize that this is another matter altogether."

He gave a mirthless laugh. "Have you ever been among the *ton*, Miss Harwood?"

"I've rarely left Yorkshire, let alone moved with the *beau monde*."

"Then you do not know where the real work of politics is done."

"Where?"

"At parties and soirées given by the wives of political men. And I must tell you, my dear, that you would not be sent invitations to any of these, let alone be received."

Now even her lips were pale. That had gone home, he thought with an odd mixture of satisfaction and disappointment. "Would David be ostracized, as well? I know that things are often different for men."

"I doubt it, this time. The merest whisper of scandal has been known to ruin someone. This, of course, is far worse."

"Oh." She glanced away, though he suspected her gaze was inward. "Is there anything I can do to help?"

She sounded sincere enough, he'd say that for her. "Yes. You can stay away from London."

For the first time, she looked defiant. "That, Your Grace, will be a problem."

He raised his eyebrows. "Oh?" he said, in what he knew was his most quelling manner.

"Yes. You see, I design clothes."

He looked at her blankly. "I beg your pardon?"

"I design clothes, like this frock." She pinched the sapphire material for his inspection. "Quite stylish ones, for the best London modistes."

"Forgive me, but I still don't understand."

There was the faintest of smiles on her face. "I know 'tis not done to go into trade, but I have a talent for design and a good eye for color and line. It seemed the natural thing to do at the time."

"I see," he said, still mystified. "Sabrina has wondered who your modiste is."

She laughed at that. "Madame Jeanette and I have a partnership. Lately I've had some commissions from Celeste, as well."

"Good God!" He stared at her. "Sabrina has patronized them both."

She smiled impishily. "So has Lady Sherbourne."

"But I always understood those to be the modistes' own designs."

"Oh, no, not always. Obviously I can't set up as a dressmaker myself, but what I can do is work with one. She, of course, sells it as her own, and we both make a profit. And you may believe that I keep a sharp eye on the books, so I receive what I'm owed."

He rubbed his fingers over his eyes. "Why?"

"For the Manor, of course. Which you may have noticed it needs. Sheep farming is not so profitable as it once was."

"But surely there must be money from your income from Stowe."

Her lips tightened. "My brother wouldn't touch that. Nor do I, if I can help it."

He blinked, now totally confused. "Why ever not?"

"I am keeping it in trust for my daughter, so that she may have money of her own someday." Her smile faded, and she suddenly looked much older. "Women haven't much power in this world, Your Grace. Money can help."

"Of course." He ran a hand over his face, and then, somewhat to his own surprise, laughed. "A scandalous marriage, and a wife in trade. Good God."

Her eyes gleamed. "It can hardly be worse, can it?"

"Hardly." His smile faded as he eyed her. "Tell me. Does he know of your mother?"

She drew in her breath. "You know, then?"

"I am some years older than Stowe. I was still in school when it happened, but even I heard of it, though when I came here I didn't remember it right away."

"Oh, heavens." Her face was in her hands. "And the other guests?"

"I've heard some talk about it. Everyone in the neighborhood must know."

"Oh, certainly." She sounded oddly detached. "It

was a great scandal. The first great scandal," she amended.

"Does he know?" he repeated.

"He does now." She leaned back. "Somehow he found out about it last night."

"But he hasn't figured it out yet, has he?"

"What?"

"Why you asked for the separation."

She stared at him blankly. "I beg your pardon?"

" 'Tis obvious, my dear. You still love him."

This time her teacup fell onto the rug, where it rolled. "Where—what makes you think that?"

Oliver gave her a real smile for the first time. "It's all over your face when you look at him."

"No." She shook her head, so that her curls danced. "I've had no feelings for him for years."

"Miss Harwood." He leaned forward. "Sabrina and I aren't the only ones who have noticed it."

Tess lost what remaining color she had, and her shoulders sagged. "Does he know?"

"Not to my knowledge, no."

"I—had no idea. None." The collie had his head on her knee, as if he sensed her distress, and she absently scratched his ears. "I thought I covered my feelings so well."

"For the most part you do." He leaned back, while she struggled to regain some composure. "It shows when you are together as a family, with Jennie."

"Oh, no—Jennie! If I could spare her all this . . ."

"I know." As a parent himself, he knew what he was prepared to do for his own child.

"What do I do?" She leaned toward him. "I know he doesn't love me. He cannot possibly," she went on, as he opened his mouth. "I destroyed all chances of that years ago."

Better not to say what he thought, Oliver decided. It would be meddling, and he knew how disastrous that could be. Sabrina wouldn't agree, but fortunately she didn't know Stowe as well as he did. "Try to make it work."

"How?"

"You have Jennie, and you're both good parents. Few people in the *ton* could say as much."

"If he intends to be dictatorial about her and forbid me to see her—"

"Do you think Jennie would allow that?"

For the first time in some moments, Tess smiled. "No. No, I don't think she would."

"You've that to start, and whatever it was you had in common when you first married."

"Ye-es." She plucked at the skirt of her gown, and then, taking a deep breath, looked up at him. "I'll have to be honest with him, too, about everything."

"Will you tell him why you asked for the separation?"

"No. I doubt he'd believe me if I did."

He set his lips. "I suspect you're right." He rose, crossed the room, and then paused at the doorway. "A pity, really. I think you would have made a good political wife."

She laughed. "Me?" she said, rising as well to accompany him to the door. "Why, doubtless I would have made a dozen *faux pas* in one day in London. I don't know how to get on at all. In fact"—her face darkened—"I sometimes wonder if that was what made me so appealing to him."

"No, Miss Harwood. That, I sincerely doubt." He shrugged into the greatcoat Bailey held out for him. "I do wish you happy," he said.

"Thank you, Your Grace. Until tomorrow?"

"Yes. Tomorrow."

Outside, Oliver swung up onto the saddle, feeling his mount, frisky after his stay in the stable, prance under him. He felt for Stowe; now he felt for Miss Harwood as well. Whatever happened, they had a number of obstacles to clear before they could find any sort of happiness.

Tess and David were married the following morning in the little stone church in the village, where they once had been married before. Though it had been cold that day, the church had been banked with flowers, and Tess had felt warm and glowing inside. Today, however, the walls gave off a palpable chill, so that she shivered in her creamy white velvet gown. In attendance before had been the entire village; today there were only Richard, the Duke and Duchess of Bainbridge, acting as witnesses, and, of course, Jennie. She watched the proceedings with wide-eyed wonder, as well she might. It wasn't every day, Tess thought wryly, that one had a chance to see one's parents being married.

There would, of course, still be a wedding breakfast at Stowcroft, even though there were so few in attendance. The newlyweds spoke little to each other on the way to the Hall, but then, they didn't have to. Jennie chattered enough for all of them. She had never been to a wedding before, and she had questions about everything, from the purpose of the witnesses to the meaning of the gold ring which now lay so heavily on Tess's finger. Tess and David exchanged a glance. Daily life with their daughter would be a challenge, they admitted without a word being spoken between them. That jolted her. So had it been once before, that often they had not needed words to communicate. In spite of herself, her hopes rose. If it was still like that between them, there was still a chance they might be able to find some contentment. She would settle for that.

Most of the guests at the house party had left the day before, going to their own estates or to London. It was, after all, an embarrassing situation their host had found himself in. Without their presence, Stowcroft suddenly seemed large and echoing, and the dining room table too long, although many of its leaves had already been removed. Tess fully expected to be seated somewhere at David's side. It jolted her, then, when he escorted her to the foot of the table, before taking his own place at the head. This was where she belonged as mistress of the house, she thought, dazed, now that she was David's wife again.

A lavish repast had been laid on, as was only fitting for a wedding feast. There were lobster patties and a joint of beef and a rich wedding cake, which, considering the circumstances of the wedding, astonished Tess, along with the finest of wines. The duke even rose to toast the newly wedded couple. Tess pushed her meal around on her plate, barely able to swallow a morsel. This was not the usual nervousness of a bride, however. Not when the husband and wife had been married to each other before, and not when this particular marriage was beginning in less than auspicious circumstances.

Eventually, the seemingly interminable meal came to an end, and the party rose from the table. Since the Bainbridges would be setting off for their home near Reading once the breakfast was finished, today there would be no ceremony of the women withdrawing from the room while the gentlemen remained behind, sipping port and smoking cigars. Instead, everyone moved into the hall, Tess standing next to David, while yet somehow remaining apart from him. It was already plain he wanted little to do with her, she thought. He'd barely looked at her since they'd returned to what would now be her home.

"Oh, I do wish you happy," the duchess said, her gloved hands capturing Tess's so that she could draw her aside, exactly as her husband had asked her to.

The duke gave the two women a look before drawing near to David. "I hope you have a care as to what you and I discussed," he said, while the two women talked.

David glanced at Tess. "About my future, you mean?"

"Yes."

"Such as it is."

"I believe it can be salvaged, Stowe." Bainbridge's voice was quiet. "If we proceed slowly."

David shrugged. "I believe I might become a gentleman farmer. Not here, of course. The winters are too cold and I never did care for sheep."

"I think you're being too hard on yourself, and on Lady Stowe."

David blinked, startled. Tess was a marchioness again, after having been stripped of her title in the past. "Spare me the fatherly lecture, Bainbridge. Just because you and your wife are happy—"

"Do you think we've never had any problems?" the duke said, suddenly fierce. "Good God, I was nearly ruined because of her. Yet we worked it through."

"You didn't speak like this yesterday," David said, frowning.

Bainbridge glanced away. "Yes, well, I've had a chance to do some thinking. Best thing for you to do is avoid London for a time, until the dust settles."

"Nothing will change, Bainbridge."

"Perhaps not, but perhaps it will." He turned away.

"Are you ready, my dear? We should be leaving if we hope to make Leeds today."

The duchess looked momentarily startled. "Certainly, Oliver," she said, hugging Tess one last time and then turning away.

Farewells were exchanged, the Bainbridges drove off in their gleaming carriage with the ducal crest on the door panels, while inside the house Nurse came to take charge of Jennie and the footmen seemed to disappear. Stowcroft was, ironically, a honeymoon cottage again, except, of course, for Jennie. Except, the couple who stood in the hall, man and wife again after many a year, were no closer than they had been before.

Eleven

For a long moment, they stood facing each other. David was the first to break the silence. "Well? And what do we do now?"

For some reason, that struck Tess as being funny. She let out a throaty chuckle, and, after a startled glance, David smiled. "Heaven knows. But then, neither of us expected to be like this again."

"Bainbridge seems to think we could rub along tolerably well, if we tried," he said, holding her elbow as he escorted her upstairs.

"He does?" Tess stopped on the landing. "When did he say this?"

"Just now, before he left."

"Ah."

"What is that supposed to mean?"

"Nothing very important." Apparently, though, the duke no longer saw her as quite so much of a liability, she thought, sitting in the drawing room. The Yule log still burned in the hearth, as it was meant to do until Twelfth Night, and the holly and ribbons still graced the room, but the holiday feeling was gone. Christmas was over.

David crossed to a table to pour himself a drink, and Tess shook her head when he held up a decanter of sherry in a questioning way. "Lord knows I didn't want this to happen, Tess."

"Why not?" she retorted, stung. "You certainly acted as if you had feelings for me the other night."

"A moment's foolishness." He drained his drink. "And you are still a desirable woman."

Tess sucked in her breath. "Is that all you wished from me?"

"Mayhap 'tis all I ever wanted."

She looked down at her hands, biting the inside of her lip against the sudden pain. "David, I know there's much between us we never dealt with. All that old pain."

"That, and the fact that you never loved me."

"I'm not talking about that! All that came between us after—could we not try to put it behind us?"

David, standing again at the table holding the decanters, paused and then looked at her over his shoulder. "No."

"Oh." Her fingers were pleating the material of her dress, wrinkling it, she noted dispassionately, and forced herself to relax. "Then I think 'tis only fair to warn you. I will not share your bed."

"I do not expect you to. But, madam, I warn you. I won't stand by and watch you cavort with other men."

"Cavort!"

"Particularly not Rawley."

She sucked in her breath again. "You're being unfair. Adrian and I are merely friends."

"A friendship I will not tolerate."

"Good lord, David." She stared at him. "Why do you feel so threatened by him? I've never given you cause."

"Oh, haven't you," he bit out. "You flirted with everyone."

"Yes, I did. You, too, as I recall."

"I remember." Now his voice was quiet. "You entranced everyone and then chose the man with the highest title and the most money."

"David!"

"And I was taken in by you, fool that I was."

"It wasn't like that," she protested.

"No? You told me you never loved me. And I . . ." He let the words trail off.

"What?" she prompted warily.

"You're an intelligent woman, Tess. Think on it."

"You're saying you never loved me," she whispered, through lips that felt suddenly stiff and bloodless.

"As I said. Think on it."

"Oh!" she bolted to her feet. "I must—I can't—excuse me," she said, and fled the room, leaving David with the impression that her eyes held the sheen of tears.

Devil take it. David raised his glass to take a sip, saw it was empty, and then, slowly, deliberately, lowered it. Now why had he done that? It wasn't what he had planned when they had come in here. Of course he had loved her. If he hadn't, he wouldn't have been so devastated when she had declared their marriage to be a mistake. That love had died, of course, he assured himself, never to be resurrected. Still, he had taken Oliver's words to heart. He had hoped that perhaps he and Tess could make something of this forced marriage. Now, though, he knew it wasn't possible, though he wasn't quite sure why. All he really knew was that, in spite of the past, in spite of all that had happened since, there were times when his need for her became a great, empty ache inside him.

The daylight was fading and the room was growing dim. David rose at last. There was naught to be done about his desires. He was not about to make the same mistake that he had years ago. Fortunately, he would only have to endure the situation for a few more weeks. Soon he would return to London, to prepare for the opening of Parliament. Once there, he could go on as he once had. Perhaps.

David crossed to the door and stepped into the hall. How, though, would he survive until then? He didn't know, he thought, his heart as heavy as his tread as he began to ascend the stairs to his rooms. He simply didn't know.

After dinner David disappeared, Tess presumed to his study, to work on estate accounts or whatever it was he did there. Marriage was lonely, she thought, lonelier than being divorced had been, once she had become accustomed to it. David had made it quite clear he wanted nothing to do with her. Very well, then. She would simply have to find a way to make her own life.

Jennie had long ago been tucked up into bed, and so on impulse Tess went to her sitting room and pulled out pencil and sketch pad. Jeanette would expect new designs for the spring soon. Already Tess's mind was brimming with ideas for gowns that were far beyond the current styles. She could hardly wait to see them made up as garments.

Time passed quickly as she drew, as design after design took shape on her pad. Stopping only to sharpen her pencil, she sketched on, knowing that if she didn't capture the ideas, she would lose them. So immersed in her work was she that when she realized someone was knocking at her door, she had the impression that whoever it was had been there for a while. "Come in," she called, and was startled when David walked in.

"David!" She rose, instinctively covering the sketches with a piece of paper. Someday she would have to tell him about her work, but surely not now. They would only quarrel more, and she was so tired of it. "What do you here?"

"I wanted to talk to you about something." He gestured toward a chair. "May I?"

"Of course." She turned on her chair as he passed.

"What is that?" he asked, indicating the sketches.

"This? Oh. Just some dresses I'd like to make."

"Very nice, though you don't have to do that any longer," he said, dismissing her work, but making her relax in relief. "Tess."

"Yes?" She watched him as he settled into the blue brocaded tufted chair. The marchioness's suite of rooms hadn't changed, she'd noted when she'd come in here yesterday. It was still decorated in the style a much younger Tess had liked.

"We need to talk about Jennie."

She drew back, wary. They had had all of dinner to discuss this. Why now? "What about Jennie?"

"About what happens when I return to London. You do realize you'll have to stay here."

Tess's lips set in a straight line. "Yes. I'm doubly fallen now, aren't I, and you don't wish to be seen with me."

"It isn't that, Tess." His voice was surprisingly gentle. "The *ton* will cut you. I'd really rather it didn't happen."

"Oh." She stared at him. He cared about that? It was a surprise. She felt touched, until suddenly she understood. "It would reflect on Jennie."

"I'm afraid so, yes."

She leaned forward. "David, you know I'd never do anything to hurt her."

"No, not intentionally, of course."

"I've told you, I'm not so impulsive as before." She eyed him balefully. "As to that, you've been known to be impulsive yourself."

"Not anymore."

"No. Now you've gone the other way."

"I am capable of making changes when necessary," he said through gritted teeth.

On the brink of answering, she suddenly closed her eyes. "This avails us nothing, David. Please, let us not quarrel again."

David looked away. "My apologies, Tess," he said, finally. "This wasn't what I intended when I came here."

Tess smiled a little. "I didn't mean to snap, either."

"Well." He settled back. "Are we actually in accord for once?"

"Apparently."

"Good. We do have to discuss Jennie."

Tess's stomach felt hollow. "Yes?"

"When I return to London, I'm taking Jennie with me."

"No!" she howled. "David, you can't do that to me! Oh, please, not after all these years—"

"Tess, I've every right—"

"By the law, yes. But please, oh please, don't separate us. Not yet. Oh, you'll be doing so much damage."

"You did without her for six years."

"Not me, David. Jennie. She needs me." Tess leaned forward, trying to make him see, to make him realize. "We've grown so close in this short time."

David's lips were set now. "She needs a father, too."

"I'm not denying that, David. Please." She bit back tears. "Don't punish her for what I've done."

He raised his eyebrows. "I've no intention of punishing anyone, Tess. Not Jennie, not even you. But we both know we don't really have a marriage."

Tess looked away, biting her lips. "Yes, we do."

" 'Tis also the way of the *ton,* for couples to live apart."

"And for parents not to see their children." Her voice grew bitter. "And sometimes for a mother to elope with a painter, and another mother to neglect her son."

He drew in his breath, sharply. "Unfair, Tess."

"True, David," she shot back. "Which is why it hurts so much. Oh, David, think." She gripped the back of her chair. "If we fight over Jennie, what harm will it do to her? Will she have to end up choosing one parent over the other? I don't want that for her. Do you?"

"Tess, that's not what I'm proposing."

"But you said you'd bring her to London—"

"For part of the year, yes. I must be there when Parliament is in session, no matter how little I'll be allowed to do, and that means Jennie will come with me. Other times, however, we can make different arrangements."

Tess sat still, hardly daring to hope. "You'd let her come here?"

"I'd bring her myself."

"Of course." Her voice was bitter. "That way you can ensure that she isn't corrupted by my bad influence on her."

"Tess, you persist in switching around all that I say."

She looked away. She would not—would not!—let him see how much this hurt her. Yet, there was hope. Watching Jennie leave might nearly kill her, but knowing she would be returning would keep her strong. There would also be her own, quiet trips to town. "David, about London—"

"There are a great many opportunities for her there that just aren't present in the country, Tess."

"While she'll have more freedom in the country than in town. But that isn't what I wanted to say—"

"Tess, this is what I am prepared to offer you. If it isn't enough for you, perhaps you'd prefer other arrangements."

She frowned at him. "I don't like it when you go all autocratic and rigid. You never used to be this way."

"No. I was impulsive once. It cost me dearly." He rose. "Do you agree to what I've proposed?"

She raised her eyes to him. "I haven't a choice, do I?"

"No. I'm sorry."

Odd. She suspected he meant that. "Then, yes, of course I agree."

"Good." He stood a little awkwardly near the door, and for a moment she had another odd feeling, this time that he was waiting for a sign from her. Shy suddenly, afraid of rejection and its pain, afraid as well of where any sign might lead, she instead kept her head down, kept her voice silent.

"Well," he said, after a moment. "Good night, then."

"Good night, David," she said without looking up, for if she did, she knew she would call him back. She knew she would invite him into her bed. And that would be disastrous.

So. She looked blankly down at her sketches, and

then rose to go into her bedroom. She had won another victory over her impulsiveness. An empty victory, when she kept looking at the door that separated his bedchamber from hers.

Her maid helped her undress and then garbed her in a night rail far more suited to a new bride than to the woman Tess had become, all frills and lace and ribbons, with a long row of buttons down the front. She could see a man's hard, brown fingers undoing those buttons—*no*. She smiled at the maid and sent the woman away, not arguing about the choice of nightclothes. The less the servants knew of her private life, the better.

Finally alone, she climbed into bed and pulled the eiderdown firmly around her. Even with a fire going in the room, nights were cold in Yorkshire in winter. Far better to have a man beside her, warming her bed. She had, however, sent him away.

The only thing for it was to endure. Snuffing out the candle, she lay down and pulled the pillow over her head. She was alone again, as she had been for so much of her life. Her fault, this time. Thus, she thought before sleep mercifully claimed her, ended her wedding night.

It was snowing again. Jennie could tell by the quality of the light, a pinkish gray, filtering into her room, even though the draperies were tightly closed against the night. It seemed to snow a great deal here. Of course, she preferred that to London's fogs and dampness. Yorkshire air was somehow clean, if sharp, while London's had a raw chill that often made her shiver uncontrollably. All in all, she preferred to be here, she decided, especially since Mama and Papa had married again. At least, she would have, if they were happy.

She sat up in bed, hugging her knees. Something was wrong, she thought, as she had the day they'd told her they were marrying again. On the outside all seemed well, and if Jennie didn't know better, she'd be happy. In the last few days, Papa had taken her about the estate with him when he visited with tenants or on the Home Farm, and Mama was supervising her lessons. Both of them frolicked in the snow with her, engaging in spirited snowball fights and building a whole family of fantastic snow people. If Mama were stricter than she had been before she and Papa married, well, Jennie didn't mind too much. At least they were together. Or so it seemed.

Jennie couldn't put her finger on what, exactly, was wrong. Mama and Papa were always perfectly pleasant to each other when they chanced to meet, or on the rare occasions when Jennie was allowed to dine with them. There were never any raised voices or quarrels that she knew of. Yet she couldn't help feeling that, like the parents of most of her friends, they lived separate lives, if under the same roof. She'd heard the servants whispering about it, when they thought she couldn't hear. Mama was usually to be found in her sitting room, they said, sketching or sewing, while Papa spent his time in his study. And what, Jennie wondered yet again, was so very wrong about the fact that they had kissed in Papa's bedchamber?

She frowned. So much of the adult world was beyond her comprehension. It should all have been easier once her parents remarried, but it wasn't. Sometimes she had the sense, when she was with the two of them, that there were things not being said between them, things that baffled her, even had she known what they were. Only now was she beginning to understand that parents were people, separate and individual from herself, with lives of their own. The problem now was how to get those separate lives to merge with each other.

And that brought her back to herself. Before Christmas she had tried to bring them together, making sure there was enough mistletoe hanging in enough places in Stowcroft, though she'd never seen Mama and Papa stand under it. Then, on Christmas night, she'd held her angel up and wished on it, wished that somehow her parents would reconcile. She'd had to. She didn't know what she'd done wrong as a baby, but since that was when Mama and Papa had become divorced, it must have been terrible, no matter how much Mama reassured her she'd done nothing. Thus she had to find a way to undo that wrong. Though her original plan hadn't worked, in the end she had managed to bring them together, though she'd been unaware of it at the time. Now it seemed as if would be up to her again.

Hm. Sleepy now, she lay down again. Maybe she had another chance to undo the damage of the past; after all, she was, for the first time ever, living in the same house with both of them. It shouldn't be that difficult, not if she put her mind to it. Maybe she could find a way they could all be happy together. Her angel's wish hadn't completely come true.

Caught in that strange world between wakefulness and sleep, Jennie abruptly opened her eyes. She had had an idea. Not an original one, perhaps, but something that might work. Something she could put to the test very soon.

* * *

Tess was just putting the finishing touches to a sketch of a spencer one evening when there was a knock on the sitting room door. Instinctively, as always, she hastily drew a piece of paper over the sketch. David didn't yet know of her career. She had tried to tell him, had even come close once or twice, but when it came to it, she'd always pulled back, remembering the Duke of Bainbridge's remarks. She was in trade, and that could only hurt David more. "Come in."

"Oh, madam." Jennie's nurse came in, simultaneously bobbing a curtsy and wringing her hands, a process Tess watched with fascination. "I'm sorry to disturb you, but Lady Jennie is missing from her bed."

Tess's head came up sharply. "Sleepwalking? Again?"

"Yes, ma'am, I believe so."

"I thought she'd stopped—has Lord Stowe been informed?" she asked, rising.

"Yes, ma'am."

"Good." Tess draped her shawl more closely about her shoulders and picked up a candle, shielded by a glass globe. "I'll wait for him before we start looking—oh, David." She hurried toward him, some of her panic lessening. "Have you any news of her?"

"No." David's hair looked as if he'd been dragging his fingers through it, and his eyes held the same worry she herself felt. "Were you aware of her doing this again?"

"No." She preceded him into the drafty corridor, shivering despite her shawl. "So far as I know, she hasn't been."

"I've set people to searching the usual places." He began walking by her side. "Has anything upset her lately?"

She thought about that for a moment. "No, I really don't think so, unless it's that we're not celebrating the twelve days of Christmas. She asked me about that yesterday." She frowned. "Or . . ."

"What?"

Tess, letting Nurse get a few paces ahead of them, lowered her voice. "She may be feeling the tension between us."

"Tension, madam?" He regarded her with feigned surprise. "Is there tension between us?"

"You know there is. Poor child, her life hasn't been happy."

"She has more than most children," he said tersely.

"In material goods? Yes. But not necessarily in other ways."

"We managed to survive our childhoods, Tess. She will, too."

"So we did, but must Jennie suffer the same way?"

"She may be in here again," he said, and she realized that they had reached the door to his bedroom. *Oh, no. Not again,* she thought, trying to see beyond the glow of the combined light of their candlesticks. Together they approached the bed, and only when they could see past the shadows of the draperies hanging from the canopy did Tess release the breath she hadn't known she'd been holding. "She isn't here."

"Obviously."

"You needn't speak to me in that tone." She looked at him and regretted her words; he appeared as worried as she. "Where can she be? You know Stowcroft better than I do."

"I don't know. Unless . . ."

"What?"

" 'Tis just a thought. Come." He grasped her wrist and she had no choice but to follow into the corridor. She tried to ignore the little tingle of awareness where his skin met hers, but she couldn't quite manage it. Thus it had always been between them, and thus, she supposed, it would always be. She wondered if he felt it, too.

David stopped. "We'll try in here."

"My room?" she said in surprise, as he opened the door. "But I don't know why she'd come in here. You're still more familiar to her—oh." She went quiet as she looked down at her daughter, asleep in her bed. "Doesn't she look like an angel?"

"Mm. If you haven't noticed, madam, she has become quite comfortable with you of late."

Tess frowned. There was that acerbic tone to his voice again, and she wasn't quite sure why. "I am her mother, David."

"I realize that."

"But you don't like it, do you." His face became more wooden, if that were possible, making her look at him in surprise. "My heavens, you really are jealous!"

"Don't be more foolish than you can help," he said in a sharp whisper. "And keep your voice down, else you'll wake her."

That made Tess look down at Jennie. Perhaps it was a trick of the wavering candlelight, but she thought Jennie's lashes moved. So the child was waking up. Or, was she? Tess looked again, harder. There was that blink again, unmistakable this time. Why, the little fraud! Jennie was awake. "David—"

"I wonder where her nurse is."

"She'll be along," Tess said, and nudged David in the side, hard. He looked at her, startled, and she indicated Jennie with a jerk of her chin, mouthing at the same time what she had just discovered. At first he looked blank, but then an expression of comprehension came over his face.

"Pity she's started to sleepwalk again," he said, holding his hand in a staying motion to Nurse, who had just come into the room. "I'd thought to tell her that we'd agreed to give her her own pony if she didn't do so again."

Jennie's eyes started blinking furiously, and Tess had to bite the insides of her mouth to stifle her laughter. "Yes," she said. "One of those little Dartmoor ponies you spoke of would have been just the thing for her."

Jennie moved her head, though her eyes were still closed, and Tess and David exchanged a look brimming with laughter. Then her eyes opened. Had she looked at them blankly enough, they might almost have believed she'd been asleep. "Mama? Papa? What are you doing in my room?"

"Watching you sleep, angel." Tess sat on the side of the bed. "You walked in your sleep again."

"No, did I? Papa, I had the funniest dream."

"Yes, Jennie?" he said.

"I dreamed you said I could have my very own pony if I didn't do that again."

That made Tess turn her head sharply, again to hide laughter. "I fear not, not now." David looked suitably grave as he shook his head. "You mama and I have discussed taking you to a London specialist if this continued. I didn't want to, but . . ."

"We have no choice now, angel," Tess said, before Jennie could speak. "After all, we can't let you wander around Stowcroft by yourself, asleep. You might get hurt." She took Jennie's hand. "There's one surgeon we've heard of who is said to be very good at curing this kind of thing. Very gentle too, I understand. He only requires his patients to be bled a few times, and he uses leeches only as a last resort—"

"I was awake!" Jennie said hastily. "Mama, Papa, I was awake the whole time."

David shook his head. "Mm, no, I know sometimes 'tis possible to dream that you are."

"But I was! I heard you and Mama come in here. You said you didn't know why I'd come in here, and then that you thought I looked like an angel."

David looked at Tess. "We had best get her to that specialist soon. Now she is not only walking in her sleep, she's hearing as well."

"But I was awake!" Jennie climbed hastily to her knees. "I really was. I was awake."

"We know," Tess said, very gently.

Jennie's face fell. "You did? But how? My eyes were closed."

"Never you mind. What did you mean by this trick, Jennie? Don't you know how much you worried your papa and me? Not to mention Nurse."

"It worked once before," she muttered.

"What? What is that supposed to mean?" David demanded.

"Nothing, Papa. I thought it would be a good jest."

"Well, it wasn't, Jennie, not one bit of it."

Jennie's eyes brimmed with tears. "I'm sorry, Mama. I didn't mean to frighten you."

"We'll talk about that in the morning, miss," David said, helping her down off the high bed. "Now, back to bed with you."

"Yes, Papa," she said meekly, and left the room with Nurse.

David turned to stand beside Tess, watching Jennie go, and then looked at her, appearing baffled. "What in the world do you suppose that was all about?"

"Heaven knows. I am beginning to wonder how parents survive their children's childhood."

"By letting other people raise them, I suspect."

" 'Tis not something I'd wish to do."

"I know. You've always been different, Tess. It's one of the things I liked about you."

She turned to him, startled. "You actually liked something about me?"

"I must have, mustn't I, to marry you? No, wait, Tess, I didn't mean that the way it sounded."

Tess looked down at his hand on her arm, holding her back from fleeing from the sudden pain of his careless words. "We can't go back, David."

"I'm aware of that. Surely, though, we can deal together better than we have, can we not?"

"I don't know." Her eyes were troubled in the dim light. "There's too much between us, David. I can't live with someone who holds me in contempt, and then goes off to London." _Leaving me so alone._

"I don't hold you in contempt, Tess," he said, startled, and was quiet for a moment. "I'm not the person I once was, either."

"I know."

"Perhaps we've been going about this all wrong. Perhaps we should simply forget about the past."

"Could you do that?"

"For Jennie's happiness? Yes. I could do anything for that."

"Yes, of course," Tess said, somewhat crestfallen. "I believe we both agree about that. Most parents in the _ton_ don't seem to care about their children's wellbeing at all. And we do have one advantage, from having been married before."

He turned toward her. "What?"

"We work well together, don't we? All that nonsense you spouted just now about a pony."

He grinned, too. "Yes, that did work, didn't it? So did what you said about the surgeon."

"I nearly disgraced myself, you know, when I saw Jennie's face."

"Lord, yes. She was completely taken in." A curious silence fell between them. "It was almost as it used to be, when our minds worked as one."

"Yes," she whispered.

"It wasn't all bad, was it, Tess?" he said.

"No, David," she said gently. "It was a good time."

"Sometimes I think the best time."

"Do you?"

"There's never been anyone quite like you since."

"Even with . . ." She forced herself to go on. "Even with the way it ended?"

He reached out to touch her cheek. "Even with that. Lord, Tess, there are times I find myself thinking about you, and I don't know why."

"I'm the same."

"Are you?"

She leaned her face into his hand, so glad to feel his touch again. "Yes."

"How strange." His other hand had possessed hers and was caressing her fingers. "How very strange."

"Yes. No! David." She pulled back, looking at him accusingly. "You are doing it again."

"What?"

"We are in a bedroom," she said pointedly.

His smile was slanted. "So I noticed."

"Oh, no. You'll not catch me that way again."

"Catch you how, Tess?" he asked, grabbing her wrist as she would have pushed past him.

"I think you know. Why must you always behave so in a bedchamber?"

"Why not?"

"Because the last time we found ourselves in a world of trouble. And I've told you I will not share your bed."

He raised her hand to his mouth and pressed a kiss on it; unwillingly and unwittingly, her eyes closed. "I know. I was hoping I might change your mind."

She swallowed. "You surely cannot be serious."

"But I am, very much so. If we're to have a new beginning, why not start here?" He looked at her intently. Even in the darkness, his eyes seemed to gleam. "Tess, I want to make love to you."

Twelve

"Oh, David!" A part of Tess yearned toward him even as she backed away. "You know that we cannot."

He stepped toward her, so that it was as if she hadn't even moved. "Why not? We are married."

"In name only."

"I want you, Tess."

"You'll be returning to London. What if you leave me with child?" she said, just as he moved again.

"Mayhap it will be a son this time."

She stared at him. "You cannot be serious."

"Would it be so terrible, Tess, if we had another child?"

"Yes! You'd take him away from me."

That stopped him. "I cannot stay here, Tess."

"I know. But is it fair to take children so far from their mother? I'm not the terrible person you think I am."

He looked searchingly at her. "When I'm with you . . ."

"What?" she asked, when he didn't go on. She could not believe this conversation was happening, especially in light of what they had just been discussing. It was unreal, dreamlike, and she kept expecting almost to wake up with the morning sun

streaming into the room as her maid pulled the
drapes back. Oh, but this was a sweet dream, one
that she'd had so many times before. A dream in
which David still loved her.

He shook his head, at the same time reaching out
to touch her cheek. "I want to believe it," he repeated.

As she had before, she leaned into his hand, letting his fingers caress her skin. Would it be so bad?
she asked herself suddenly. 'Twould be only for this
one night, that she'd make clear to him. One night
for her to remember, when he and Jennie returned
to London. Though nothing had been said about that,
she knew her time was short. Soon they would be
gone, and her life would be far bleaker than it had
ever been. She would need her memories.

Tess looked up at him. "Tess?" he said, and she
went into his arms.

In the early morning, Tess awoke alone, and
stretched luxuriantly, content for the first time in
years. Though she didn't know when David had left
her during the night, she had no doubt that all was
well. She belonged in his arms, rather than living
alone and lonely as his estranged wife. Now she
knew that he felt the same way, too, and that this
would not be, as she had thought, for one night only.
Oh, she realized that she'd damaged his career, probably beyond repair, but she never had meant to,
surely he knew that. She would do anything she
could, she thought now, to help him repair it and to
build his reputation and esteem back up. If that
meant staying in Yorkshire while he went to London
without her, so be it. She would do anything she had
to, so long as they could be together again.

It wouldn't be easy, that she knew. She would probably have to give up her enterprise designing clothes, she thought with a grimace. He could probably survive her scandalous background, but not the fact that she was in trade. That would be difficult for her, not just because of the money her work brought to Harcourt Manor, but because of the personal satisfaction she took from it. From now on the only work she would be able to do of that sort would be for herself and for Jennie. Yet, it would be worth it, for what she would receive in exchange. She would have Jennie again, and maybe more children. Most of all, she would have David again. The thought brought with it both tremendous excitement and a deep peace such as she hadn't felt in years.

Tess turned over as her maid came in and softly opened the drapes, letting in the light. The light of a new day, she thought, and smiled. How very lucky she was to have this second chance at happiness. This time, she knew how fleeting it could be. This time, she was not going to let it slip away from her again.

David sat in his study, his head in his hands. He had awakened this morning, dazed, disoriented, and then it had all come back to him. The work he had been doing last night in this very room. The news that Jennie was missing from her bed again. The long, nightmarish search, ending with finding her in Tess's room. And, finally, holding Tess, loving her. Making what had to be the second biggest mistake of his life.

There was a knock on the door, and before he could answer, Tess sailed in, smiling. "Good morning," she sang, bending to kiss his cheek. He couldn't help it; he flinched, and her smile wavered a bit. "David? What is wrong?"

He looked up at her. "You need ask?"

"Yes. I thought, after last night—"

"You thought wrong," he said, his voice suddenly savage. "Last night was a mistake."

Tess dropped into a chair, the glow on her face gone. "Why?" she asked, reasonably enough.

"Why? After all that's happened between us, you have to ask me that?"

"But what happened last night—"

"Was the product of memories and dreams. It was a mistake, Tess. Our marriage is a mistake."

"I don't understand."

"Don't you? Then let me explain it to you." He leaned forward, and she flinched again, surprise in her eyes. "I am married to a woman who doesn't care the slightest for me. Is that not a jest, Tess? Because of that, I can no longer do as I choose with my life. I cannot remarry to provide myself with an heir. My career is in a shambles. I have nothing in particular I want to do with my life, I'm the focus of scandal, and I have a daughter I'm not even sure is mine!"

That brought her to her feet. "You know that's not so!"

"How do I, Tess? Prove it to me."

"I came to you untouched. You know that yourself."

"And how can I be certain you were faithful to me, with Rawley always sniffing about?"

"Oh, for heaven's sake! I've told you time and again he is only a friend."

"A friend. Hah."

"He is. David, you have only to look at Jennie to know she's yours. Look at the shape of her face, at her nose, at her ears—the resemblance is there, if you would but open your eyes. I saw it immediately when I was in London to . . ."

"To what?" he demanded, when she didn't go on.

"Well." She raised her chin and pushed her hair back. "Since you are enumerating my sins against you, I suppose now is as good a time as any to tell you."

"Tell me what?"

"I design clothes."

He looked at her blankly. "Yes, so?"

"Not just for Jennie and myself, David."

It took a moment, but it began to sink in. "For other people? Is that what you are saying?"

"Yes."

"Who?"

"People in London."

"What?"

"No one knows." She stared almost defiantly at him from across the room. "I am in partnership with a modiste. That is how I happened to go to London the times I saw Jennie."

"My God." He sank abruptly into the chair, staring at her. "You're in trade?"

"In a manner of speaking, yes."

"How the devil did that happen?" he demanded.

"Almost by accident, really." She sat down again. "Please don't be annoyed, David. I didn't do it to hurt you."

"Annoyed! A wife in trade. Do you realize—"

"Yes. But I wasn't your wife when this started."

He was silent for a moment. "When did it start?"

"Not long after you left." She looked away. "Not long after you took Jennie away from me."

"I will not apologize for that."

"Of course not," she said bitterly, and then

stopped herself. Arguing about past hurts would avail them nothing. Pleading about the future would avail her nothing. "It hurt so much, David. You cannot know how much it hurt, to see you go. To have my daughter taken from me. For a long time, I just— drifted. Richard told me later he feared for me."

He frowned. "What do you mean? That you'd go into a decline?"

She looked up at him. "No. Not that passive. I was still an impulsive person."

"My God," he said, his eyes widening. "That you'd take your own life?"

"That one day I'd go out onto the moors and never return."

He was the one to flinch this time. "Did you—did you walk on the moors?"

"Yes. When I wasn't sleeping, which was quite a bit. Oh, don't look at me so. What I just said was Richard's fear, not what I would have done. I could not have hurt Jennie in such a way."

"My God," he said again. "I never knew."

"No." *And you wouldn't have believed it, were you told. You wouldn't have believed I cared.* She sighed and brushed some hair away from her face. "I came out of it eventually, of course. And when I did, I went into the partnership with the modiste."

He rubbed at his face. "I cannot believe this."

"I needed to stay busy, so I started sketching. Day dresses, evening dresses, bonnets, spencers—anything you can think of."

"For yourself?"

"For no one, at first. Then, yes, for myself." She took a deep breath. "What happened, though, was that I made more dresses than I could possibly wear. When I finally realized what I was doing, I stopped and looked at what I'd done, and I discovered something, David."

"What?"

"That I was very good at it. That I knew about the right lines for a dress, and what fabric it should be in, and the color. Also that what I'd made was more stylish than anything I'd seen in *La Belle Assemblèe* or *Ackermann's Repository*. That was when I had the idea that I could make clothes for other people besides myself."

He stared at her. "You considered setting up as a dressmaker?"

"No, of course not. I considered doing just what I am doing. Believe me, David, I thought it over carefully. I knew quite well what people in London would say if they learned I was trying to sell my designs to a modiste there. And they would have, because it would have been so unusual."

"They would have talked."

"Oh, yes. It would have hurt you and Jennie, and I'd hurt you both enough."

"How kind of you to care."

"You needn't talk in that tone of voice."

He rubbed at the bridge of his nose. "So why the devil did you consider it at all?"

"Because I needed it, David. I had to have something, if I didn't have a family."

"You could have married again."

"No. That, I could not."

"Why not? Did not Rawley want you then?"

She held onto her temper by a great effort. "This has to do with me, David. Not anyone else."

"My apologies," he said, though he didn't sound as if he meant it. "Go on."

"There was a dressmaker in York I'd patronized

when I needed to." She paused. "She made my wedding dress, when I married you."

His face darkened. "Go on," he said again.

"She had mentioned to me once that her dream was to work in London. I brought her some of my designs, and before we quite knew it, we had decided to become partners. So. I do the designing, and she makes the ensembles, and it has worked quite well."

"Who knows about this?" he asked, finally.

"My brother, of course, and the Duke of Bainbridge."

"Bainbridge?" He frowned. "But he never said a word."

"No. 'Tis between us."

"And the world! My God, if this ever became known—"

"Why should it?" she asked calmly.

"Why? Think of the fame this modiste would have, being associated with a peer's wife—"

"The scandal, you mean," she retorted. "Which you claim is all people know of me."

"Scandal, fame, it matters not. What if she were to say something?"

"I hardly think 'tis likely, David. Think of the blow it would be to her esteem, to have that known. Not to mention, as I said, the scandal. Who would think she would wish to be associated with me?"

"Why do you do it?"

"For the satisfaction of it, and the money, of course."

"Why? Isn't the allowance I make you enough?"

"Of course it is! It isn't that, David. Harcourt needs extra income. What I make, I give to Richard, except for my needs."

"Which is why I make you an income."

"I've saved that for Jennie."

"I can provide for our daughter," he said stiffly.

"I'm not saying you can't. This will be something I can leave to her someday. Lord knows I've given her little else."

"By your own doing. My God." He shook his head. "You have utterly ruined me."

"I hardly see that, David."

"Do you not? Good lord, Tess! My career is ruined, but I thought I had a chance of regaining some of it. To work in the background, as before. But to have a wife who is in trade would take away all chance of that."

She stared at him. "I never meant to hurt you, David. I swear to that."

"Did you not?" he said bitterly. "It matters not. The result is the same."

"Let me remind you that you were the one who wanted the divorce!"

"After you told me you had never cared for me. My God, I had never felt so rejected since . . ."

"Since when?" she asked, and then drew in her breath. "Since your mother said those terrible things to you. Is that what you were going to say?"

"It hardly matters now, Tess." He rose. "We won't speak of this again. It will be as if never happened."

"I don't see how that can be." Her arms were crossed at her chest. "It's a part of us, just as the way our mothers hurt us is."

"We recovered from that, madam. We'll recover from this."

"Will we, David?" She looked up at him. "Sometimes I think about what my mother did, and it's as if it just happened. Poor Jennie."

"Why?"

"We've done the same thing to her. I wonder if you realize that."

He looked at her, struck. "But I'm a good father. At least, I try to be. And," he added unwillingly, "you're a good mother."

She blinked. "Why, thank you. Jennie means the world to me. I hope you know that."

"I do," he said, grudgingly.

"I'd do anything for her." She paused. "David, last night you said we could deal together better than we do. Do you think—is it possible we could start over? Make something of our marriage?"

His face hardened. "No," he said baldly.

Tess rocked back in the chair. "Well! That's honest, I suppose." She looked away, not wanting him to see the tears that had come, unbidden, to her eyes. Likely he was right. There was too much between them, too much pain, too much that had been said and done, to allow for a clean start. That he had spoken last night of dealing better together didn't mean anything. They had been alone in a darkened bedroom that once had seen their greatest happiness, as well as their greatest misery. It was perhaps no wonder if the past had overwhelmed him for a time. Except, for her, it hadn't been the past. It had been now, as well as the future. A month ago, she hadn't thought her future would ever include Jennie, let alone children not even dreamed of yet. Now she didn't know how she could let any of them go.

She looked back. David had picked up some papers and seemed to be busy with them. "I'll go then, shall I?"

"Yes," he said, not looking at her.

"Very well." She rose and went to the door. "I suppose I'll see you at luncheon."

"Yes."

Oh, David, she thought, and took a deep breath. "Yes," she said, and went out.

Hardly seeing where she was going, Tess stumbled upstairs to her sitting room. There she sat in the tufted blue chair, looking out over the snow covered moors, hurting, aware that she was not the only one. One thing had been made clear to her this morning. David's dealings with her had only been disastrous, and promised to become worse. No wonder if he didn't wish to have any more to do with her than he had to. To him it must seem as if anything she did was calculated to hurt him, and yet she'd never meant to do so. She loved him, and Jennie, too much. Not that he'd believe that if she told him.

Was there any chance, then, of saving their marriage? Though they were bound together, they were still somehow apart. It wasn't what she, or doubtless Jennie, wanted. She wanted them to be as they once had been, in love and freely expressing that love. Oh, she realized they could never return to the heady innocence of those early days, but there was something David didn't know. He didn't know why she had behaved as she had so long ago. Telling him might make a difference. Maybe. If he believed her.

She glanced at the door leading to her bedroom, and memories of the night before flooded her. There had to be some feeling remaining inside him for him to have behaved as he had last night. Even desire for her had to be motivated by something, didn't it? Maybe, then she had a chance. Not that it would be easy. Admitting how foolish one had been never was. Perhaps, though, if he would realize what her motivations had been, he would forgive her. She prayed it would be so. Because if he didn't, the alternatives were unthinkable. She would have to let him and Jennie go.

* * *

She designed clothing! Waiting for Tess to come down for luncheon, David prowled the drawing room, fuming, as he had all morning. Good lord, what she did was only one step better than being a modiste. She might as well be taking people's measurements, she, the wife of a marquess. Oh, this would finish him in politics if it became known. She never had meant to hurt him, he thought sarcastically, no, not her. All that she had done, and she could actually say that. And she had asked him, just this morning, if they could begin anew. How could she ever think such a thing?

The door opened and Tess stood there, pausing just a moment when she saw him. Then, head held high, she came in. "David," she said.

"Madam," he answered, just as tersely.

An awkward silence fell. "David, I—"

"Tess, if—" he began at the same time, and they both stuttered into silence. "Go ahead."

"I'm sorry, I didn't mean to interrupt—"

"Tess, for God's sake, just say what you want to say and be done with it!"

She closed her eyes and took a deep breath that made him look away from her chest. "Very well. I've been doing some thinking."

"As have I, about what we discussed this morning."

She looked up, and he was stunned to see a hopeful gleam in her eyes. "Oh, David, have you?"

"Yes. Tess, you do realize you can't continue in trade."

Her shoulders sagged. "Oh. That."

"Yes. What did you think I meant?"

"I thought—it doesn't matter. David, I never told you why I asked you for the separation in the first place."

He closed his mouth on a hard exhale. "For God's sake, Tess. Can we not leave the past where it belongs?"

"When it matters so to the present? No. I never did tell you, David. I think it's important that you know."

"I hardly think it will make me change my mind."

She sat down, keeping her gaze on him. "It might."

"I doubt it." He leaned his arm on the mantel. "But if you feel you must tell me, then just please do so."

She looked doubtfully at him for a moment, and then nodded. "Very well. You're right. Nothing will be served by putting it off. It's just—it's hard." She fell silent, and this time he didn't try to hurry her along. "David, do you remember when you learned about my mother—my heavens, that wasn't so very long ago, was it?"

"No. Keep going."

"Yes. Well. You asked me why I'd never told you about her. What I told you wasn't the real reason."

He looked at her with the first real interest he'd felt in whatever she had to say. "Which is?"

"I told you it was because she'd hurt me, and that much is true. What I didn't say," she closed her eyes, "is how ashamed of her I am. And of myself."

That made him blink. "Why?"

"The scandal. The thought at first that maybe I caused it. Then later," she looked at him, "that I'm like her."

"Tess—"

"When I went into the village, when I went to church, I was always aware of people whispering behind my back. When I go into the village now, 'tis the same. I've tried to become accustomed to it."

Sympathy stirred within him, and he pushed it ruthlessly down. "I hardly see, though, what this has to do with us."

"Don't you? Do you remember, when we married, my brother was from home on estate business?"

"Yes, so?"

"You had told me of what you wanted to do politically, but I had no idea of how my mother's background might affect that. Ah. Do you begin to guess what I'm trying to say?"

"Are you telling me that you asked for the separation for my own good?"

"Yes."

"I don't believe it," he said flatly.

"Oh, but I did." She leaned forward in the chair, as if to prove her earnestness. "When Richard came home he took me aside and told me I was a little fool, didn't I have any idea what I'd done? That the scandal we'd gone through would be yours, too. Well." She took a deep breath. "I knew I had to fix it. The only thing I could think of was to give you up."

He stared at her. "You could have told me."

"No. At the time I really don't think I could have, not feeling as I did. I didn't want you to stop loving me."

"Yet you asked for a separation. Tess, it doesn't make sense."

"I know," she said in a small voice. "Don't you remember how impetuous we both were? We married by special license that time, too, but not because we had to. Just because we wanted to." *Because we had gone up on the moors, and we wanted the freedom to do that again. Together, in our own house, for all the rest of our lives.*

"My God." He rose to pace behind his desk. "This is all absurd."

"Is it? Is it any more absurd than what you did? I asked for us to live apart, so that the stain of my past wouldn't reflect on you. You wanted a divorce."

"Tess, people would have remembered about your mother, whether we stayed together or not."

"I know, but I wasn't thinking straight then. I was in love, David, and I was young, and I believed in making grand, dramatic gestures. I simply never expected it to go so wrong."

"What did you expect I'd do, when you told me you'd never loved me?"

"I told you. I thought you'd go—no." She straightened. "If I'm to be honest, I think I hoped you'd try to convince me."

He rubbed at his nose. "My God," he said quietly. "You were naive."

She nodded. "Yes."

"I was angry, Tess. Didn't you ever think of that?"

"No. I know it now, though. David." She held out her hands. "I never stopped loving you."

"Do you truly expect me to believe that?"

"I never did! David, it's true."

"You must think I'm a fool."

"No. But I do think you love Jennie, and I hope you'd want her to grow up in a better family than her parents did."

"I don't think that's possible, Tess," he said, and even to him it had the ring of finality.

"No?" she said, after a moment.

"No."

"Oh." She looked away. "I suppose it isn't."

The bell rang for luncheon, and they looked at each other. If he touched her, even to take her arm to escort her, he didn't know what he'd do. "You realize I'll be leaving for London soon?"

"Yes." Her shoulders heaved, and then she rose to cross to the door. "I find I have no appetite for food."

"Tess—"

"I won't try to hold you when you want to leave," she said, and left the room, leaving him more alone than he had ever been in his life. It had to be this way, he knew, but it hurt with an ache he doubted would ever quite heal. For with Tess had gone their marriage, all in a quiet whisk of sound.

Thirteen

Parliament wouldn't be starting session for some time. Even so, Papa was planning to leave for London soon. He'd told her so. Jennie was excited, because surely this time her mother would be coming with them. And surely in London, matters between her parents would get better. They had to.

Sitting on the window seat in her room, looking over a garden deep in snow, Jennie frowned. Her trick of sleepwalking hadn't worked, that much was obvious to her now. In fact, it was much the opposite. As before, her parents didn't quarrel, but they shared no underlying friendliness, either. She could sense it. She didn't know what had caused it, or what she could do about it. She only hoped that in London, where there was so much to do both day, for her, and at night, for adults, things would improve.

There was a brief knock on her door, and then Mama and Papa came in. Jennie's spirits lifted briefly at the fact that they were together, but then fell again; they didn't touch each other, not even their hands, nor were they looking at each other. "Hello, Jennie," Papa said.

"Papa. Have you come to hear my lessons, the way Mama does?" Jennie asked.

"Er, no. We want to talk to you. No, sit back down, poppet."

She sat on the window seat, her hands folded in her lap. "Yes, Papa?" she said, looking at them expectantly. Maybe they were going to tell her she was going to have a little brother or sister, she thought, suddenly. One of her friends had told her about her parents doing that, and Jennie had been ever so jealous.

"Do you remember that we talked about returning to London?"

"Oh, yes!" She leaned forward, excited now. "And I'm so glad. It's not that I don't like Yorkshire," she explained quickly to her mother, "but there's ever so much to do there. I can't wait to show every place to you. Papa, do you think we might all go to Astley's Amphitheater?"

"Jennie, there's a problem with that."

Jennie went still. "What problem?"

"I'm not going to London," Mama said, speaking for the first time.

"Not going!" She looked from one to the other. "Of course you're going."

"No, angel, I'm afraid I'm not."

"But why? I thought that since you were married, you'd live together again."

"We've decided that's not the right thing for us," Papa said.

"Why not?"

Mama and Papa looked at each other, and he took a deep breath. "It's hard to explain, Jennie. It just is. You'll have to trust us."

"But it's not right, it can't be. We belong together. As a family."

"Jennie, I know you think so, but—"

"I know so," she said stubbornly, "and nothing you can say will change my mind."

Again her parents exchanged looks. "Jennie." Mama went down on one knee before her. "I know this is hard. Believe me, there are reasons, but they're grown-up reasons. You wouldn't understand."

She crossed her arms on her chest. "Grown-ups always say that."

"Yes, I suppose we do." Mama came to sit beside her on the window seat, and gathered her close, though Jennie tried to pull away. "Unfortunately, sometimes it's true. They aren't always good, logical reasons, angel."

"But where will you live?"

"Harcourt, with Uncle Richard, as before. And you'll come to me to visit. Think of that, Jennie. You've never been here in the summer. Oh, just wait until you've seen the lambs. They're so funny, all long legs frolicking everywhere—"

"I don't want to just visit you!" Jennie said, tearing herself away and standing up, facing them both. "If we can't all be together, then I won't go back to London."

"Jennie—"

"I won't, and you can't change my mind." She nodded, once. "I just won't."

Mama and Papa looked at each other yet again, this time startled. Jennie saw other emotions, too, but she couldn't name them and didn't care. All that mattered to her was that it was all falling to pieces around her. She'd be without her mother again, but this time it would be worse. This time, they'd actually met.

Mama chose to laugh a little, definitely a mistake. "Don't be silly, Jennie. Of course you can't stay here."

"I could, if I ran away."

"That's enough, Jennie," Papa said sharply. "No threats, and no games such as hiding or sleepwalking. We've made this decision, and that's it."

"You've made it, but I haven't." She put up her chin to them. "And I'm not going."

"You'll do what we say." "We're your parents and we make the decisions. If I have to carry you, Jennie, I will, but you will come to London with me."

She looked up at him, so tall above her, until now her hero and her god. "You can do that," she said, "but I'll hate you for it, Papa. I will."

Tess bit her lip. For the first time, David looked truly discomposed. "Jennie, it's for everyone's good—"

"No, it isn't," Jennie interrupted. "It's not for my good."

That was so clearly unanswerable that Tess could see David struggling for something to say. "Jennie," she said, "you wouldn't really hate your father."

"Yes, I would, for this. Wouldn't you?"

Tess sucked in her breath. She had never hated her mother—no, that wasn't true. There were moments when she had been younger and scared, times when she had cried in the lonely night, when she *had* hated her mother for leaving her. What had been done to her had left a scar that had never really healed. If they forced this on Jennie, they might be doing something similar to her.

"David," she said, and he brought his troubled gaze up to hers, "I think we need to talk about this some more."

"Hmph," Jennie said, sounding very much like a disapproving old lady and looking like a parody of one, with her arms still folded over her chest.

"We've made our decision, Tess," he said, sounding just the slightest bit helpless.

"Yes, but when we did so we didn't consult Jennie. 'Tis only fair, since it involves her."

He simply looked at her, and she could almost hear what he was thinking. Part of deciding as they had was so that her reputation wouldn't damage Jennie's. Yet would that matter, if the child grew up without her mother? Visits would not be enough. Tess herself knew that too well; David should, too. "And what will people think?"

"Do they matter?"

"Tess. You know that they do. What will happen in twelve years, when it's time for her to find a husband, if her reputation isn't spotless?"

"The truth is that she will always be my daughter, David. Her reputation could be white as snow, and it wouldn't matter. People would always whisper about her. I should know."

"What will they say about me?" Jennie demanded.

Tess shook her head. "Not really about you, angel. About me."

David's lips were set; she knew he hadn't heard the whispers before their marriage. Would they have mattered to him if he had? "Are you saying we should give in to her?"

"I'm saying we should consider her happiness. And you yourself told me that she can be stubborn."

"Does this mean I'm going to stay?" Jennie said, looking up at them.

"No, poppet." David looked tired suddenly, and no wonder, with all the tension there had been between them lately. "It simply means that your mother and I have to discuss this matter over again."

"Papa, why can't we all live as a family?"

"I know you want that, poppet. I'd give it to you if it were possible, but it's not."

Jennie looked from David to Tess, and suddenly her shoulders sagged. "But—but I thought . . ."

"Oh, angel, I know," Tess said, kneeling again and opening her arms to her daughter. "Unfortunately things don't always work out the way we'd like."

"It's not fair."

"I know. Life isn't fair, Jennie." Tess rose. "Nurse will be bringing your tea soon."

Jennie looked up. "Will you take it with me today, Mama?"

"No, angel. Your father and I are going to discuss this again."

"I won't go," Jennie warned.

Tess smiled. "We'll keep that in mind," she said, and she and David went out.

"She'll go if she has to," David said in a low voice when they were in the passageway outside the nursery.

"Perhaps. And perhaps she'll run away first. Knowing Jennie, anything is possible."

David rubbed at the bridge of his nose. "I suppose it is."

"I will tell you one thing," she said as they reached the stairs. "If we force her, she'll hate us for it."

"But, being Jennie—"

"She'll be stubborn and we'll have no choice," Tess finished for him.

"Did you ever hate your mother for leaving you?"

"Yes," she confessed after a moment. "Once in a while, I did. I must say, David, I don't like the idea of Jennie feeling that way about me at all."

"Yet, what can we do?" he asked, stepping aside

to let her precede him on the second floor. "We can't let her stay here."

"Why can't we?"

"Her life is in London, with me."

"You mean it always has been in London, with you."

"Yes. I see no reason for that to change now."

"Of course you don't."

"I won't stand discussing this with you in the hall." His lips were set in a thin, angry line.

"Your study, then," she said, and, opening the door, swept into it.

Once inside, she went to the pair of chairs set near the hearth. David paused for a moment, and then joined her. "You know all the reasons we decided it was best," he began without preamble.

"I do. But things have changed. Jennie's seen to that. She's right, David. It is her life," she said, before he could interrupt.

"She's a child. How can she make a decision like this?"

"Sometimes children see things clearer than adults do."

"What is that supposed to mean?"

"Jennie is thinking with her heart."

"Which is why we have to decide for her."

"No. Which is why her decision might be wiser than ours. This once, anyway. David, listen. All those things we discussed, about her education, her reputation, they're not really the important things."

"They will be."

"Not if her parents fail her. And we will fail her, if we make the wrong choice."

"Are you really saying that we should give in to her?"

"No. I'm saying that she doesn't want to live without a mother."

"So it comes back to that, does it? Whether you win, or I do."

"Oh, David." She looked at him sadly. "Don't you realize it? There are no winners in this. Only losers."

He looked into the fire for a few moments. "I don't want to lose her, Tess," he said in a low voice.

"Do you think I do?"

"No. But I think you're capable of using every weapon you have to keep her."

"That's unfair!"

"Life isn't fair," he said in a mocking refrain of what she had told Jennie only a few minutes ago.

"I don't want to keep her from you. I think that's as wrong as keeping her from me for six years was."

"Ah. So that's what this is about."

"No! David, for heaven's sake, open your eyes! We both risk losing Jennie if we make the wrong decision."

"The right one being that she stays here with you."

"It might very well be, yes. At least, for a time."

"Damnation, Tess, I don't like this!"

"I wouldn't like seeing her leaving me, either," Tess retorted. "But I'd let her go, if I thought it was the right thing."

"You did."

"Yes, well, Jennie's rather changed my mind, I'm afraid."

David rose and walked to a window. "Damnation," he said again. "One of us has to give her up."

Tess didn't say anything. She had reached that conclusion upstairs, when she had seen Jennie and David with their gazes and their wills locked, both looking alike in their stubbornness. To point that out to David now, though, would only rub salt in the wound. "David, I'm sorry—"

"Don't." Something about his eyes told her he wouldn't have seen anything out the window, even had the glass in this room in the old part of the house been clear and not thick and wavy. "I've never had to do without her before."

"You've done a good job with her, David. Most fathers in our class don't even know what their children look like."

"I know. I've tried to make it up to Jennie, but . . ." He let his words trail off, but she understood him anyway. A child wanted both her parents. "Very well." He turned to her, his shoulders squared. "How do we do this?"

"The way we agreed before, I suppose."

"Except I'll be the one she visits."

"Or you could come here."

"No." There was finality in his voice. "I won't be returning to Yorkshire. I also think she needs to visit London from time to time."

Tess thought about that, then nodded. "I agree. When I bring my designs to the modiste, I can bring her."

"Good God, no!"

"I won't contaminate her, David." Her head was high. "You need only specify a place and time where we can meet, for you to get her. A hotel, perhaps."

He nodded, slowly. "Yes. That isn't such a bad idea."

"Then all that is needed is to go through with it."

"Yes." He moved away from the window. "Well. Congratulations, Tess. You finally have won."

"David," she called after him, but too late. He had already left the study, and, though her heart ached for him, she knew better than to follow. This wasn't

what she wanted; how could he think that? She
wanted them to be together, a family, as Jennie did.
She wanted to be his wife. Since he'd ruled that out,
though, neither was possible. There were only impossible choices.

Suppressing a sigh, she rose. The decision had
been made, and, no matter what he might think, there
really were no winners in this. There were only losers.

The carriage stood ready in the drive, the horses
blowing and stamping in the cold. Although the
weather was still uncertain and he knew he might
have to stop on the way, David had decided to
chance going to London. It was too painful to remain
at Stowcroft. If he had to make the break, he wanted
it to be a clean one. Tonight would be Twelfth Night.
Christmas was over.

Jennie had refused to change her mind, no matter
what he or Tess said. He supposed he couldn't blame
her. After all, her parents had been together again.
She had the right to expect that they'd stay that way.
Unfortunately, circumstances prevented it, no matter
how much she might want it. What he didn't quite
understand was that he wanted it, too.

Everything was packed, stowed in the baggage
coach, except for any papers he thought might be
important and so carried with him. It remained only
for him to don his greatcoat and step into the carriage. Still, he looked around the study one more
time, ostensibly to check for missing or forgotten
items, but in reality to delay the leave-taking. He
had had Jennie with him since her birth. Leaving
her, and Tess, behind would be the hardest thing he'd
ever done.

Might as well do it, he thought, and, after pulling on the heavy greatcoat, stepped into the hall. There Tess and Jennie awaited him, Tess with her face serious and her eyes large and somehow bruised-looking; Jennie in tears. "Ah, poppet," he said, going down onto his knee before her, and it apparently was too much. With a sob, she threw herself into his arms.

"I wish you didn't have to go," she said, clinging to him.

"I do, too, Jennie, but it's necessary." He held her away from him. "There's still time for you to change your mind."

Jennie's mouth took on the mutinous cast he knew so well. "No. I'm staying here."

"I've tried talking to her, David," Tess put in softly, and he glared at her. Just now he didn't want to hear a word from her. She might not have started this, as she claimed, but she was the one benefiting from it.

He rose. "I'll write, of course," he said stiffly.

"So will we," Tess said just as formally.

"Every week, Papa," Jennie put in. "I have the papers you franked and the wafers and everything."

He forced a smile. "Good. I'll be looking forward to reading them. Well." He looked at Tess again. "If there's anything more?"

She shook her head. "No, I don't think so, David."

"Well, then." He bent to kiss Jennie on the head. "Be a good girl."

Jennie was in tears again. "I will, Papa, I promise."

"Good." There really was nothing left, nothing to hold him, except his own, strange unwillingness. "Keep well," he said, suddenly gruff, and strode toward the door, held open for him by a footman. Behind him he heard a sudden choked sob. It made him pause for a moment, but only for that. There was really nothing for it but to keep going, across the frozen drive. If he looked back he would be truly lost.

Blindly he stepped up into the carriage, and the door was closed behind him. Just as blindly he rapped the roof with his stick, signaling to the driver to start. He was aware of seeing in a blur through the window, Tess, holding Jennie by the shoulders, and then he was past them. Stowcroft, and all it represented, was behind him.

For the first few miles of the journey he saw nothing of the passing scenery, so lost in his own thoughts was he. There was no order to what he thought. He was aware only of a terrible well of misery inside him, and an ache he didn't think would ever go away. Eventually, though, he began to come out of himself to put a name on what he was feeling. He wanted his daughter beside him, laughing and pointing out things on the road. He wanted Tess, which was odd. Weren't his difficulties with her at the root of all his problems? Yet, there it was. He wanted Tess.

Well, perhaps that wasn't so surprising, after all. She was still an attractive woman, with the power to stir him. Hadn't he discovered that twice, to his own disaster? The first time had led to marriage; the second, to intimacies that shouldn't really matter. They were only of the flesh, and Tess was just like any other woman. That she moved him in a way no woman ever had was beside the point. Any feelings he had once had for her had died long ago.

Still, if there were one effect from this enforced separation from Jennie, it was that he realized the sacrifice Tess had made, all those years. She had said it herself. A child should not be kept from her mother. Yet he had made certain that that very thing happened. For Jennie's own good, he hastened to add to himself, and even though he'd occasionally had doubts as to the child's parentage.

That thought made him frown. No, he had to be fair. Maybe Tess had shown some partiality to Rawley all those years ago, teasing and flirting with him, but she had done so with other young men of the neighborhood. In his anger then, David had thought her capable of being a wanton. Nothing in her behavior since, though, had borne that out. She had had ample opportunity to marry Rawley had she wanted to, yet she had remained single, living with her brother instead. True, she was still friendly toward the man, but there was nothing more in her attitude than that. There was also the fact that Jennie did have some of his features, something he had been reluctant to concede, because Tess had pointed it out. Now that she had, though, he could see that his daughter's nose was indeed shaped like his, and her ears, as well. There was no question. She was his daughter, of the body and of the heart. And yet here he was, in this carriage, being taken away from the two people he loved.

The *two* people he loved? He rubbed tiredly at his brow. He was thinking of Jennie, of course, no one else. Of course he didn't love Tess. He had once, he wouldn't deny that, but that love had died when she had told him she didn't love him, had never loved him. The tale she'd told him recently about her motives, about wanting to protect his political career, was just that, a tale. Tess was duplicitous, capable of twisting the truth to suit her own needs. He, of all people, should know that. It didn't matter that she really did have a mother who'd caused a scandal, a fact she'd tried to keep from him. He didn't believe her. He didn't love her.

Except. Laying his head back on the squabs of the carriage, he closed his eyes and remembered too much. He remembered his mixed emotions at seeing her again for the first time, his anger mingling with the startling realization that she was still beautiful and desirable, that even then she stirred him in a way no other woman ever had. He saw her with Jennie, far better a mother than he would ever have expected. He remembered, God help him, but he remembered the feeling of her in his arms, so warm and soft and giving. And he remembered something else, something that still might have been only a dream. Later on in that night when he'd given into madness and desire, when he'd been so near to sleep, she had whispered something. She had whispered that she loved him.

He sat up straight. How could it possibly be true, after all this time, after all that had passed between them? Even more astonishing, how could it be so that he loved her? Because he did. He thought that perhaps he always had.

Lord, help me, he thought, closing his eyes again. This was madness. This was something he could never in his wildest dreams have expected. Yet, it explained so much. Tess herself had pointed out that he had been the one to take the steps toward divorce, not her. He had been the one to ruin his career. He faced that now. Had he not acted as he had, he might have been more than a nameless person working behind the scenes. Oh, certainly he seemed to have a certain sense where politics and government were concerned, and certainly people in the party were beginning to listen to him. Without the divorce, though, and the scandal it had caused, he might have taken his seat in the House of Lords by now, and been more than someone in the shadows. He might very well have been his own man. It had been an over-reaction of the worst sort, giving Tess a divorce. Even now he didn't want to admit to himself, or to anyone else, why he'd done it, though he knew. He'd always known. It had hurt, the thought that she might not love him. The divorce, as impulsive an act as hers, had been his way of striking out at her, of hurting her. That it hadn't stopped him from loving her was something he rarely let himself think, either.

His anger toward her, from the beginning of the visit to Yorkshire to now, was rooted in the same feeling. If he were angry, he could forget about what he truly felt. It was only now, when it was too late, when he was in a carriage being borne away to London, that he admitted the truth. He loved her. The feeling was so immense, so strong, that he wanted to shout it. He loved Tess.

Then why, he asked himself suddenly, was he going to London? Lord knew there was little enough for him there, with Jennie staying behind and his career in a shambles. Any credibility he'd managed to build up during the past six years had been destroyed, and he would have to start again. In the meantime, he would also be facing the worst of the scandal, as both fashionable and political London gossiped and tittered about the fact that he and Tess were married again. It was best to let it blow over, to wait until some other scandal had come along to supplant his own. Tess, though, would unfortunately never be received by the hostesses who mattered, and he himself would be suspect. London, he thought, looked damned bleak.

If that were the case, then he didn't want it, he

decided. He could bear the whispers for himself; he didn't like the idea of starting over again in politics, but he was young, and peoples' memories could be short. What he didn't like was the idea of Tess, his Tess, being ostracized because of his own foolish actions in the past. True, she had hurt him, asking for a separation instead of telling him the truth, but her motives had been good. She had done nothing except try to spare him pain. In so doing, she had brought it upon herself, more than she could ever have imagined, more, certainly, than he had ever realized. Not only had she borne the weight of the scandal, but she had lived without him, and without their daughter, for a very long time. She was, he thought humbly, far stronger than he was.

He was foolish to go to London, then. Instead, he owed it both to her and to himself to go back and try to make something of their marriage. Perhaps someday they would go to town, but not yet. Not now. When they did, it would be as a family. A career that demanded he leave his loved ones behind wasn't worth it.

With his stick, he rapped on the roof of the carriage again. Slowly it came to a stop, and then the small door in the roof opened, showing the driver's curious face. "Yes, my lord?" he said.

"Turn around," David said crisply.

"My lord?"

"Turn the carriage around. We're going back."

"Back? But, my lord—"

"You heard me. Turn around."

"Yes, my lord," the driver said, and closed the door.

In a minute David felt the carriage slowly turning and backing on the narrow road, until it was at last traveling in the other direction. *Good*, he thought, sitting back and resting his hands on the head of his stick. He was returning to Stowcroft, and his anticipation made it feel like Christmas again.

Fourteen

Jennie was inconsolable. Tess, sitting on the window seat in Jennie's room with her daughter's head on her lap, could do little beyond stroking her hair and murmuring soft, meaningless words of comfort. There were, Tess had found, less pleasant aspects of parenthood than the ones she had envisioned. Imposing discipline was one of them; teaching about life's lessons was another. Jennie was learning very young about the hard choices one sometimes faced. Better now, though, than later, Tess thought, and sighed.

"Jennie," she said, and Jennie looked up, her eyes red and swollen with tears. "This is what you wanted."

"But I didn't know it would be so hard!" Jennie wailed. "I knew if I left you I'd . . ."

"What, angel?" Tess asked, when Jennie didn't go on.

"I'd cry just as much," she mumbled.

"Oh, angel." Tess put her fingers under the child's chin, forcing her to look up. "This is what you decided. You have to learn to live with it somehow."

"Can't you make it better?"

"No, I fear not. Only you can do that, and time."

"Oh." Jennie moved away from her, wiping at her face with the back of her hand.

"Here." Tess took out her handkerchief and handed it to her. "This is a difficult situation, Jennie."

"Why does it have to be so hard?"

"Life is hard, Jennie. And it's not fair, either, before you say that."

"Well, it isn't."

"No," she said, smothering a smile, though in truth she felt as desolate as her daughter. David had left her again. She didn't know how she would bear it.

That one night, that one magical night, she had poured all her love into her every action, hoping he would see, hoping he would know that she never had stopped loving him, no matter what she had once said. Hoping later, against hope, that he would realize she had been motivated by love so very long ago, when she had set into motion the disastrous chain of events that had so affected their lives. He hadn't, though. Now he was gone, and, like Jennie, she longed to wail and weep. The only problem was that she was the adult. She would have to do her mourning in private, and be strong for her daughter.

Jennie had moved away and was leafing desultorily through the pages of a book, though Tess suspected it was the last thing she cared about. "Mama," she said suddenly.

"Yes?"

"Why have you and Papa lived apart all this time?

Oh, no, the difficult question. Tess had thought about the day when Jennie would ask her this, had dreaded it. She still didn't know what she would say. "There were reasons," she said carefully.

"But didn't you love him?"

"Oh, yes, very much."

"Then, why?"

"It seemed like the best thing to do at the time."

"But what about me?" It was a cry from the heart. "I wanted you, Mama. I wanted you."

Tess bit the inside of her lip, hard. "I know you did," she said, her voice unsteady. "I wanted you."

"Then why? Was I really so very bad?"

"Oh, Jennie." Tess opened her arms. "I told you before. It didn't have anything to do with you. It was between your father and me."

"And now?"

"It still is."

"It's silly," Jennie declared. "You love him, and he loves you—"

"Nonsense, he does not."

"Yes, he does. I've seen him look at you."

"How?" Tess asked involuntarily.

"I don't know. He just does." She looked up at Tess, her eyes wide and candid. "Why did you let him go?"

Just like that, Tess decided. Maybe it was wrong, but she suspected Jennie was suffering more from not knowing than she would if she knew the truth. "You know your father and I were divorced."

"But you're not now."

Tess smiled. "Yes, Jennie, I know. That's part of the problem, too. You must know that divorce is something people disapprove of. You must have heard people talk about it."

"Well, yes," Jennie said unwillingly, as if by listening she was being disloyal. "But I don't understand why."

"You know yourself why. People are supposed to stay married. Yes, I know you know other children whose parents live apart. You've told me. They stayed married, though, didn't they?"

"Yes."

"It was the divorce that kept us apart, Jennie. It caused a lot of talk and it hurt your father's career. It would have hurt worse if I'd lived in London, and it certainly would have hurt you. So I stayed in Yorkshire."

"Oh." Jennie appeared to be digesting this. "But you're married now."

"And people are talking all over again." Tess smiled, though without amusement in it. "You see? More damage done."

Again, Jennie took time to think about what Tess had said. "It's silly," she pronounced finally.

"Maybe, but it's the way things work. I'd rather be in London with you and your father, but I can't be, Jennie. I'm sorry."

Jennie wiped at her face with her fingers again and went to stand beside Tess, leaning her head on her shoulder and looking out at the garden. "I know."

"We'll have to get used to being without your father, angel. I'm afraid we've no other choice."

"I know." She raised her face to Tess's. "Mama, will it get easier?"

"In time. 'Tis amazing what one can become accustomed to."

"I won't."

"You'll see." Tess paused. She didn't quite believe what she was about to say, but she had to go through with it. If she didn't make the suggestion that had occurred to her, it would always bother her. "Jennie, you do know that what you did to your father wasn't very fair."

"But life's not fair."

"Oh, now wait a minute, miss." Tess put Jennie away from her, her face stern. "I don't like hearing you say things like that."

"I'm sorry," Jennie muttered.

"I should hope so. Your father's done a lot for you. Think of how he must be feeling now. I think it just about killed him to leave you behind."

"He could have stayed."

"No, Jennie, he couldn't, and you know it. His work is in London."

"I don't care."

"I do. If it makes him happy, it's what he should do. But you, miss, were very hard on him, refusing to go."

"I wanted all of us to go."

"I'm well aware of that. Since we couldn't, though, you should have gone along."

Jennie's mouth took on that mutinous pout. "Are you going to make me? Because I told you I'll hate you forever."

"I know." Tess's face was grave. "I take you seriously on that, Jennie. 'Tis why I won't force you."

"Oh." Jennie frowned. "Then why did you say it?"

"Because I think you should decide it yourself."

"No."

"No?" Tess angled her head. "Your father's very unhappy now. Do you want that?"

"No, but—"

"You're the only one who can change it. Unless you want him to be unhappy?"

"No! But, Mama." Jennie's eyes were desperate. "If I went, I'd miss you, and you'd be unhappy, too."

"Yes, angel, I would be." Tess smoothed back tendrils of hair from Jennie's face. "But there's something you're not thinking about. It wouldn't last forever."

"But I'm afraid it will!" Jennie launched herself at Tess, who gathered her close. "Papa said he's never coming back to Yorkshire."

"Oh, but Jennie—"

"And I'm afraid if I go, he'll find some reason to keep me with him, and I'll never see you again."

"He wouldn't do that, Jennie! That wasn't what he and I had arranged."

"But what if it happened?"

"Then I'd go to London after you."

"You would?"

"I would, but it wouldn't come to that. I trust him to keep his word. Don't you?"

"I—yes."

"Have you ever known him to break a promise?"

"No."

"Then you shouldn't start thinking that way now."

Jennie leaned back against her. "Do you really think I should go?"

"Yes, angel, I do."

"I don't want to."

"I know, but we'll see each other in the summer. And we'll write. You will write to me?"

"Oh, every week!"

"Good." Tess hugged her child fiercely, her eyes squeezed shut. She was losing her daughter again. That this time it wouldn't be permanent didn't ease the pain. The thought of being separated from Jennie was devastating.

"Well, then." She straightened, freeing herself from Jennie's clinging embrace. "All that remains now is to have Nurse pack your clothes and have a carriage ready to go."

"Will you go with me?"

"Of course I will. I wouldn't let you go alone."

"Then maybe you could stay in London for a few days with me."

"No, angel." Tess shook her head. "I'm afraid not."

Jennie looked away, and then nodded. "I know."

"Will you go tell Nurse, or should I?"

"I'll go." Jennie straightened, looking, Tess thought, just a little bit older. Without looking back, she crossed the room. At the doorway though, she paused. "I love you, Mama."

"I love you too, Jennie," Tess said, and watched her go, the lump in her throat threatening to choke her. She was losing her daughter again, and she didn't know how she would survive.

Another carriage stood ready in the drive of Stowcroft Hall, this one borrowed from Richard. Tess and Jennie, both wrapped well against the cold Yorkshire air, and with hot bricks to warm their feet, were already inside, each holding to the strap as the carriage started up to bring them to London. Although their eventual parting was days away, their faces were glum. Saying good-bye, especially for Tess, was not going to be easy.

Tess glanced out the window as the Hall disappeared from sight, and then faced resolutely ahead. She had made her decision and would abide by it. It was made from love and thus couldn't be wrong, could it? So it was best for all concerned, she told herself again. At least, it was best for Jennie and David. They'd never been separated from each other for any period of time before, while Tess had become accustomed, in some measure, to being without her daughter. She could become so again, she told herself. She would have to.

Since they had started their journey late in the day, they wouldn't make much progress today and so would have to stop at an inn in York. From her past journeys to London, Tess was familiar with all the posting stops, and when they would have to stop to change horses. She wasn't really surprised, then, when the carriage began to slow. What did startle her was that, when she glanced out the window, all she saw were trees.

The door in the roof opened, and she saw the driver's face. "Why are we stopping?" she asked, more than a little anxious. She'd never encountered highwaymen in the past, but she knew there was still some crime on the road. Instinctively she put her arm around Jennie to protect her.

"There's another carriage ahead, signaling us," the driver said. "Looks like—aye, 'tis Lord Stowe."

"Stowe!" Tess exclaimed. David? What in the world?

"Papa?" Jennie said at the same time. "Why is he coming back?"

"I don't know, Jennie." Tess held onto the strap as the carriage jolted to a complete stop, her brow furrowed. Dear heavens, she hoped nothing was wrong with David.

The carriage door opened abruptly, and David sprang inside. "Papa!" Jennie hurtled herself at him as he sat opposite them, and he pulled her tight. "Why did you come back?"

"I had to," he said, though he was looking at Tess as he answered.

"Is all well?" she asked.

"No." He shook his head. "How could it be, when I was leaving the two people I love?"

It took a moment for that to sink in, and then Tess simply stared at him. "The two—"

"I never stopped, Tess."

She blinked. "Never? But—"

"Didn't you ever stop to think about what I did? Didn't you realize that it was as much an overreaction as what you did?"

"Yes, but—oh, my heavens!" She put her hands to her cheeks.

"You were impulsive, Tess. So was I. You acted to save me pain; I was too hurt to see it." He shrugged, a sheepish look on his face. "I had no idea that I would be wasting so much time. Time we can never get back."

"Oh, but we can, David." She leaned toward him. "It's in the past now."

His gaze was intent. "Is it?"

"We'll put it behind us and start again. We can do that."

He held out his hand. "Yes. We can."

Tess looked at him, her gaze as focused as his, and then her hand crept out. They met, palm to palm, fingers to fingers, halfway, and then David's hand clasped hers warmly. Something cold and stiff within Tess, something that had been there since he had left her, but that she hadn't even been aware of until now, let go, loosened, and was gone. It was Twelfth Night, and she had just been given a marvelous Christmas present, the best Christmas present. She and David were together again.

"Are you still going to London, Papa?" Jennie, a silent witness until now, asked.

"No." He still looked at Tess. "I'm returning to Stowcroft."

"But, David." Tess protested. "Your career. Don't you have to go back to try to salvage it."

"At some point, probably yes. But, Tess, what good is a career, what good is London, if they don't include you?"

"Then what will you do?"

"I expect Bainbridge will keep me informed of all that is happening. If I have any ideas, I can relate them through him. Eventually, perhaps they'll be accepted as mine, and not someone else's."

Tess leaned forward even more. "Oh, I'm sure of that, David. Your ideas are too good to be ignored for long."

"And we will go to London someday, Tess, all of us. I promise you that." He smiled. "As for now, I might try my hand at being a sheep farmer."

"Mama says the lambs are funny when they're little," Jennie put in.

David looked briefly down at her. "I'm sure they are, poppet." His gaze returned to Tess. "We talked once about dealing together better than we had been. Do you think we can?"

"Yes." She squeezed his hand. His gaze became serious, and he raised her hand to press a long, warm, openmouthed kiss on her palm. Tess's breath caught. "Yes," she gasped, and he smiled, warmly, intimately, the David she had once known and always loved. "Yes. I'd like that."

"Good," he said. "Then let's go home."

Jennie lay in her bed at Stowcroft, comfortable and warm with the quilts piled about her. Nurse thought she was asleep, but she had long ago managed the trick of appearing to be asleep while actually awake. At least, she thought she had. One day she would figure out how her parents had known she was feigning sleep, that time she had appeared to sleepwalk.

For now, though, such things didn't matter. She was home, and all was well. Both her parents were here, together again at last. Once they had returned home, Nurse had taken charge of her, as both Mama and Papa disappeared in the direction of their suite of rooms. She had wanted to follow them, but Nurse had held her firmly back. She hadn't understood that. Nor had she understood all that had been said in the carriage this afternoon, but she'd seen her mother's face and felt the warmth of her father's embrace. For some reason, whatever had kept them apart was gone. All that she had hoped for had happened.

Pulling the top quilt from the bed, she wrapped it about herself and padded over to the window seat. It had snowed since they had returned home, and outside was a world of diamond icicles and lacy white branches. Tomorrow, perhaps, she would go out into the snow with Papa and Mama. Maybe they would have a snowball fight again, and build a snowman, and go skating. For now, though, she was content only to look. She was safe and warm inside. All was right with her world.

From the folds of the quilt she pulled out the crystal angel, her father's Christmas gift to her. At least, it was the gift he'd thought she'd prize the most. What she'd always wished for, though, what she'd always wanted, was to have a mother, just like her friends. If Mama had turned out to be different from the person she had imagined, well, that was all right, too. Mama might scold her occasionally, and insist that she do her lessons and eat food that she didn't like, but she also played with her and fixed her hair and hugged her. Mama made her feel safe and secure, complete in a way she'd never felt before. They would always be together now.

The angel glittered in the moonlight, the colors reflected inside its facets pale imitations of what they would be in sunlight. Jennie held it up, admiring it as it dangled on her fingers on its silken cord. It truly was a lovely addition to her collection, but that was all it was. It was a figurine only, just a thing. Her Christmas angel was something that wouldn't fit on a shelf. It was warm and alive and was hers to keep. It was truly all she'd wanted.

It had startled Papa, being told what she'd really wanted for Christmas, she remembered now. What she hadn't told him at the time was what she secretly dreamed, that once he saw Mama again, they would make up whatever had kept them separate and the three of them would be a family again. For a long time, it had seemed as if that wouldn't happen, though she had tried her best to make it come true. Something had happened, though. It didn't fit the logical way she had planned things, but that didn't matter. Maybe some things just defied logic, as Mama had once said.

Jennie smiled at the thought and leaned her head back against the window casing. She didn't have to make any plans anymore, didn't have to wonder about the future, didn't have to try to take care of Papa or of Mama, either. It had taken some time, but it had happened. All was truly well. Her angel's wish had come true, at last.

More Zebra Regency Romances

Celebrate Romance with one of Today's Hotest Authors
Meagan McKinney